Crescent
Shadow

Peter Boczar

Cover design and formatting by www.ebooklaunch.com

ISBN 978-988-14331-3-8

Distributed by
MobiShow Ltd.
GPO 4616
HONG KONG

For Mustapha
Who got me home

Dedicated to
The U.S. Marines
Who do their job against all odds

Acknowledgements

Special thanks to Quentin DeMarco, James Gessling, Robin Heid, Kingsley Smith, Jason Sylvester and Alexander Thomas for their support and insights. Additional thanks to Dave Sametz for sharing important words to live by:

"Don't Die Until You're Dead."

About the Author

Peter Boczar started writing in the 1970s for magazines and newspapers in Hong Kong, where he also dubbed Chinese kung fu movies into English and made a cameo appearance in the Bruce Lee movie *Game of Death*. As a writer, he traveled extensively throughout the world and notably covered conflict zones in the Middle East, Southeast Asia and Central America.

Chapter One

"Mrs. Smith?" the male voice asked the woman who answered the phone.

"Yes?"

"My name is Steven Brown. I'm a consular officer with the United States State Department. I have news about your son Adam."

"Adam? Is he all right?" Mrs. Smith asked anxiously.

"We believe so, but he's been kidnapped."

"Kidnapped? Let me get my husband," she replied and shouted into the room behind her. "Hank! Come to the phone. Adam's been kidnapped."

"Hello? What's that about Adam?" a surly male voice shouted into the receiver.

"Hello, Mr. Smith," the official reiterated. "My name is Steven Brown. I'm a consular officer with the United States State Department. Yes. We believe your son has been kidnapped in Beirut by Muslim terrorists."

"What do you mean 'believe?' He is or he isn't," Mr. Smith answered back angrily. "Is he ok?"

"We have reason to believe that he is," the official replied.

It was 1983 and the Lebanese civil war raged on. Christians, Muslims, and all others were fighting each other. There were armies within armies and militias within militias. Everyone was changing sides on a regular basis. Adam Smith was an engineering professor at the American University of Beirut.

"So what do they want and what are you doing about it?" Mr. Smith interjected.

The U.S. official said they were doing all they could. That was government-speak for not doing anything at all, but that wanted to make the family feel a bit better. The shock to families in these situations was devastating. They suddenly felt guilty and helpless. Guilty because they were helpless. And helpless because they were.

The State Department, also known as "State" in government lingo, wasn't interested in spending resources on Americans stupid enough to live in the chaotic hot spots of the world, be it Beirut or anywhere else, unless it considered them a useful intelligence, political or public relations asset.

"The kidnappers want five hundred thousand dollars in ransom for his release," the official explained, but he advised them not to pay.

"We don't have that kind of money, anyway," Mr. Smith returned. "We live on a small pension. Our house is not even worth one-third that amount. We pay our taxes. You're the government. Why can't you pay?"

"We don't negotiate with terrorists," the official responded. "Kidnapping is a business for them. The more we pay them, the more hostages they will take."

That was a pretty self-serving policy. It meant that the bureaucrats could just ignore these situations and not bother themselves.

At the same time, the policy of the terrorists was to not negotiate with anyone who wouldn't pay. And they held the hostage.

As the saying goes, possession is nine-tenths of the law.

The assumption was that all Americans were rich and if they didn't have the cash, they would mortgage everything to pay up.

"So, what will you do?" the father asked the State Department official.

"Everything we can," was the reply.

"What does that mean?" he asked again anxiously. "Adam is an American citizen. We are not rich folks but believe in our government and pay our taxes every year. So I want to know what you are doing about this."

"Everything we can," repeated the cold official, now irritated by the question. "You need to be patient. Don't call us. We'll call you."

The family wanted to trust the government but didn't want to just sit around waiting for the phone to ring. Also, the press reported that some foreigners had already been kidnapped earlier. And there was still no news about them.

The official hung up on Mr. Smith without another word.

The Smith family decided that they had some options of their own. They were living near Detroit and the Detroit area had one of the largest Middle Eastern populations in the U.S. Before World War II, many came to work in the auto industry. And more followed.

The family's immediate instinct was to turn to friends. And the Smith family had a number of Lebanese friends. It seemed everyone from their neighborhood was from Lebanon. They didn't know their politics, and didn't care. They were all friends. They grew up with the Danny Thomas television series and enjoyed watching the reruns together.

Danny Thomas was an American-born Lebanese actor. His parents were Maronite Christian immigrants from the Middle East. He started out in stand-up comedy and radio, then made it big on U.S. television. He had his own show and partnered with other television giants at the time such as Lucille Ball, Desi Arnaz and Dick Van Dyke.

Their son, Adam, attended school and played with Middle Eastern kids in the neighborhood. The children had innocent, trusting friendships. Nobody thought of asking their friends about religion. It didn't even occur to them. And the Smith family always welcomed the Easter and Christmas gift of the honey-sweetened pastry known as *baklava* that the families of Adam's friends sent them. In return, the Smiths sent traditional Christmas fruitcake, that dry, tasteless, horrible tooth-breaking pastry that was more of a rock than a sweet, but it was graciously accepted.

Baklava was a few layers of paper-thin pastry sheets with chopped nuts in between. Pistachios, walnuts. Sometimes almonds and hazelnuts.

Sometimes all of them were stuffed between the thin sheets of pastry. It was held together by thick honey and was often the finale to dinner in the Middle East, along with a thimble of thick, rich, almost granular black coffee.

The Ottoman Turks claimed credit for it, but the rest of the Middle East quickly adopted it and developed its own regional varieties.

So the Smiths immediately called a friend who owned a Lebanese restaurant in Detroit.

"Joseph?" Mr. Smith asked of the voice at the other end of the phone.

"Mr. Smith," Joseph replied, recognizing him. "I haven't seen you in a long time. Maybe you don't like our food anymore. Or maybe it's the prices. But we have to push them up to pay the rent. Sorry to say it."

"No, Joseph," Mr. Smith answered. "It's nothing like that. I just got a call from some U.S. government guy who said that Adam's been kidnapped by Muslim terrorists in Lebanon. I don't know what to do. And I don't know what they're going to do."

"I'm so sorry to hear that," Joseph replied. "Lebanon is a dangerous place. But let me tell you this. There is no such thing as a Muslim terrorist. There are terrorists who are Muslim, Christian, Jewish, Japanese, Spanish, German and on and on. Even American. That's what happens when you don't spank your children.

"I'm a Christian, so I have no reason to defend them, but in my soul, I am first Lebanese. What made Lebanon great was that it accepted everybody and everybody accepted everybody else. That was the idea of Lebanon. It was home to everybody and everybody respected each other. Then the big powers came in and turned it into a battlefield.

"I apologize, Joseph," Mr. Smith interjected.

"No need to apologize," Joseph replied. "We are old friends. We grew up together. We watched Danny Thomas together. Your family is my family.

"Let me see what I can do. I will call a friend who will call a friend who will call a friend and on and on. You know how it is.

"Meanwhile, I will send you some *baklava.*"

That friend of a friend of a friend knew Eric Ketch from his days in Hong Kong when he hung out at Byblos, a Lebanese restaurant along Lockhart Road in the Wanchai, "Suzie Wong" girlie bar district.

The friend only knew Ketch as a journalist, not an undercover operative. However, everyone seemed to assume that journalists were powerful people who could investigate things and help those in need.

Byblos was a favorite of his because it was on the main bar strip and the owners always gave him a front-row seat on the sidewalk.

He drank beer and ate thinly sliced lamb *shawarma* right off the vertical grilling spit with pita bread and olive oil while watching the street action and sympathetically listening to stories of "the Lebanon" from the owners.

Ketch never knew why they called it "the" Lebanon. Maybe like Americans call their western mountain range, "the Rockies."

The Lebanese owners of Byblos explained that it came from the French.

In long ago history, the French used to call all the Mediterranean geography east of Italy *le Levant,* which meant something like "the lands where the sun rises," depending on who you asked.

And in modern French it was, *le Liban,* still with "the" as a prefix.

They also noted that, in French, Beirut was called *Beyrouth* and many restaurants used that name to give them some cachet.

The Byblos owners were more down to earth and did not use the name *Beyrouth,* because they felt nobody would understand it.

One of them even noted that *Beyrouth* sounded more like a German epic poem than a city in the Middle East.

He had never been there, but to Ketch, it was just Lebanon.

Lebanon had been the home of a Phoenician maritime empire that flourished for over a thousand years.

The Phoenicians were distinguished sailors in the Mediterranean. They dominated trade between the eastern Mediterranean, the North African coast and Ancient Greece and Rome.

They had established trading colonies in Carthage, Tunisia and Cadiz, Spain. Culturally, they gave the West the concept of an alphabet, though the Latin alphabet looked very different from the Phoenician one.

But they remained one of those mysteries of history. No one knew where they came from or how they reached such heights of power.

A key strategic city was Carthage.

Carthage was along the coast of modern Tunisia and a choke point between North Africa and Sicily for trade between the eastern and western Mediterranean. And the Phoenicians already had a powerful, well-trained navy to control the narrow straits.

Interestingly, one of the most important goods traded between the Phoenicians and Western Europe was the purple dye they produced from shellfish, which the Roman elite classes used to tint their clothes.

As unlikely as it seems that wars would be fought over purple dye, it was not too different from trading empires that were built on pepper, soft drinks or hamburgers many years later.

Bottom line, the consumer rules.

In more modern times, Lebanon fell under the Ottoman Empire, which controlled much of the Middle East and North Africa.

However, the Ottomans made a bad strategic choice during World War I and allied themselves with the Central Powers, led by Germany and Austria-Hungary.

According to the history books, Austria-Hungary was trying to dominate a neighboring country, Serbia, but the Serbs, who had an alliance with Russia, resisted.

When a Serbian extremist shot the visiting Archduke Ferdinand of Austria-Hungary, the Astro-Hungarian Empire used it as an excuse to invade.

Germany stepped in to back its alliance with Austria-Hungary and Russia stepped in to back its alliance with Serbia.

Then France and Britain stepped in to support their alliance with Russia and before long, you had great nations fighting each other from stinking, squalid trenches in Belgium and France.

Historians dubbed it the Great War.

But there was nothing great about it.

There was also nothing practical about it in terms of money, territory or resources. It was a war of pompous, arrogant, egotistical, European aristocracy at its best and failed diplomacy at its worst.

The Central Powers were defeated and the Ottoman Empire paid a high price for its alliance with them.

It was dismembered.

The League of Nations was established, presumably as a neutral body that would adjudicate the post-war order and arbitrate conflicts around the world.

They proclaimed the lands of Lebanon and Syria as the French Mandate and the lands of Palestine as the British Mandate.

Initially, Lebanon did well under the French.

For many years, Beirut was known as the "Paris of the Middle East" and Lebanon as the "Switzerland of the Middle East." Its multi-ethnic, multi-lingual population, speaking English, French and Arabic, created a dynamic diversity that promoted banking, trade, tourism, and culture.

In the 1920s, the French formed the Lebanese Republic with a democratic government under a parliamentary system, although the French did not give up their mandate in doing so. They did not give up the mandate until after World War II under international pressure.

The system was called "confessionalism." Allegedly, it allowed all sects to be involved in the government and appeared to be very democratic. However, the so-called democratic parliamentary system the French set up was not very democratic at all. Under the system, the president was required to be a Maronite Christian, the speaker of the parliament a Shiite Muslim and the prime minister a Sunni Muslim.

At first glance, that seemed fair, but when you really looked into it, you realized the Maronite Christians held all the cards.

In 1948, the Lebanese government made its own strategic error. It supported its Arab neighbors in their war against Israel, although Lebanon did not invade.

And after the conflict, Lebanon and Jordan accepted a flood of Palestinian refugees. Mostly Jordan. The Jordanian monarchy not only supported their presence, but also their use of Jordan as a base to attack Israel.

However, over the years, the Palestinians in Jordan became a state within a state and started to challenge the monarchy that had supported them there.

This led to civil war.

The monarch appealed to the British for assistance. The king and his father had a long relationship with the British. However, the British abandoned them, despite the fact that Palestinian terrorists had been bombing targets in London.

The Brits decided that they wanted to be on what they perceived to be the winning side. The Palestinians. And British public relations agents sought to disassociate the Palestinians from the London bombings, claiming they were done by rogue factions.

To paraphrase one of Britain's leading statesmen, "Britain has no long-term friends or enemies. Only long-term interests."

That summed up British morality and foreign policy for decades to come.

However, the Jordanian monarchy prevailed and the Palestinians retreated into Lebanon.

In Lebanon, they were able to establish themselves as another state within a state, forming a formidable political and military power base there.

That should have been a warning to the Lebanese.

But, like all national tragedies, nobody saw it coming. Those who did, didn't know how to act, or their governments wouldn't listen to them, or it was too much trouble to act and they just wanted to protect their offices through the next election.

It turned into war.

In 1975, full-scale civil war erupted in Lebanon, as all sides jockeyed for control of the country. Christians, Muslims, Palestinians and others all fought each other and fought among themselves. Ironically, Syria initially entered the war to support the Palestinians, but later switched sides and joined the Christian militias.

It was total war. There were many civilian casualties. Probably more than military ones.

Snipers took pleasure in cutting down unarmed pedestrians just crossing the street coming back from the market. All sides showed that they had no morality, and whatever religious or political ideology they claimed to be fighting for, they only proved that they were heartless, sadistic gangsters without scruples.

The civil war dragged on for many years, but all parties acted like the state of chaos they had come to know was something of a state of peace.

Although all sides battled each other, they seemed to accept their places on the game board and killed each other's soldiers and civilians within a framework of twisted, sadistic rules that everyone got used to.

However, in the 1980s, the Palestinians in Lebanon saw the chaos as an opportunity to assert their power even more and make a bid for the country.

Unlike what was reported in the press, the Palestinians were not a coherent cultural or political unit with clear objectives. The Palestinian Liberation Organization, the PLO, under Yasser Arafat, claimed that it was the spokesman and political entity that represented all Palestinians. But it was not.

The PLO was a confederation of various Palestinian organizations, initially organized by the Arab League. Arafat's *Fatah* organization, which meant "Victory," was the largest group within the PLO and he ultimately got elected chairman.

However, there were various rivalries among the groups and some acted independently of the confederation. Arafat positioned himself for or against them based on their policies and when he saw it to his personal advantage to claim or deny credit for their deeds. It was not just tribal or sectarian politics, but PR on the world stage.

Sadly, the Palestinians had been betrayed by Arab politics as much as European politics and were wandering refugees in the Middle East.

Their Arab supporters cheered them on and funded their budgets, but didn't want any more participation than that. In fact, they probably only funded them out of fear that they might launch the same terrorist activity in their own countries that they were doing in others. It was blackmail money. And it was just easier to write a check to make them go away than to get involved.

The Palestinians wanted a home. And they were justified.

They held the moral imperative.

However, their leaders wouldn't settle for any home. They wanted their old home back, Palestine, which was now Israel. So all peace talks offering them lands here, there or elsewhere, were not satisfactory. They wanted Palestine. And that meant dissolving the state of Israel.

They hoped that their terrorist attacks on Israel would create sufficient fear and instability to drive the Jews back to where they came from.

However, the Israelis made it clear they were there to stay and would respond to any violence with massive retaliation.

Meanwhile, as the Palestinians increased their influence in Lebanon, the Beirut government felt increasingly threatened. Lebanese leaders had also become cynical about the Palestinian cause. The Palestinian people were living in squalid refugee camps while their leaders were living in luxury villas and enjoying the "high life" of Beirut.

Meanwhile, they were dictating to the Lebanese leaders how to run their country with veiled threats of assassinations and bombings.

The Lebanese had enough.

They recalled the unappreciated generosity of Jordan some years earlier and decided to take action, lest the Palestinians take over Lebanon.

So in 1982, the Lebanese president invited the Israelis to come in and push them out.

The Israelis justified the action to their public based on the fact that the PLO was using Lebanon as a cross-border sanctuary to launch attacks on Israel. Particularly Israeli civilians.

It was real. It was credible.

So the Israelis accepted the invitation and seized the opportunity.

In a typical Israeli-style lightning strike, they invaded Lebanon at full throttle and pushed Yasser Arafat and his boys up against the wall.

They could have wiped them out.

However, at that point, the international powers got involved and complicated things. They negotiated that the Palestinians would be evacuated by ships to Tunisia.

Not only that, but ironically, U.S Marines and French troops would provide security for them to the port of Beirut.

It seemed that peace had been restored to Lebanon.

It was the Israelis that kept the peace. But they were continually pressured to pull back by the international powers. They were Jewish and Lebanon was not, so it was considered politically unacceptable for them to be there and they were constantly prodded to go home, despite the fact that many Lebanese wanted them there.

The response of the West was to send in an "independent multinational force" to keep the peace.

It quickly assembled a team of American, French and Italian forces on the ground to achieve that objective.

But nobody defined the rules for "keeping the peace."

Chapter Two

Eric Ketch happened to be on assignment in the Middle East at the time.

Pakistan.

Karachi, Pakistan.

A port on the south coast.

Historically, Pakistan had been part of India. But British politics after World War II changed all that.

Ironically, most of the Indus River, which India was named after, fell into modern day Pakistan as a result.

In the pre-World War II period, a charismatic Hindu religious ascetic named Mohandas Gandhi started campaigning for Indian independence from the British Crown. After the war, he gained considerable momentum.

He was originally trained as a lawyer and spent some time practicing law in South Africa where he witnessed the worst abuses of apartheid, before returning to India.

Although he was Hindu, he preached a secular India, given its significant populations of Muslims, Sikhs, Jains, Christians and other religious groups. He also pushed for equal voting rights for all the castes.

The caste system constituted the social hierarchy that Indians were born into, but could not get out of. It defined their position and role in life. The system originated in India over a thousand years before, but continued to be promoted during Islamic Mughal and British rule as a way of sustaining social order and controlling the population.

At the top were the Brahmins. Priests. Then Kshatriyas. Rulers, government leaders, administrators and soldiers. Then the Vaishyas. Merchants, craftsmen and farmers. Next to the bottom were the Shudras. Laborers. And at the bottom, the Untouchables. Street sweepers, garbage collectors, toilet cleaners and funeral cremators.

It was India's form of apartheid.

But Indians accepted it. And unlike South Africa, the West also accepted it.

It was positioned to the world as a religious tradition and, under their various traditions, Indians embraced the concept of "duty." That is, accepting your role in life, regardless of what role you were born into, and making the most of it.

The West, especially the U.S., was under the spell of India. Its ancient pedigree, its spiritual literature and Gandhi's non-violent tactics captured Western imaginations. Many Indians were vegetarians, and Indians let cows freely roam the streets because they considered them sacred. Some Indian religious sects wore masks over their mouths to prevent them from accidentally inhaling insects. In the eyes of the West, India was a sacred, spiritual country that respected life. Something that offered hope for humanity.

But the reality was very different.

Despite all its natural resources, literacy, education and technology, India was controlled by powerful elites that used religion and the caste system to keep themselves in power and exploit the poor.

A nineteenth century American writer visiting India for the first time once commented, "All life is sacred in India except human life."

The elite bullied the castes below them and used violence whenever necessary to achieve their ends.

Then came Partition.

Despite Gandhi's vision for a secular nation, the Muslims were cynical about it and didn't believe they would ever be fairly represented.

They rallied behind Muhammad Ali Jinnah, a lawyer turned politician who founded the Muslim League and preached a separate country for Indian Muslims.

He proposed that the western and eastern provinces of India, which were predominantly Muslim, become their own states respectively called East and West Pakistan.

"Pakistan" meant "Land of the Pure."

The British mediated the situation and received great international praise for providing a seemingly peaceful solution to an intense sectarian political issue.

But the situation on the ground was very different.

Muslims and Hindus entered into a bloody rampage of ethnic cleansing.

So much for spiritual India.

Muslims traveling to Pakistan were butchered on westbound trains, while Hindus were slaughtered on eastbound trains traveling to India.

The British made the genocide easier for both sides.

During their rule, known as the *Raj,* they instituted ID cards for everyone. The ID card indicated your caste and religion.

The implications were tragic.

Anybody could be stopped along the road and asked to present their ID. If they weren't on the same team as the checkpoint boys, they were brutally murdered, often just with clubs or knives. The women were typically raped before being killed.

After the bloody Partition was completed, both sides became rivals for power in the region.

Despite extreme poverty in both countries, they managed to find enough money to develop missile programs that they enjoyed taunting each other with.

National pride has no morals.

And they continued to squabble over a northwestern province known as Kashmir. During Partition, the British gave the reigning maharaja there the opportunity to choose sides. But he was a Hindu reigning over a Muslim majority, and hesitated. At that point, Pakistan sent in militias to help convince him. But it backfired. Instead, he appealed to the British, who then assigned Kashmir to India.

Pakistan claimed that Kashmir should be part of Pakistan, because the majority of the population was Muslim. India claimed that was irrelevant because India was a secular state.

More than thirty years later, they were still squabbling over it and the province remained divided. Later, China and India clashed forces over a northern piece of it and China won. So Kashmir ended up in three pieces managed by Pakistan, India and China.

In the meantime, East Pakistan got caught up in its own bloodshed. Although technically part of West Pakistan under the Partition agreement, the Bengalis of Bangladesh never felt that they were truly represented in the government or got their fair share of national resources. They also spoke Bengali and not the Urdu of

West Pakistan. In the history of conflict, language often divides.

So they sought independence.

Depending on the source, hundreds of thousands to millions were killed in the conflict.

Ironically, although the Bengalis were predominantly Muslims, their primary support came from Hindu India, which was instrumental in helping them defeat their Muslim brothers from West Pakistan.

Unfortunately, independence did not bring stability. Poor governance, coups, floods and famines continued to bring tragedy to the new nation.

What remained of Pakistan, was West Pakistan. Unfortunately, it see-sawed between elected governments and martial law. It also later defined itself as an Islamic Republic which sent a message locally as well as regionally. In the meantime, corruption was rife and the gap between mega rich and mega poor widened. And outside influences started to become more involved in the country.

Chapter Three

Ketch was bored beyond belief.

There was not much to do in Karachi. Maybe that's why they posted him there. His favorite pastime was to go down to the harbor and hire a dhow, the lateen-rigged sailboat that was the workhorse of Arab fishermen and traders.

He'd cruise out into the bay with a small crew of three and fish for crabs. The crew would steam them up on board and he'd wash them down with cold beers. It never made for a better day.

He'd be bobbing along eating crab and downing beers while freighters with imposing names like *Male Climax Guardian* steamed through. Ketch wished he got a picture of that one, but photos were not allowed in the harbor and the slightest move towards his camera got him swamped by the crew with hands and shouts of "Forbidden!"

Although the Indo-Pakistani tension over Kashmir and Bangladesh happened many years earlier, both sides were still super-paranoid. Anyone taking pictures in the harbor was considered to be taking pictures for Indian military intelligence. In reality, if the Indians wanted such pictures, they could just ask one of their allies to give them satellite photos.

But that was the paranoia of Pakistan.

Aside from crab fishing, Ketch made a point of jogging around town, not just to keep up his stamina but also to get to know the streets and the neighborhoods. He did this twice a day. Once in the early morning when the shops were closed and the streets deserted. Again in the late afternoon.

The morning jog, when all the shops were closed with their shutters down, forced him to make a map in his mind of the area with no obvious landmarks for reference. The late afternoon jog allowed him to get to know the neighbors and the shopkeepers.

He always made a point of stopping to buy some small staple at shops where the managers spoke English.

Almonds, dates, figs, cinnamon. Something he could use as a topping for his breakfast.

They were all piled into bottomless sacks that decorated the sidewalk with their color and scent.

"Where did you learn English?" he asked one of the shopkeepers.

The usual reply from the old men was "British army."

"What is your native language?" Ketch would ask out of curiosity.

"There are so many native languages in this country, no one can say," one store manager explained.

"But Urdu is the national language. British India made it the official language of Muslims so we could all take commands in their army. Many of the troops from India were Muslims," he explained.

"We fought all over the world for the British," he continued. "World War I, World War II, Hong Kong, Singapore, Burma. Go to the cemeteries there. Many of the names are Muslim ones."

Once, during a jog, Ketch was stopped by a shopkeeper at an incense shop.

"Hey, American," the manager shouted at him. "You always run past my shop but never stop to look."

"No need to buy, just look."

"Why do you think I'm American?" Ketch asked.

"Everybody knows you here as the American runner," the manager replied. "Everybody knows everybody who comes into the market. And you come everyday from the American office building in the city."

Ketch stopped and went inside.

The air in the shop was overwhelmingly aromatic with unique, sweet-scented smells burning in the background. Smells that Ketch could not identify but that excited his senses.

However, there was one scent that reminded him of his childhood.

"What is that?" He pointed at the burning fragrance.

"That is frankincense," the shopkeeper noted. "You must be Christian."

"Why would you say that?"

"Because that is the incense Christian priests burn when they enter the church. In the Roman Catholic Church they burn it only during special occasions, but in the Eastern Orthodox Church they burn it at every service.

"It comes from an ugly tree or bush grown in the Arabian Peninsula. I don't know whether it is a tree or a bush. I've only seen pictures of it and it is ugly. It is interesting how something so ugly can produce something so beautiful.

"You have heard of the Silk Road from China. Well, there was also an Incense Road from Oman through Yemen and Saudi Arabia to Egypt, then elsewhere in the Middle East. These incense also comes from Somalia and Ethiopia.

"This incense is supposed to purify the air and produce a calming effect. The churches made the Arab traders rich from it. At first, nobody but the churches bought it. Now everyone buys it to purify their homes."

"How do you know so much about what incense the churches buy?"

"I am an incense merchant. My father and his father and his father and his father going back hundreds of years were incense merchants," he answered. "We know our business."

Ketch had no interest in buying incense but was taken in by the merchant's friendliness and candor.

"Ok. Let me buy some frankincense," Ketch answered. "But not too much."

"No problem," the merchant replied. "But you must also buy something to burn it in. I will give you the cheapest one. Two dollars American.

"But you don't burn it directly," he explained. "You heat it from underneath with white-hot charcoal.

"Some people eat it, but I don't recommend," he added. "If you want to try, first crush it into a powder, then mix it with wine."

"Ok," Ketch agreed.

"Are you Christian?" the merchant asked, as he wrapped up the nuggets of frankincense in a piece of newspaper with Arabic script all over it.

"Catholic," Ketch replied.

"Well, then you cannot leave without buying the incense of Jesus."

"What's that?"

"Myrrh," the merchant replied. "When the Three Wise Men came upon the baby Jesus in the manger, they offered gifts of gold, frankincense and myrrh. I can't sell you gold, but I have myrrh."

"Ok. How much is the myrrh?

"I will only give you a small amount. Only one dollar American," the merchant replied. "It is very strong and very oily. I urge you not to put it in your clothes or suitcase. They will smell of myrrh for years.

"It also comes from the Arab lands. According to the Bible, Jesus was offered myrrh and wine before his dying on the cross. It is supposed to relieve pain. But he refused it. The Bible said that the people mocked him by satisfying his thirst with vinegar. But the Bible writers only said that to make his suffering more tragic. I know they offered him myrrh mixed with wine to be merciful, but it was cheap wine, so the Bible writers claimed it was vinegar.

"Myrrh mixed with frankincense is supposed to make you high."

"Maybe that's why people went to church," Ketch laughed.

"Burn a little to see if you like it. In fact, you don't even need to burn myrrh. It is that strong," the merchant added.

"So, what made these incenses so popular?" Ketch asked.

"The Bible stories," he explained. "But before, only the churches were buying them. People were afraid to because they believed them sacred. And they didn't want to offend the churches.

"But now everyone is more relaxed about it and using them as what you might call air fresheners. But incense is more healthy and cheaper than what you buy in a can."

Chapter Four

Ketch told one of the guys at the consulate who was attached to State about his run each morning and suggested that he come along some time.

His name was Ed.

Ed was a junior official just out of Foreign Service school. Typically, State posted its new young officers to the shitholes of the world to test their mettle and commitment. It was a form of hazing, just like initiation to a college fraternity.

Ed really had no choice but to accept the Karachi assignment and hope the sacrifice would get him a posting with a better lifestyle on his next rotation. Each rotation was only two years. He looked at it like a prison sentence. He had no interest in the country, the people or the region and was very demeaning about all of it. It was most noticeable when he referred to the Pakistanis at the "Paks" or the "Pakis."

Ed graduated from a prestigious U.S. university with a degree in history. He passed the Foreign Service exam, both written and oral, with minimum scores. But he passed.

The exam had nothing to do with your international experience, only your knowledge of history and your ability to test well. In fact, when Ed took the exam, he had never previously traveled outside the U.S. so he wasn't a foreign affairs expert by any stretch of the imagination.

Ketch also assumed he was a member of his university's secret society known as Quill & Blood.

Allegedly, the society tapped the elite of the elite that fed an elite coterie of America's wealthy and powerful. They weren't necessarily the best and the brightest, but were loyal soldiers with family or business connections who were sworn to protect the elite's interests.

The rumor was that they invited you to join when you were taking a pee in the bathroom. Someone would put a hand on your shoulder from behind and announce, "Quill & Blood, in or out."

That was the easy part. Apparently, the initiation process required you to masturbate in front of all the other members.

Small price to pay for referrals to high-powered jobs, offices in politics and the wealth, power and prestige that came with them. Rumor was that American presidents belonged to the society.

Initiates were pledged not to reveal their membership, but the organization's officers allegedly videotaped the initiation proceedings to be used against them if they didn't comply with future demands from the society.

If they accepted you, you then had to prick your finger with a quill pen and sign a statement of loyalty in your own blood. They called each other "Quillons." Interestingly, a quillon was the name given to the cross guard of a sword.

Ketch once asked Ed outright if he was a member.

"I can't say," Ed replied.

In Ketch's mind, that confirmed it.

"So what are you going to do if they go public with the initiation videotape of you wanking off, because you didn't want to do something they asked?" Ketch taunted.

"If that was truly part of the initiation, as you suggest, and if they went public with it, they would damage the reputations of all its members which would include corporate CEOs and some American presidents.

"As I said, I can't say," Ed said speciously, "So if that was part of the initiation, videotaping it would not be in anyone's interests."

Ketch chuckled to himself.

All these schoolboy organizations had some stupid initiation that shamed candidates into camaraderie and loyalty.

Ketch learned camaraderie in the Special Forces. They taught you camaraderie by pushing you to do your best, beyond your best, working with your team, performing under fire and taking care of your fellow soldiers. Not stupid schoolboy pranks.

Wanker, Ketch thought every time he saw Ed. It was a great British word. It didn't just mean someone who jerks off all the time, because he couldn't get a lady. It meant a pathetic, limp-dick idiot who couldn't get his act together or make anything happen but tried to impress everyone with his over-educated, intellectual pronouncements. He was a talker, not a doer and always covered his butt. A quintessential passive-aggressive bureaucrat or over-educated intellectual with no real world experience.

The American English translation might be *twit* or *dork*. But where Ketch grew up in New Jersey, the guy would be called a *douche-bag* or *douche* for short. However, none of them carried the full flavor and power of the British insult *wanker.*

"So, how did you make it into State?" he once asked Ed. "What was the toughest part?"

"The oral exam," Ed replied. "They really pushed you to answer hard questions on the spot."

This reaffirmed to Ketch that the guy was a *wanker*. Hard questions did not impress him. As part of Ketch's Special Forces initiation, he was thrown off a boat in full combat gear and told to swim three miles back to shore. Then the boat sped off. Nobody would be there to rescue him.

If he didn't make it, then he didn't make Special Forces.

In fact, during the Normandy landings of World War II, there were concerns about dropping troops in only six feet of water out of fear that they would drown because of their heavy combat packs.

The drill instructors also didn't tell him the rules and whether he was allowed to dump his combat pack or boots and strip down to his shorts for a lighter swim back to shore. That mental exercise and the decision choices were part of the drill.

Ketch knew he couldn't make it in full combat kit without drowning, but didn't want to fail.

He relaxed, controlled his breathing, took a moment and decided what he really needed.

He peeled off his clothes except for his shorts and T-shirt. He threw away everything from his combat pack except the water bottles, first aid kit and rifle. He was trained never to give up his weapon.

Also, he also didn't know what to expect on shore. Would it be a bunch of guys greeting him with beers, or rifle fire? Never assume.

He took off his boots and socks because swimming with his boots on would just hold him back and his socks would get water-logged and do the same.

But he didn't toss them away, knowing he needed them later. He knew how much he would cut up his bare feet getting through the surf if he made it to shore.

After he emptied the pack, he waved it over his head, inflating it with air, then tightened all the fasteners to make it into a float. He put his boots, socks and first aide kit inside. He attached the water bottles to the outside and put his rifle on top then slowly paddled his way toward shore at a relaxed pace.

Ketch heard stories of the brutal training that the Russian Special Forces, *Spetsnaz,* went through.

They were beaten up regularly by their instructors and all drills were under live fire.

According to one story, a *Spetsnaz* candidate got tangled up rappelling down a cliff. It looked like he couldn't work his way out of it and would fall several hundred feet to his death.

One of the other candidates, frightened for his comrade, badgered the training instructor, "We need to help him. He is trapped and will fall and die."

"If he dies," the training officer coolly replied, "then he is not *Spetsnaz.*"

He fell and died.

"So what was the hardest part of the oral exam?" Ketch asked again. "Giving the guy a blow job?"

"Funny," Ed responded. "There were two hard parts. One based on history, the other based on situational analysis.

"The history part was easy. Name any three-year period in American history and explain why it was significant from a foreign policy standpoint," Ed indicated.

"So how did you answer?" Ketch asked.

"Well, I threw them off a bit, which got them irritated," Ed offered. "They expected me to talk about

World War I, World War II, the Korean War or Vietnam.

"Instead, I talked about the American Revolutionary War and the French support for our cause. It was my undergrad thesis so I had most of the facts in my head.

"Of course, the French were only supporting us at the time because they were feuding with the Brits in their colonies all over the world. So it was a totally *realpolitik* scenario. The examiners didn't get the idea of *realpolitik* and seemed to suggest I was not diplomatic material.

"When I mentioned Henry Kissinger and the concept, they responded that he was only a political appointee and not career State."

"I'm surprised they didn't fail you for calling it the American Revolutionary War," Ketch commented. "I'm no history expert, but I thought it was called the American War of Independence since there was no revolution."

"Point taken," Ed sneered.

"At the end of the day, the examiners seemed to be looking for people who could smooth-talk any argument and make all parties feel good about it, even if it was a bunch of fluff.

"A friend who took the test before me noted that all our foreign diplomatic counterparts were considered clients and just wanted to feel good about us telling them how to run their countries in America's best interests. Just like selling any product to a client.

"The way to get ahead with those clients and within the organization was to be somebody that makes everyone feel good about what your bosses want to do. Right or wrong. Just like any corporation.

"Anyway, the examiners had no idea what I was talking about. I made up a lot of stuff along the way.

"I assume they passed me based on my logical argument. I think that was what the test was really all about.

"That and presentation skills," he added cynically. "Showing confidence in your presentation, whether you were bullshitting or not, was key."

"And what about the situation analysis," Ketch asked. "What was that all about."

"Oh, they put you in a potential real life scenario and asked how you'd respond," Ed added.

"So, what was your scenario?" Ketch continued.

"I'm the duty office in the embassy of country XYZ. Some local national comes in, waving a pistol and demands to see the ambassador. The guy's in the main reception area where people are applying for visas and renewing passports. There are 30 people in the room and the goal is to bring this to a peaceful resolution and minimize loss of life. What should I do?" they asked.

"Well, in the first place, I'd ask how some guy off the street got through embassy security with a gun," Ketch responded.

"Yeah. But the fact of the matter is that he did and you're not allowed to ask questions about the scenario, but only describe how you'd respond to it," Ed answered.

"Well, I'll tell you how I'd respond," Ketch replied. "I'd instruct the Marine guards to blow that mother fucker's head off. If I was armed, I'd take him down myself."

"Well, that's what makes you an operator and not a diplomat," Ed continued. "My response was that I'd calm the guy down and stall him for time while we got any potential hostages out of the area to minimize loss of life. We'd talk about his anger, his family and maybe give him an understanding hug."

"Yeah, well my solution drops one wacked out bad guy and keeps 30 innocents alive and it's over in a few seconds," Ketch replied. "Your method strings along some maniac who could go ballistic at any second. And in the meantime, everyone is traumatized by the drama of it. The local police show up, then the media show up. Then you get command conflicts between the police and the embassy guards. Nobody wants to make a decision because nobody wants to take responsibility for it. Then media drama and all the rest. The bad guy is lovin' it cause he gets all this free media time and spouts off about whatever he wants. He ultimately surrenders to the local police for illegal possession of a firearm and gets certified as mentally ill, spends a week in jail, then walks away on a suspended sentence. And shoots somebody else two weeks later."

"Maybe," Ed responded, "But they liked my answer and I got the job."

Ed did not want to join Ketch for an early morning jog or an afternoon jog. Ed was not into jogging, but he was interested in Ketch's scan of the neighborhood and a sightseeing trip around town. Although he had been posted in Karachi for almost two years, he had never walked the streets.

On a typical day, a security-cleared driver picked him up at his apartment, took him to the consulate, then back home again.

When there was an evening event, it was typically at one of the few five-star hotels where State employees were allowed to mingle with a select list of locals. Again, an approved driver picked him up and took him home.

He was given a car but it got him into trouble.

"You've never walked around town before?" Ketch asked in amazement.

"No. We are instructed to avoid contact with the Pakis," he sneered.

"So how do you know what is going on?"

"We get reports."

"From where?"

"Reliable sources."

"Have you met these sources?"

"No."

"So how do you know they are reliable?"

"Various agencies tell us they are."

Ketch shut up.

They walked around town, then stumbled into a filthy market where freshly cut meat was hung out for the flies.

"So why are you allowed out now for sightseeing?" Ketch asked.

"One of the agencies approved it and said that you'd be responsible for my security."

"What?" Ketch exclaimed, "Nobody told me that. I invited you out as a friend. I don't even have a gun."

"Sorry," Ed smirked. "But anything that happens to me is now officially your responsibility."

Ketch's instinct was to immediately make something happen to him. At least a bloody nose.

"Sorry, but I was pointing out one of the sights and his face got in the way," Ketch would explain.

They continued to walk down the alleys. All the streets were muddy, dirty and smelled of urine and feces. When the wind blew dust up from the streets, Ketch instinctively turned his head in the other direction and covered his eyes.

He didn't want flecks of cow shit, horse shit, dog shit, human shit or whatever kind of shit from the streets getting into his face.

Ed didn't take any notice.

In the middle of one alley, someone had set up a block of ice in a metal washtub and was pouring milk over it for sale by the cup. Everyone drank from the same cup.

"Thirsty?" Ed asked.

"Yeah, but for a cold beer," Ketch returned. "Better to get it back at my hotel."

As they walked around the market, speakers suddenly started blasting some sing-song message in a local language. Ketch guessed it was Urdu and a call to the Muslims' midday prayer.

"What are they saying?" Ketch asked Ed.

"I have no idea."

"They could be calling on everyone to kill all the foreigners right now, and you wouldn't know it."

"I thought you were here for a two-year assignment," Ketch noted. "Didn't they give you any local language skills?"

"My training language was French," Ed explained. "When I joined the service, they gave me a choice of French, Spanish, Chinese or Russian.

"I chose French so at least I could impress women in French restaurants. You need to be careful about becoming a country expert, otherwise you could get stuck in the country of your nightmares.

"I thought the worst I could do with French was get posted to some shithole in Africa. However, Africa has always been a fascination for me, so I went with French.

"Even if they sent me to the shittiest of the shitholes there for two years, I could use it as a base to explore the continent."

"You know," Ketch responded, "I try to take a two-week immersion course in the language of my next op, if possible. At least I can order a beer and tell the taxi drivers how to get me back to the hotel."

"That's the difference. You're an operator, but I am a diplomat," Ed explained. "You are thinking short-term, while I am thinking long-term."

"So did you study a few phrases of Urdu?" Ed asked.

"No. They told me I'd only be here a week. I went through an Arabic language course. But it was the wrong course. First, they don't speak Arabic here.

"Second, I learned that Arabic has as many dialectical differences as Chinese and they put me through the one for Moroccan Arabic. So nobody understands me anywhere else. Except *habib* or *habibi* which means 'friend,' I think.

"The most interesting thing I got out of it was learning how to read and write the Arabic alphabet. Right to left. Unfortunately, outside the textbooks, nobody puts the vowel markers over the script, so you're always second-guessing what everything means and can't find the words in a dictionary."

"Welcome to the Middle East," Ed snickered. "Second-guessing what everything means. Sounds about right."

As they walked back to the consulate, they passed the incense shop where Ketch had bought frankincense and myrrh.

"Hey, my friend," the shopkeeper called out. "Did you try my incense?"

Ketch walked into the shop with Ed and engaged the shopkeeper.

"I tried the frankincense but not the myrrh. You scared me about that one. I can smell it, even in the plastic bag you gave me."

The shopkeeper suddenly turned his eyes to Ed. The look was very serious.

"Is this your friend?" he asked.

"I don't know," Ketch answered tactically, noting the look. "I just met him on the street, and I am walking him back to his office."

"He is not a good man," the shopkeeper advised.

"Last month, he was drunk in his car," the shopkeeper explained. "He hit another car but refuses to pay the damages. He claims he is an ambassador, so he doesn't have to pay anything."

"Is that right?" Ketch asked, turning to Ed.

"Listen, you don't need to know and best you just get me back to my office."

Chapter Five

Ketch then decided he didn't want to make friends with Ed or anyone else at the Karachi consulate.

He also decided he didn't want to be there anymore. He spent his time reading reports filed by all kinds of people on all kinds of affairs but nothing related to his assignment to find poppies in Pakistan. It was a big waste of time.

So Ketch decided to do some sightseeing.

Officially, he wasn't cleared for travel, so he couldn't go out and investigate beyond the city limits of Karachi or the crab-fishing area of the dhows in Karachi harbor.

But Ketch, being Ketch, decided to take matters into his own hands.

He didn't see himself on any kind of investigation, just a sightseeing trip to northern Pakistan and the famous Khyber Pass.

The Khyber Pass was a rough road from Pakistan into Afghanistan through the Spin Ghar Mountains. It was an important trade route between Central Asia and South Asia. It was also a strategic route. Over the centuries, armies used it to come and go in both directions.

It was managed by a variety of tribes who controlled the area. Typically Pashtun clans known as the Afridis and Shinwaris.

Like other passes around the world, the tribes levied tolls for safe conduct. Not too different from American states setting up toll booths along their highways.

The Khyber Pass was symbolic of all the conquerors who tried to enter Afghanistan from British India, or into British India, which then included Pakistan, from the opposite direction. Ketch was sure that Rudyard Kipling must have a poem about it, but didn't know.

The last Kipling poem he remembered from boyhood was about Gunga Din. He didn't know whether Gunga Din, pronounced "deen," was a real person or a product of Kipling's imagination.

Nevertheless, he was a symbol of the inequalities of British Rule in India and the arrogance of its officials and soldiers there regarding the natives.

Gunga Din was an Indian local attached to one of the British regiments. He was a *bhishti*, pronounced "beastie."

His job was to carry water to the troops, even in the heat of battle. Despite that vital function, the Brits constantly insulted him, pushed him around and made him feel like he didn't even have the right to carry their water buckets because he was a low-caste Indian.

He was enamored with the idea of joining the British Army as a soldier but was constantly rebuffed.

According to Kipling's poem, Gunga Din was killed in the midst of battle saving a British soldier. It ends with the British soldier regretting his poor treatment of Gunga Din. "You're a better man than me, Gunga Din," he said.

However, Hollywood got caught up in the story, and, of course, changed it to suit their purposes and the drama of the big screen.

The Hollywood film featured Cary Grant and Douglas Fairbanks Jr. They are attached to a British regiment in India during the period and portrayed as adventurers looking out for an opportunity to plunder riches from the country.

Gunga Din, still a water bearer, tells Cary Grant of a golden temple, and offers to take him there.

In the meantime, Gunga Din acquires a bugle and teaches himself some of the regimental calls which Gunga Din hopes will get him a place in the army.

However, the British commanders still scoff at him and don't even allow him to blow his horn at parade events, though he keeps practicing and is as good as any other bugler in the regiment.

Meanwhile, Grant is enticed by the promise of a golden temple. But when Gunga Din leads him there, they find the temple is controlled by the *Thugs,* pronounced *Thugs, Tugs or Toogs* depending on who you ask and what flavor of English they speak

The *Thugs* are a criminal fraternal organization of professional assassins that terrorize India. They kill, then rob their victims, and worship a cult goddess called Kali who forbids them to draw blood. So, they kill their victims by strangling them with silk scarves.

The cult worship deems the killing more important than the robbing and every victim enhances the killer's standing with the goddess.

They refer to their actions as the "Art of Thuggee."

Cary Grant gets captured while investigating the temple but Gunga Din escapes back to the regiment to get help. Unfortunately, Gunga Din only comes back with Douglas Fairbanks Jr. and they are all taken hostage.

Fortunately, Fairbanks told his commanders to bring the full regiment if he doesn't return in a couple of days.

Finally, one morning, they awaken to the sound of the bagpipes of Scottish troops with the full force of a British regiment in tow.

This delights the Thugs, who expected them and already prepared a combined trap of infantry, cavalry and artillery from their mountain stronghold and the British troops are walking right into in it.

Grant and Gunga Din fight their way to the roof of the stronghold, killing several Thugs along the way, but get shot and stabbed in the process.

The British continue marching confidently towards the mountain with its Scottish contingent blowing loudly on their pipes, oblivious to the threat ahead.

Gunga Din spies a bugle on a dead Thug and, despite his wounds, struggles to the top of the spire above him.

There, he sounds his horn, signaling the British regiment with a call that alerts them to the trap.

The regimental commanders are at first confused by the signal, but then take heed. They separate their troops and organize them into attack formations.

Gunga Din keeps blowing his horn until he is shot by the Thugs.

The Brits take over the stronghold, and against all regulations muster Gunga Din's dead body into the army with the rank of corporal, and give him a full soldier's burial complete with uniform.

Cary Grant and Douglas Fairbanks Jr. survive to share in the happy ending.

Chapter Six

Ketch caught a flight to Peshawar, the unofficial capital of the North West Frontier Province and gateway to the Khyber Pass, which led into Afghanistan.

He had the wild idea that he was going to drive across the Khyber Pass, all the way to the Afghan capital of Kabul.

He picked up a rental car from the airport and headed west along a narrow two-lane highway.

At this time, the Soviet-Afghan war was in full swing and Ketch hoped to get a glimpse of it. Several years earlier, the Soviets had replaced the leadership in Kabul with someone loyal to them and their ideology.

But the local tribes rebelled, took to the mountains and waged a guerrilla war on the Russians that took a heavy toll. The press called it Russia's "Vietnam."

The similarities were telling. Low-tech, but highly motivated guerillas with basic weapons fighting a high-tech superpower.

Just before Ketch entered the pass, he noted a huge billboard along the road.

"You are now entering the North West Frontier Province. The Pakistan government assumes no responsibility for your safety."

He continued. The road wound its way through rugged heights and occasionally passed concrete blocks alongside the road and in the valleys. The locals called the blocks "Dragon's Teeth" which were meant to thwart a tank advance through the pass during World War II.

Ketch could easily see how any army marching along this route was vulnerable to the heights. Any defender on the cliffs just needed to roll a few boulders down the hill to thwart the troops marching below.

Ketch made good progress until he got to the Pakistani border town of Torkham.

The frontier guards would not let him pass because he didn't have a visa for Afghanistan.

Kabul, the capitol of Afghanistan, was maybe only two hours down the road and he kicked himself for his oversight. Americans think they don't need visas and can go everywhere. But that was not the case. And given the war footing, he probably wouldn't have gotten one anyway. If he had, he'd probably be taken by the Russians along the road. So, it was probably a blessing in disguise.

Ketch pulled into a truck stop along the border and ordered some lunch. Finely cut goat meat, cheese and pita bread.

He sat at a round table along with the other drivers that plied the route and also ordered a beer. He was surprised that the restaurant had any.

Heineken.

His best friend all over the world, from the best bars to the worst shitholes. Heineken was always there for him.

Although the taste required some getting used to, it was available everywhere, even the most remote locations, and was consistent and trustworthy.

When Ketch first arrived in Karachi, he once pulled a Coke out of a five-star hotel mini-bar only to gag. Fortunately, he reacted quickly and spit it out. It tasted like rusty water. it wasn't "The Real Thing."

According to his colleagues there, it was in fact rusty water. The locals would retrieve the empty bottles from the trash, fill them with rusty water, recap them and sell them back to the hotels at a discount.

Ketch tried switching to cans figuring that they couldn't tamper with the pop-top but had another near-fatal experience. The locals drilled a hole in the bottom, drained out the real stuff, put in more rusty water and soldered up the hole before selling it back to the hotels, restaurants and bars.

There were no forks or knives at the truck stop. The meat and pita bread were in separate dishes. The protocol was to tear off a piece of bread with your hands and use it to scoop up the meal.

The locals claimed that the only way you would really taste the food was if you ate it with your hands.

The beer was cold and that helped. He gulped down one bottle and ordered another. For a moment he relaxed.

But Ketch also noted that the drivers at the table were eyeing him suspiciously.

"What brings you to Torkham?" one prompted.

"Just sightseeing."

"You must be British. Many British come here to live the dreams of the *Raj*," he suggested.

"No. I'm an American. Just curious."

"Ah, just curious. It is dangerous to be curious in this part of the world," he advised. "Do you know why the other men are staring at you?"

"No, tell me."

"They don't trust you because you are taking food with your left hand."

"What's the difference?"

"The difference is that we wipe our bottoms with our left hand, so we only touch food with the right one."

Ketch laughed and noted that he was right-handed, so he wiped his bottom with his right hand and therefore was eating with his left. He stood up and mimicked the action for the others and the driver translated.

They got a big laugh out of that and bought him another bottle of beer.

"I wish you a safe trip home," the English-speaking driver offered. "You shouldn't come back,"

"Why not?"

"This is a tribes area. We all have our customs. You are a foreigner and can never be part of our customs. You must be born to it. You must be blood.

"Even the tribes do not talk with the other tribes unless it is a matter of business. Many foreigners, including the Pakistan government, have been trying to tell us how to live our lives.

"They have all failed.

"Look at this table. We have several tribes here. They are not talking to each other, only eating.

"They will finish their food then go about their business. They don't want to know you and don't want to know each other.

"Look at them. They are watching each other with a hawk's eye, just like they are watching you.

"They liked your joke, so they bought you a beer. But they would easily kill you for the few dollars in your pocket or steal your car if they found you alone along the pass.

"Look at this land. There is nothing. Life is hard. But we have survived here for many hundreds of years.

Not because of the government, but because of our customs.

"Just leave us alone. Play your games of politics somewhere else."

"So why are you so curious about me?" Ketch asked.

"Many years ago, I served in the British Army. They let us go when they were done using us.

"I am old and trying to find some friends from those days. I thought you were British and could help me."

"I'm sorry."

"No need to be sorry," the old man said. "But on your way back, you should visit Darra. It will show you something," he suggested.

Ketch watched various people crossing the borders in either direction.

Typically, women dressed in *burqas,* balanced huge sacks of all their worldly possessions on their heads or struggled under loads strapped to their backs like mules. Meanwhile, the men, carrying nothing, led the way.

The *burqa* was a full-length gown down to the feet with a head covering that also covered the face. There was a small mesh screen in front of the eyes to allow the wearer to see where she was going. But she typically needed to be led by her husband or children.

In that regard, it was more conservative than other Middle Eastern head coverings, because you could not see the woman's eyes.

He asked the driver about it.

"Women commit many sins with their eyes," he replied. "They use their eyes to tempt men and lead them into wrong doing. So they must be covered."

Ketch also noted that they were not stopped by the border guards. He asked the driver about it.

"That's because they are locals," he explained.

"They are tribes people. They belong to one of the tribes in this area and the tribes have no boundaries. They graze their goats and follow the grasses, the wind and the rain. The tribes give them their identities, they take them in and accept them into their family. The tribes will protect them and take responsibility for them.

"Do you think that little book you carry, your American passport, will do the same for you? Will it protect you? Will it give you food and a place to sleep? I don't think so.

"The life of the tribes is better."

The drive back to Peshawar sent up an alarm in Ketch's mind. He didn't know why he hadn't seen them on the drive out. But they were too obvious to be missed.

Poppies.

Fields and fields of them in plain sight along the roadside.

Again. Something was wrong. Very wrong.

He had been sent to Pakistan to find poppies and shut down the production. But here they were presenting themselves for all to see. It was too easy. Something was wrong. Way wrong.

Why was he sent to Pakistan to find poppies everyone already knew about?

He felt that someone was playing him.

Obviously, his bosses. He no longer knew what he was doing there or how it would end.

In his mind, it would end badly.

Chapter Seven

Ketch took the road to Darra, a village in the North West Frontier Province, south of Peshawar. Darra was famous for making guns from nothing.

Blacksmiths would cast a gun barrel from scratch using local steel and a backyard furnace. Then they'd turn it over to young boys, who would bury it in the ground and bore out a barrel with a hand screw.

Darra consisted of one street lined with shops. All the shops sold guns, opium or hashish. The guns were mostly locally made hunting rifles, muskets and imitation AK-47s. The genuine AKs were imported from across the border and bought with hashish or opium. Most of them were sold by Russian soldiers who were completing their deployment and heading back home.

Men with guns and yards of ammunition dangling around their shoulders, bandolier-like, walked the streets.

Ketch popped in and out of a few shops but didn't see what he was looking for.

However, one shop caught his attention.

Gadget guns.

Pens and cameras that fired bullets.

Ketch inspected some of the gadgets in one of the shops and was immediately engaged by the manager.

"Please sit down my friend," he said in perfect English. "Have some tea."

The manager withdrew to the back of the shop and re-emerged with a steaming pot of mint tea and a bowl of brown sugar.

He poured some tea into a filthy cup, swished the hot liquid around, presumably to kill any germs, then spilled it out onto the dirt floor.

He then poured a fresh amount into the still-filthy cup and offered it to Ketch.

The shopkeeper was keen on selling him a camera gun. It looked like a standard 35mm single-lens reflex camera but was in fact a pistol that fired off one .22 caliber round.

Ketch was intrigued, but the workmanship was not very demanding and it would never pass for the real thing, even though "Nikon" was sloppily stenciled across the front of the case.

It was obviously fake, and most importantly, there was no glass in the lens. The lens housing contained a two-inch barrel. You flipped open the back as if you were adding film and slipped in the cartridge. The firing pin was cocked by the film advance lever and the bullet was fired by pressing the shutter button.

Also a .22 caliber round was not likely to do much damage unless you hit the guy right between the eyes. Unlikely with only a two-inch barrel.

A fun toy, but not a serious weapon. You only might kill someone with it, if you got close enough to put the bullet through his forehead. However, at that point, you'd be quickly shot dead by all of his bodyguards.

Caliber referred to the diameter of the bullet. It was mostly an American measure. It meant hundredths of inches, so .22 caliber was .22 inches and .50 caliber would be half an inch.

Gun measures were a mix of measurement standards between the British Imperial system, which was transplanted to the U.S., and the metric system later adopted by Europe and the rest of the world where millimeters became the standard.

It was all very confusing. The Americans held out for the British Imperial standard across many industries, simply because they didn't want to invest in the retooling required to align their products to the metric system.

Meanwhile, the British, who originally provided the Americans with their product standards, were very critical of the U.S. for not joining the metric system. However, British industry itself did not wholly follow suit.

Ketch recalled the car he owned in Hong Kong which had half the parts measured in metric and the other half in British Imperial units.

Similarly, it was not uncommon to find a gun, whose bore diameter was presented in millimeters while the barrel length was measured in inches.

Bottom line, the .22 caliber was a small bullet, typically used in training rifles and pistols.

Ketch recalled that's what his high school rifle club used to poke holes in paper targets.

It had no stopping power but also had little to no recoil which is why it was a good training weapon. However, not much more than a BB gun.

In the early twentieth century, the U.S. military adopted the Colt .45, Model 1911, specifically for its stopping power.

However, the .45 was just a bit too big for many men to handle and the compromise was the 9mm round, which became the European standard. European arms manufacturers and their overseas salesmen quickly made it the world standard, so the round was easily bought everywhere on the planet.

British armament makers were second to none when it came to marketing their products overseas, particularly low-technology items like small arms, grenades, mortars, tear gas, web gear and clothing.

They weren't restricted by their government, like American manufacturers, and were pretty shameless about pushing their products and bribing the right people in governments to get the deal done. On the contrary, Americans were held back by their Foreign Corrupt Practices Act, which severely punished U.S. companies and individuals for similar activity.

While Americans were exporting self-righteousness, the rest of the world was exporting lethal products without qualms about making a lot of money from it.

Bottom line, the 9mm round still produced a big kick. The pistol barrel typically flipped up on discharge, even when the gun was held with two hands. So the shooter needed to re-aim each shot at the target.

"Only fifty dollars American," the manager said with a smile referring to the camera gun.

Ketch ignored the sales pitch and picked up one of the pens.

It was an imitation Mont Blanc writing pen. He immediately knew something was not quite right because of its heavy weight. It also sported "Made in America" English script under Arabic letters that said who knows what.

"How much?" Ketch inquired.

"Only twelve dollars, American," the manager replied.

"Can I give you Pakistan money?" Ketch inquired.

"Only dollars, deutschmarks or pounds sterling," the shopkeeper answered. "But I prefer dollars. If you pay in dollars, I can make a discount and will give you two bullets at no extra charge.

"It would also be better if you gave me small dollars. All one dollars," he added.

"Can I test it first?" Ketch asked.

"Yes, but you must pay first."

Ketch reached into his pants and pulled out his wallet.

"I only have fives," he noted.

"Ok. I make discount. Two fives. Ten dollars."

Ketch handed over the money and the shopkeeper handed over the pen.

He then instructed Ketch in its use.

"It is better if I shoot first so you will know how," he advised.

The shop keeper took back the pen and they went outside to the back of the shop, which consisted of a dirt lot that extended about twenty feet with sand bags piled up at the end against dirt walls.

The shopkeeper twisted off the middle like a normal pen. He put in a .22 caliber bullet and tightened it closed. He then twisted off the front nib which actually had a cut-down ballpoint pen cartridge in it so it could still write to fool anyone suspicious.

The trigger was in the clip. The firing pin was actually the plunger you normally pressed to extend the ink cartridge. However, in this case you pulled back the plunger at the end until it clicked into the clip. Then you held it very, very tightly.

"You must hold on very tight," the shopkeeper warned him. "It is very dangerous."

The shopkeeper shot off a round then handed it back to Ketch.

The metal was still hot from the blast.

Ketch mimicked the process, put the pen in his left hand, then pointed it at the sandbags and was about to press down the clip with his right hand.

"Stop!" the shopkeeper shouted at him urgently. "You must hold it much more tight and close to the back. It is very dangerous."

Ketch pulled his fingers back on the pen further from the front end and held on as tightly as he could. He then pushed down on the pocket clip and fired it. Despite his tight grip, the barrel still slipped back a couple of inches in his grip from the recoil. He could have easily blown off his fingertips if he had held it too close to the end.

Nevertheless, Ketch bought it as a "souvenir." Ten dollars American included two rounds of .22 caliber ammunition.

What he really wanted was a pistol. But Darra didn't seem to have any.

"Pistol no good," the shopkeepers told him. "Short range, short accuracy. No good."

Most of the shops supplied guys going across the border to fight the Russians or men hunting game for the family meal. Ketch just wanted something that would protect him in his hotel room.

He was directed down the road and found a shop that had boxes full of junk. The shopkeeper invited Ketch to sit down.

The shopkeeper offered him strong mint tea and some unidentifiable pastry while Ketch sifted through the boxes. They contained mostly junkyard pistols, unpolished and rusty, as well as some grenades, including German stick grenades from World War II.

The shopkeeper jumped in when Ketch dragged out a Colt .45, Model 1911 pistol.

"U.S. Army," he shouted excitedly. "I will give you special price."

Ketch ignored the sales pitch and kept digging. He was looking for a Browning Hi-Power. One of Ketch's first training weapons.

It was love at first sight. It fit like a glove, was double-action and held 14 rounds. Despite the 9mm recoil, Ketch was comfortable firing it with one hand.

The Browning was originally designed as a single-action pistol, taking a 13-round 9mm magazine. Although 9mm was the world standard for pistol ammo at the time, it came in various lengths and you needed to know what you were buying to make sure it worked in your gun. Although designed by an American, it was primarily manufactured by the Belgium firm Fabrique Nationale, famous for their assault rifles. The rifles were not just distinguished by their long barrels sticking out of the front stock, but also by a wire carrying handle on top.

They were known colloquially among troops as the "FN."

For years, the FN was the standard assault rifle. Most notably during various colonial conflicts in Africa.

They took a twenty round magazine that fired very high velocity cartridges. High school physics taught you that force equals mass times acceleration squared, so even if you had a small mass, you could create tremendous force by making it go faster.

Bottom lime, someone hit with an FN round was essentially dead. Even a badly aimed shot. Any peripheral hit produced hydrostatic shock that caused a fatal wound.

The Browning Hi-Power pistol name came not from a super-charged cartridge, but from the fact that its magazine held 13 cartridges.

For years, it was the standard sidearm of the British SAS and many other military and police professionals throughout the world.

In the 1980s, Fabrique Nationale introduced a Hi-Power double-action version known as Model BDA, which stood for Browning Double Action.

That's what Ketch was looking for in the junk boxes.

Ketch armed himself solely with "double-action" or "dual-action" pistols.

The alternative was a single-action pistol.

Like double-action pistols, single-action pistols required you to chamber a round by pulling back or "racking" the slide.

With a single-action pistol, the user could then drop or "de-cock" the hammer to make the gun safe. But it wouldn't shoot unless the hammer was once again pulled back and cocked. That meant you had to take the extra step of cocking the hammer before you could shoot. The alternative was cocking the hammer in advance and putting on the safety, to prevent the hammer from releasing prematurely.

The position in which the hammer was cocked and the safety engaged was referred to as the "cocked and locked" position also known as "Condition 1."

Ketch never felt comfortable carrying a cocked and locked single-action pistol on his person. Mostly, because he typically didn't wear the gun in a holster. When he carried the gun, it was typically in a jacket or pants pocket or inside his waistband.

Given his international travel, he typically had to sneak the gun through security. The gun could be disassembled into various parts and hidden in all kinds of stuff. The holster could not and would be a dead giveaway. The holster was a "smoking gun," so to speak.

Ketch was always afraid that the safety would snag on something, arm the hammer and he'd shoot himself as he pulled the gun from his pockets. It happened even among highly trained professionals.

A "double-action" pistol allowed you to chamber a round, but then you could drop down or "de-cock" the hammer so the gun wouldn't fire until you pulled the trigger.

The first trigger pull would cock the hammer and fire the round. You didn't need to manually pull back the trigger. Two steps. Hence double-action. However, the much heavier trigger pull on the first round meant it might not be that accurate in the heat of the moment.

Ketch finally found a Browning Hi-Power pistol, but not the one he was looking for. This one was single-action. Also the slide was missing and who knew what else.

"This is what I want," Ketch shouted at the shopkeeper. "You have the rest of it?" he asked.

"We need to look," he replied. "Please have some more tea."

The shopkeeper brought out more boxes, dumped the contents onto the table and employed Ketch in the search.

In addition to tea, he offered Ketch a strong liquor served in a thimble. He poured himself and Ketch a round. The shopkeeper downed his quickly then poured himself another.

It smelled flavorful and sweet like licorice, but potent. Ketch sipped his.

After much digging, they found a slide and the rest of the pieces of the Browning.

"You really want this old gun?" the shopkeeper asked.

"Yes."

"One hundred dollars American."

Ketch produced a one hundred dollar note, which satisfied the shopkeeper.

"Thank you," he said. "But I must tell you. It is not worth it."

"To me it is," Ketch replied.

"Can I take this on my flight back to Karachi?" he asked.

"No problem," the shopkeeper replied. "Just put it in your check-in suitcase."

The shopkeeper then detail-stripped, cleaned and oiled the weapon.

Ketch couldn't believe how quickly the shop manager disassembled the entire gun into every single piece. He not only pulled out main items like triggers but also pushed out pins and springs, safeties, firing pins and blocks. It only took him about twenty minutes. Ketch was even more impressed when he put it all together again in about the same time. When he was done, he invited Ketch to check it out in the back lot.

There were a few sandbags out there painted with American flags. Ketch smiled to himself, and the shopkeeper gave him the Browning.

He took it into his right hand, then double gripped it with his left. His left hand supported the right hand on the grip, but he also clasped the front of the trigger guard with a few fingers for additional support. The right hand pushed forward on the grip, while the left pulled back on the trigger guard to create a stable shooting platform.

"Like a glove," Ketch noted quietly to himself. Then he let a full magazine rip into the stars and stripes.

At about twenty feet, he got a good grouping around a few of the stars.

"You have a bag or box I can put this in?" Ketch asked the shopkeeper. "I don't want to be showing it off to everyone."

The shopkeeper smiled and gave him a small cloth bag with a drawstring on the top.

Ketch bought two more magazines of ammo, then left.

Chapter Eight

Ketch assumed the drive back to Peshawar would be uneventful. He had already driven the length of the Khyber Pass without incident and expected none on the way back.

However, about an hour's drive outside of Darra, he noted two tribesmen along the road waving their hands at him. He also noted that they had built a *cairn*, or small rock barrier in front of the road.

Ketch had no choice but to stop. He thought about ramming the low-rise barricade but didn't think his rental car could take it.

In the meantime, he pulled out his Browning from the bag, racked the slide to chamber a round, but didn't drop down the hammer or engage the safety. He wanted it good to go with minimum effort. Cocked but not locked. He slipped the gun back inside the bag.

As he approached the *cairn*, he slowed down and pulled to a stop.

One tribesman was standing in front of the rock pile and waving his arms at him to stop.

He and his partner both wore long robes with leather vests, turbans on their heads and rifles slung across their backs.

One of them blocked the road, and the other stuck his face in Ketch's window.

"You give me car," he shouted in English.

"I give you ride, but no give you car," Ketch responded.

"You give me car!" the tribesman insisted. He then unslung his rifle and pointed it at Ketch through the window.

"Ok, ok," Ketch returned. "I give you car."

"Out. Out," the tribesman shouted.

Ketch turned off the ignition, put the keys in his pocket, then got out, carrying the cloth bag with the Browning inside.

The tribesman pushed him aside, threw his rifle recklessly into the car, jumped into the driver's seat and tried to turn over the ignition switch without the keys in it.

It didn't work of course and he started shouting at his partner in some Central Asian dialect, likely Pashto, the language of the Pashtun tribe.

Ketch noted that the partner guarding the *cairn* was starting to unsling his rifle.

He didn't waste a moment.

He reached into the cotton bag, grabbed the Browning and fired two shots through the cloth into the bastard's chest.

He then removed the gun from the bag and poked the barrel hard into the temple of the other tribesman sitting in the car. Hard enough to make it hurt.

"Out. Out," he instructed.

The tribesman got out and left his rifle in the car.

As soon as the tribesman left the car, he fell to his knees and started bowing and scraping.

Ketch pointed his pistol at the *cairn* and shouted, "Out, Out."

The tribesman got the message.

He crawled over to the rock pile and began pulling it apart. He threw the rocks over the cliff into the ravine beside the road.

The tribesman was still on his knees when he finished. He looked at Ketch with a big smile, put his hands together like he was praying, and shook them at Ketch saying something in the dialect Ketch couldn't identify.

Ketch guessed it meant, "Please don't shoot."

In response, Ketch shot him twice through the chest. "No mercy for murderers," he said out loud to himself.

People were shot along the road all the time. However, being the over-thinking American, Ketch felt he needed to cover his tracks. So he decided to shoot each one with the other one's rifle, then push them off the cliff. It would be a long time before they'd be discovered, but when found, it would look like a tribal feud or some personal vendetta, he told himself.

However, when he examined their rifles, he noticed they were flintlock muskets.

"Shit!" he said out loud. He had fired a flintlock musket only once in his entire life. It belonged to a friend who was a classic gun collector. Most of what he knew about them was from the movies.

The tribesmen's guns appeared to be the famous "Brown Bess" .75 caliber muskets used by the British during the American War of Independence.

Ketch fished around the clothes of one dead tribesman and found a number of paper cartridges.

The cartridges were paper cylinders cinched at each end with a twist. Each contained a pre-measured amount of gunpowder and a lead musket ball. The ball was actually somewhat smaller than the muzzle diameter, so you could still get it down the barrel after firing the musket a few times and dirty, burnt black powder built up on the inside. Typically, it was .69 caliber.

As late as the Napoleonic Wars of the early nineteenth century, muskets were used in war but still only had a limited accuracy. They were smooth bore and essentially just propelled a stone through a tube, which is why infantry soldiers felt confident standing shoulder-to-shoulder facing an enemy only yards away.

On the other hand, rifles had "rifling" inside the barrel that spun an aerodynamically shaped, machined bullet, giving it stability and accuracy in flight.

Loading a musket was fairly slow. An experienced shooter could get off maybe three shots a minute. That's why troops stood in lines behind each other. The front line fired, dropped to their knees and reloaded while the lines behind them followed up with a volley over their heads.

The basic procedure was to cock back the flintlock mechanism halfway to expose the powder pan in front of it. "Half-cocking" the musket in this way would not let it fire. The powder pan was covered by a hinged, L-shaped piece of metal called a frizzen. You then bit off the powder side of the cinched paper cartridge and primed the pan by adding a bit of powder from the cartridge into the pan. You then covered it with the base of the frizzen to keep it from spilling out. A small hole connected the powder pan with the inside back of the barrel and the main charge that would shoot out the bullet.

You'd pour the remaining powder from the cartridge down the barrel, then stuff the remaining paper cartridge with the lead ball inside down the barrel and ram it to the base of the barrel with a rod that slid out from under the barrel called a ramrod. The paper wad kept the powder in the barrel in place and helped seal the explosive gasses that would drive the musket ball out.

Some shooters preferred to first ram down only the paper wad, then drop down and ram in the musket ball. They felt they got a better seal on the explosive gasses, but this took more time. And time was a luxury in warfare.

You then fully pulled back the cock holding the flint, aimed and pulled the trigger. When fired, the flint scratched the vertical surface of the frizzen, sending sparks into the powder pan which ignited the gunpowder there. That sent flames through the small hole at the back of the barrel and set off the main charge inside. It went off with a big explosion, lots of smoke and noise but little accuracy.

Ketch mimicked the process as he best remembered it from his one experience with a musket as well as from old movies. It worked and he shot one of the tribesmen through the chest exactly through the same wound produced by his Browning. Then he rolled the body off the cliff and threw the musket after it.

However, after he did that, he realized that he should have grabbed the guy's musket to do the same in return to the other tribesman so it would look like they shot each other. It was too late but Ketch decided that forensics in this area would not be that detailed.

He reloaded the musket from the remaining tribesman using the same procedure, then shot him through the bullet wound he had inflicted with his Browning.

He rolled the body off the cliff and threw the musket after him into the ravine.

Ketch then drove back to Peshawar without further interruptions. He could have taken a flight back to Karachi, but decided to spend the night and check out the town.

He found his way to the Continental Hotel and dropped off the car with the concierge.

They had rooms available and Ketch checked in.

Chapter Nine

Ketch hadn't expected to spend the night there so had little luggage, only a small backpack, and was surprised no one questioned him about it. They didn't even ask for his name or passport. Their only concern was that he paid in advance. Cash. American dollars.

As requested, he paid one night's lodging with forty American dollars then went up to his room. Nothing special, but comfortable. The sun had not yet set, so he decided to explore the town a bit, return to the hotel for a quick dinner then get a good night's sleep.

He put the Browning and pen gun under his mattress then went down to the lobby and asked the concierge what might be interesting sightseeing.

"The market," he replied. "But get some small money from the desk. American money."

Ketch went back to the reception desk and changed a twenty dollar bill into singles then went back outside.

As he counted his change, he noted that a number of bills had red stains on them.

"Blood?" he asked the concierge.

"Betel nut juice," the concierge laughed. "Everyone chews it for energy. It's like chewing tobacco but makes your mouth and teeth red. But try not to touch the red spots. They could make you sick from other people. It is like sticking your hand in their mouth."

The concierge got him a taxi and directed the driver to the market. After a short ride, only just a couple of blocks from the hotel, the driver stopped and motioned Ketch toward a series of alleys and smells not unlike the market in Karachi.

"How much?" Ketch asked.

"One dollar American," the driver replied.

Ketch paid the driver and ventured into the main alleys trying to make a mental note of the way back out to the main road.

He decided to stay on the main alley he entered and not make any turns. But the shops there were very depressing. Most of them specialized in prosthetic devices for *mujahideen*, or "holy warriors" who had lost limbs fighting the Russians in Afghanistan. The holy warriors came from all over the Muslim world to fight the atheist Soviet infidels and Peshawar was the primary recruitment center as well as their entry and exit point.

After a quick look, Ketch decided he had enough and was about to go back to the hotel but then spied a fruit shop down another alley and decided to pick up something to top up his breakfast for the next morning.

As he pondered over sacks of dates, figs and apricots, a woman in a *niqab* with *abaya* came close by and began staring at him. The *niqab* consisted of a head scarf and veil, but it didn't cover her eyes, which were not only big and almond shaped, but had traces of makeup highlighting their exotic quality. The *abaya* was a floor-length, loose-fitting robe with long sleeves that covered her from neck to toes. Only her hands were exposed.

When Ketch looked back at her, she tilted her head motioning him to follow. He couldn't resist. He followed her further down the alley, then she turned off into an even narrower alley, which led to a dead end. Ketch stopped halfway there, but she continued to the end then turned around.

She stared directly into his eyes without so much as a blink, then opened up her *abaya* which Ketch noted was secured with Velcro. She revealed over-sized, fleshy, centerfold quality breasts bursting out of a lace brassiere and flimsy lace panties barely covering her private parts. She had big chunky thighs, muscular calves and a round tummy.

But what actually caught Ketch's eye was the white, high-top basketball sneakers she was wearing with pink socks.

"You want?" she asked still staring into his eyes, mesmerizing him.

Ketch knew it would be a mistake, but was curious enough to ask.

"How much?" he inquired.

"Twenty dollars American," she replied.

"Where?" he followed up.

"Here," she answered, nodding at the ground.

At that point, Ketch decided that he satisfied his curiosity and decided to leave, but suddenly felt a hard metal pipe-like object jabbing him in the back.

"Give me money," a voice said from behind.

The woman quickly covered up her body, but didn't run off and kept staring into his eyes.

However, Ketch didn't raise his hands up in surrender. Instead, he crossed his left foot over the right and twisted around quickly, while the back of his right forearm hit the arm of the gunman, pushing the pistol's line of fire away from his body. As he came face-to-face with his attacker, he noted the asshole was armed with a revolver. Instinctively, Ketch's left hand grabbed the gun over the top of the cylinder, preventing it from firing.

Then, with the help of his right hand, he twisted the bandit's wrist back, forcing him to release the weapon. Ketch continued to put pressure on the wrist, dropping the gunman to the ground on his back. He then kicked him in the groin, heel-stomped him in the solar-plexus, then the jaw, knocking him unconscious.

He picked up the revolver from the ground, cocked back the hammer, and pointed it at the woman as he slowly walked towards her.

She dropped to her knees, bowed her head and put her hands together, presumably begging him not to shoot.

"Off. Off," he shouted at her.

She took off her *abaya*, laid it at Ketch's feet and presumably assumed she was going to earn twenty dollars.

Ketch picked it up then ripped off her *niqab*. She immediately leaned over covering her face with her hands and started to cry.

Ketch donned her clothes and started to leave the alley, knowing it would be hard for a naked Muslim woman to explain her way out of the situation for awhile.

His original idea was to leave the market disguised as a Muslim woman. But as he was about to enter the main alley, he had second thoughts and went back. First of all, her *abaya* only came down to his shins revealing his trousers and men's shoes. Second, his broad shoulders and Western eyes were a dead giveaway. He suddenly realized how ridiculous he looked.

He returned to the woman, who was still bent over and crying in her hands. He calmly walked over to her, took off the *niqab* and *abaya* and dropped them on the ground in front of her.

"I'm sorry," he said.

As she leaned over to pick them up, Ketch shot her in the back of the head.

Harsh.

But Ketch had no time for anyone who tried to kill him or set him up for a kill. Male or female. It never ceased to amaze him how women killers all over the world thought they deserved mercy because they had big boobs or pretty faces.

He then dragged the gunman over to her body, pushed the pistol against his temple and shot him through the brain. He then put the gun in the dead man's hand and left.

Hopefully, it would look like a dispute between a pimp and his lady, Ketch reasoned.

He walked through the market as if nothing had happened and back toward the hotel. He went up to his room, put the Browning and pen gun into his backpack, then went down the emergency stairs through the fire exit into an alley full of stinking piles of garbage. No alarm bells went off as he pushed the fire door open.

After he was several blocks from the hotel, he hailed another taxi.

"Airport," he instructed.

"Twenty dollars, American," the driver answered.

"No problem."

"Women commit many sins with their eyes," Ketch reflected, recalling the words of the Pakistani truck driver in Torkham.

Chapter Ten

Ketch caught the next flight back to Karachi.

As he was buying his ticket in Peshawar, he noticed that there was no security before the gates, so he just took his backpack, complete with Browning and pen gun, with him.

As soon as he got back to the Karachi airport, he went straight to the general ticketing counter.

"What international flights are leaving Karachi tonight?" he asked the clerk.

"There are many flights," the male counter clerk answered. "Hong Kong, Paris, Istanbul, Dubai, Jeddah, Larnaca."

"Larnaca, Cyprus?" Ketch asked.

"Yes," the clerk replied.

"Ok. I want that one," Ketch returned.

"You can buy your ticket here but you need to check in with the airlines at the end of the hall."

Ketch bought the ticket and also noted that there was no security check so took his gun laden backpack with him.

The flight didn't leave for two hours and Ketch already started to stress out. For him, the wait would be excruciating.

His mind had only just started to catch up with events of the last few hours, and he started to get paranoid. Paranoid about getting out of the country and paranoid about what he would say to his bosses.

However, there was no question in his mind that he needed to get out of the country immediately. The poppies, the killings. He tried to assume that they were random events and had nothing to do with him personally, but they started to bend his perspective and play on his sense of personal security.

He needed a drink but there was no bar. So he opted for the only other refuge available.

Sleep.

He found the gate and introduced himself to one of the uniformed female airline staff there.

"Hi. My name is Kelly," he explained. "I'm on the flight to Cyprus, but I'm really tired, so I'm going to sit over there and try to take a nap. Please wake me up when you are boarding."

"Of course, sir," she replied.

Ketch knew he couldn't sleep, but closed his eyes and focused on his breathing, trying to release himself from space and time. He let his body go limp and tried to relax every muscle. A warmth started to creep over him and he embraced it. He searched all over his body for the slightest bit of tension, then released it.

After about fifteen minutes, the warmth was replaced by a numbness and he couldn't feel his body anymore. Then he emptied his mind of all thoughts. He continued to focus on his breathing. He reached the point where he felt nothing, heard nothing and thought nothing. He released himself from time and space. He became one with the universe.

Then he dozed off.

That was a mistake.

He dreamed he was being chased by naked women wearing only *niqabs* and basketball sneakers but armed with big, thick butcher's knives. He would often trip and fall as he was running, yet just as they were about to pounce upon him, he found his legs and started running again. This went on in cycles. But the last time he fell, one of the women caught up with him and stabbed him in the arm.

Ketch suddenly woke up.

Fortunately, it was only the airline staff who brought him back to reality by gently pinching his arm.

"We are boarding, Mr. Kelly," she announced as he tried to pull himself together. "I'm glad you could have a nice nap with all the noise around here."

Ketch looked at her blankly, dazed and not sure where he was at first, then started getting oriented and feeling his body again.

"Thank you," he said.

"Have a nice flight," she replied with a big professional smile.

Chapter Eleven

Paphos, Western Cyprus.

Greek Cyprus.

Cyprus was an island nation in the Eastern Mediterranean off the coasts of Lebanon, Syria, Israel, Egypt and Turkey. It was in the eye of the Middle East hurricane.

Like all those countries, it had a checkered history.

According to mythology, Paphos was also the birthplace of Aphrodite, Greek goddess of beauty and love.

Many assumed she represented idealistic, romantic love, but the cynics claimed she was essentially the goddess of sex and physical pleasure, and that she had many lovers.

Cyprus was taken over by the British in the twentieth century where it became a strategic outpost in the Eastern Mediterranean, notably protecting the Suez Canal, which was the major sea link between Britain and the rich resources of India.

Meanwhile, the Turks claimed the north of the island, while the Greeks claimed the south. Following nationalist violence in the 1950s, Britain granted it independence in the 1960s which only resulted in sectarian violence. After a coup by Greek Cypriots in the 1970s supported by the mainland Greek military, the Greeks proposed incorporating the whole island of Cyprus into Greece. Since Greeks formed the majority of the population at the time, they thought that was quite reasonable.

The Turks didn't agree and invaded northern Cyprus. The island remained divided ever since. The Turks in the north, the Greeks in the south.

The capital, Nicosia, straddled the dividing line.

Ketch flew to Cyprus for sanctuary.

He needed time and space to figure out his next move.

A sympathetic international friend from university, who was based in Cyprus to avoid European taxes, always offered Ketch a place to stay.

Marco.

Marco was born in Cairo into an Italian banking family and later grew up in Italy and Paris where the family went into the property business.

He had three passports but wouldn't tell you which ones. If you asked where he was from, he'd tell you Corsica, the birthplace of Napoleon.

Ketch was never quite sure what Marco really did for a living. At one point it was trading old masters paintings. Another time, it was investing in gold mining shares. Another time it was buying rough diamonds to sell to cutters in Israel.

However, he was a good friend. The kind that calls you once a week to see how you are. And takes your calls in return. Day or night.

Marco was in the process of fighting with his brother for custody over property that had been left by his mother's estate in France. So Ketch didn't want to trouble him. But Marco always had time for his friends. Anyway, his apartment in Paphos was unoccupied, because he was in Paris for a month fighting legal battles. So he offered it to Ketch.

Ketch had never been there before and couldn't believe how beautiful it was. It reminded him of Southern California, but without the traffic.

Small villages of Mediterranean-style homes with red tiled roofs and low-rise condos clustered around white sandy beaches. The villages sported small boutique shops and restaurants with sidewalk seating that offered a variety of international cuisine overlooking the sea.

Ketch didn't know what he was going to do there. He just knew he needed to get out of Pakistan.

He also needed to resign from the agency. Immediately. The level of gamesmanship was beyond his IQ. Important to know what your limits are and adjust accordingly, he always reminded himself.

Ketch also knew that Cyprus was a hotbed of guns-for-hire companies recruiting for security jobs in the Mideast. Maybe it could mean some work for him. It was only a ferry ride to Beirut. And in the meantime, it offered nice beaches and beautiful women on vacation from all over Europe.

Chapter Twelve

The phone rang and woke Ketch up next to some lovely Latvian girl. The night before was an episode of binge drinking and he ached from what he already knew would be a three-day, full-body hangover.

He tried to piece it together. The last thing he remembered was talking to some long-legged, blue-eyed, blonde girl from Riga about exchanging lessons in English for lessons in Latvian.

Or was it English for French? She spoke three languages and had a degree in civil engineering.

She was hanging out at a pub in Paphos with two other girlfriends there on holiday. He looked at her. She looked back and moments later they were sharing a table, talking about architecture.

He didn't even remember bringing her home or making love to her. But she was there. Long, lean, naked with a nice Cyprus tan. No white bikini lines on top and only a thin, naughty, g-string mark on the bottom. She claimed she was twenty five years old and her taut body affirmed that. However, her eyes and face showed much more maturity. The marks of growing up in tough times and tough places.

Based on her worldliness and self-confidence, Ketch assumed she was at least thirty years old.

Her name was Katrina.

The phone kept pestering the morning's rest and Ketch made the mistake of answering it.

It was Evans. His supervisor and nemesis from Washington D.C.

"Eric Ketch," boomed the voice. "You know it's so easy to find you, I'm wondering who trained you. I already sent a message to HR to find that nitwit and fire him. You want to go rogue, you need to do a better job of it.

"You should know that you can't just walk away from the agency. And you can't resign. This isn't a country club. You're a lifer until you get killed or kill yourself. We own you Ketch, until death do us part."

"What do you want, Evans?"

"Your ass back on the job, earning the taxpayers' money, like you're supposed to be doing," Evans replied. "Why did you walk out on us in Pakistan?"

"Something was wrong," Ketch responded.

"Something is always wrong. That's why we send in guys like you."

"You sent me to find poppies. They're growing all over the place. Your airplanes would have seen them. The embassy staff on Sunday picnics would have seen them. You didn't need me to find them. I was being set up."

"No, you were sent there to find the people behind the poppies. You don't listen very well, Ketch. The fact that we know there are poppies doesn't mean we know why they are there, who controls them and who keeps growing them. That was your job. Find the money guys. You missed the big picture. Once again.

"Our embassy staff can't be going around shaking down politicians and businessmen there. These people are our friends. They are our allies. We can't go offending our friends until we have a good reason to do so.

"You are our tool. Haven't you realized that by now? We can't go upsetting the apple cart every time one of our friends breaks some rules. They need to make money just like we do and we let them make it. Until they do something we don't like, then we break their necks."

"This is not what I signed up for."

"Sure you did. You signed up for everything about it. The problem is, you still think like a warrior.

"You think your job is to go out and shoot the bad guys. Wrong. That's what gets you so confused and twisted up inside."

"So what is my job?" Ketch asked.

"Your job is to do as you're told. If we tell you to shoot the bad guys, you do it. If we don't, then you don't."

"And who makes those decisions?"

"Someone who sees the big picture and makes a lot more money than you ever will."

"Ok. But why did you stick me behind a desk in Karachi when all the action is up north?" Ketch asked, showing his frustration.

"Well, maybe all the action wasn't up north," Evans shot back. "Maybe that's only where they were growing the stuff. And maybe, once again you missed the big picture. Maybe the real players, the money boys, were in Karachi. What's up north? Farmers. Who gives a shit about farmers?

"You only sat behind your desk because that's what you wanted to do. You were feeling sorry for yourself, got lazy and didn't take any initiative.

"Look, Ketch, we bring you into these situations because usually you can read between the lines, figure out what needs to be done and do it.

"This time, you failed miserably. Feeling sorry for yourself. Maybe you're not the same guy anymore. Maybe you *should* be sitting behind a desk. But next time, it will be in D.C. And you'll be living in the suburbs. Maybe screwing a few plump, bored housewives, but definitely not the exotic babes you're used to. So stop feeling sorry for yourself and get your game face on.

"Right now we are lending you to another agency for a project in Beirut."

"What agency?"

"You don't need to know. Not narcotics. Something simple."

"Day after tomorrow you fly to Cairo, where you'll be briefed on the Beirut op.

"A plane ticket is waiting for you at the Egyptair counter. The flight leaves at three. Don't miss it."

"Beirut?" Ketch asked. "I've never been there."

"A first time for everything," Evans replied coldly. "You'll like it. Just like 'Nam. Everyone shooting everyone else for no reason whatsoever.

"You're booked three nights at the Nile Hilton in Cairo. It's not the new, modern Ramses Hilton, but you'll like the bar in the basement. Jackie O's. All the Cairo spoiled rich kids hang out there, including twenty-one-year-old wannabe movie starlets.

"Make the flight Ketch or you will be dealt with," Evans threatened. "We need to maintain discipline within the ranks and you will become an example."

Ketch and Evans both slammed down the phones at the same time.

Chapter Thirteen

The loud chit-chat and phone slamming woke up Katrina.

She rolled over in bed and modestly covered her naked body with the sheet.

"It sounds like you have to leave," she said.

Ketch nodded.

"I have to leave day after tomorrow," he replied. "Beirut."

Ketch felt guilty about leaving Katrina, but she was very calm about it.

"Hey, it's your business," she said, not knowing what his business really was. "You have to go. This was a nice vacation with you. And hopefully I inspired you to come visit me in Riga."

She then kissed him gently on the forehead and said, "Let's have one more special day and night. Let's go to the beach tomorrow then have a nice dinner together.

"I need to go home now and will see you tomorrow," she added.

After she left, Ketch didn't know what to do with himself.

He walked around the neighborhood and had lunch at a restaurant overlooking the ocean.

He then grabbed a taxi and asked the driver to take him to the capital, Nicosia.

"There is nothing there," the driver responded. "Only some office buildings. The beauty of Cyprus is along the coast."

"I know," Ketch replied. "But I want to see northern Cyprus."

"Why?"

"To see the difference."

"I can only take you to the checkpoint," the driver replied. "I can't take you across the border."

"Why not?"

"I'm afraid," he replied. "Maybe they will find some reason to keep me there and ask my family for lots of money."

"How could they do that?" Ketch returned. "You are Greek. On what grounds would they hold you?"

"You are obviously an American," the driver replied. "You think like a lawyer. You think that someone needs to have grounds. These people have no grounds. They can do whatever they want with me. You Americans are still very stupid about the world."

Ketch ignored the slight and the driver took him to the checkpoint where he got out.

"I will wait for you one hour," the driver offered. "After that, I expect that something bad happened to you. But I can't help you. I have a family."

Ketch got out of the taxi and walked the corridor down the street to the North. He was surprised. He expected a dull, dreary, border crossing, but instead it was filled with designer shops and outdoor cafes.

He got to Greek immigration and they stamped his passport without even looking at it.

Turkish immigration was only about fifty feet away.

When he got there, a very friendly official in a booth, speaking perfect English asked him, "Do you want me to stamp your passport?"

Ketch didn't know how to reply.

"I don't know. Why not?"

"Well, if you do a lot of traveling around the world, it's better that we don't stamp it," the official advised. "Some countries might not like this stamp on your passport and give you trouble for it."

"And what if you don't stamp it?" Ketch asked.

"I put a stamp on a piece of paper," he explained. "But if you lose this paper, we cannot let you back into the Greek zone. So you cannot lose it.

"It is very important that you do not lose it."

"Ok, give me the paper," Ketch replied, deciding to take the risk.

Ketch got the stamped piece of paper and put it in his wallet.

He then walked into the northern side of Nicosia and looked about a bit. Since the taxi driver only gave him an hour, he just wandered about the streets close to the border.

They reminded him of Pakistan.

Shops were selling goods on the sidewalk from big, bottomless sacks, just like the market in Karachi.

Shop windows showed off *Turkish Delight*.

Turkish Delight sounded like a special service you'd request in a bath house, however it was just another sweet dessert made of nuts, but not like *baklava*. The nuts were packed in a gel, and came in small, often square, bite-sized pieces that you could eat with your hand without worrying about honey dripping all over you.

The other obvious difference from Karachi was the women.

Women were covered up, but only with *hijabs*. Not as extreme as a *burqa* or a *niqab*. The *hijab* was a combination of scarf and shawl that covered the head and shoulders, but left the face exposed.

Ketch gave the streets a quick tour, noted the time, then walked back to the border checkpoint.

He produced the slip of paper with the Turkish stamp on it and the border official re-stamped it.

"Would you like to keep it?" the official asked. "It's a good souvenir."

"Sure," Ketch replied with a smile. He accepted the paper back and put it into his wallet.

He walked down the street to the Greek crossing and the official there again stamped his passport without a word or even looking at it.

"What did you see?" the taxi driver asked.

"Not much," Ketch replied. "It reminds me of the Middle East.

"That's why we must fight them," the driver responded forcefully. "We want to be part of Europe, but they want to be part of the Middle East."

Chapter Fourteen

Katrina picked up Ketch at his friend's apartment the next morning and drove to a small secluded beach on the southeast coast of the island. It had perfect white sand and a small grove of olive trees.

She had brought along a bottle of Rosé, a long, freshly baked loaf of French bread known as a *baguette*, some sliced tomatoes and feta cheese, made from goat milk.

"Goat cheese is good for the digestion," she offered.

They added to the sandwich by picking olives off the trees in the grove behind the beach. The olives were as sweet as grapes. Along with the Rosé, it made a nice meal.

After lunch, Katrina, took off her shorts and blouse to reveal a tiny bikini underneath.

She then pulled off her bikini top and raced into the ocean, challenging Ketch to join her in the waves.

He chased after her and they hugged and kissed in the sea as soon as he caught up.

He was already very hard and started to pull off her bikini bottom, but she pushed him off.

"Have you ever tried to make love in the ocean?" she asked.

Ketch was somewhat embarrassed by the question, but honestly admitted that he had not.

"You cannot," Katrina replied instructively. "The door is closed. The salt water dries out everything. There is no lubrication. It will hurt me and it will hurt you.

"Let's go back to your room and finish this. We will have a nice meal, a nice sleep, and I will see you in Riga one day.

"You like lobster? I feel like lobster tonight," she added. "It is my treat. I know a place close to your flat.

"I am sorry to say this, but you have a problem, Eric. You are a very dangerous man. I know it from your eyes. But you are also a very kind, loving man. I know it from your touch.

"You need to figure this out. Who will you become? The dangerous man or the kind, loving man? You are more dangerous to yourself than anyone else.

"I cannot help you with that, but hope in my dreams to see you again.

"I will pick you up for dinner," she said.

They went back to the olive grove, packed up their stuff and drove off in Katrina's rental car. She dropped him off at his apartment and left.

"See you in a few hours," she shouted as she drove off.

"Take a shower," she smiled. "You smell like the ocean."

Chapter Fifteen

Katrina showed up at seven o'clock with two shopping bags.

"What's that for?" Ketch asked. I thought we were going for lobster."

"We are. But here."

She pulled two live lobsters out of one of the bags and placed them in the sink. Their claws were tied with strips of string so they could not snip anyone or each other for that matter.

"I am making you dinner tonight," she said.

She then pulled out two bottles of chilled Rosé from the other bag and an assortment of spices, ingredients, vegetables and a fresh *baguette*. She then looked around the cabinets for wine glasses.

"Fresh from Provence, France," she smiled, presenting the wine. "Pulling out the cork is the man's job."

Ketch put a corkscrew in one of the bottles and squeezed out the cork.

"You work in a restaurant before?" she asked.

"No. Why?"

"You took out the cork very professionally."

Ketch had simply centered the tip of the corkscrew into the middle of the cork, then rotated the bottle until it took hold. After it took hold, he twisted in the screw.

"No, something I learned at college," he replied. "I went to Columbia University in New York City. We were taught to be very well-rounded. We were not only required to study the Classics, but how to open and taste a bottle of wine."

Katrina laughed. "You got university credit for tasting wine?"

"No. It was what they called an extra-curricula class," he responded. "No credits. But I grew up on James Bond, and wanted to be just as savvy as him."

"What?" she laughed. "You took a wine class so you could be just like James Bond?"

"Well, James Bond was the Renaissance Man at the time," he replied lamely. "And that's what I wanted to be."

Katrina laughed again and continued looking for wine glasses for the Rosé.

The apartment didn't have proper wine glasses, but she found two brandy snifters and poured the Rosé into those.

"To new friends," Katrina toasted and downed the first helping in one gulp.

"Yes, to new friends," Ketch replied, but sipped his.

Katrina poured herself another Rosé then took command of the kitchen.

She found the pots that she needed and started to prepare a dinner of lobster and vegetables.

She turned on one of the gas burners and put a frying pan on top of it. After a bit, she sprinkled some water into it to test the temperature. The water quickly bubbled into droplets that exploded under the heat. That meant it was ready.

She poured in a few short strokes of olive oil she brought from the market and swirled it around in the pan.

She then dumped in some cloves of garlic, slices of ginger and green vegetables.

It reminded Ketch of his Hong Kong days.

"What are those vegetables?" he asked.

"Choy sum," she replied. "Also ginger and a touch of ginseng. *Choy sum* are Chinese vegetables, but now grown in Cyprus. Very healthy. Cyprus exports them to China.

"But what the Chinese really want is ginseng. They claim it cures everything and is an aphrodisiac. They tried to grow it here, but the climate is not right. Hundreds of years ago, the Americans found wild ginseng in their hills and started to export it to China.

"That's what started the American trade with China. Not opium, like the British."

Ketch was mesmerized by the food wizardry that Katrina performed over the stove.

He was a big eater, but not a big cooker. The best he could do was boiled or scrambled eggs. Tuna fish out of the can mixed with mayo for a sandwich and maybe, just maybe a grilled hamburger, but not one that tasted very good.

So Katrina's performance was all magic to him.

Katrina finished stir-frying the vegetables and put them into a dish on the side of the oven.

Meanwhile, she had a large pot with a bit of salted water boiling on the back burner.

She grabbed the lobsters one by one and crossed their claws.

"That way, they can't bite me," she explained.

After crossing the claws, she slit off the string binding them with a kitchen knife, then put them into the pot headfirst.

"You need to put them in headfirst," she instructed. "To get it over with for them. Otherwise, they will be tortured while they are cooking.

"It would be very cruel."

Ketch poured himself another Rosé and watched Katrina artfully turn all these ingredients into food.

After a few minutes, dinner was served.

Katrina brought the vegetables to the table with the fresh *baguette*.

"You don't have a bread knife then?" she asked Ketch.

"What's a bread knife?" Ketch replied unknowingly.

"The kind that has a jagged edge so you can saw your way through the crust," she explained.

"I don't know," he answered. "It's my friend's apartment."

"Obviously your friend is a man who doesn't cook for himself," she returned sarcastically.

She used the large cooking knife to cut the *baguette*. She cut it on a long diagonal to give more surface area to the slices, but had to push down quite a bit on the knife to make the cuts through the crust. Ketch watched her every move with the fascination of a novice apprentice in the presence of a guru.

"It's not even sharp," she snickered. "How do you guys eat?"

"Take-out," Ketch answered.

She went back to the stove and took the lobster pot off the burners.

She filled it with cold water to cool off the shells a bit, then pulled them out and cracked them on the sink to make them easier to eat.

She couldn't find a lobster or nut cracker in the kitchen, so she wrapped them in a towel then hit them with a wooden carving board to break open the shells.

The towel kept the shell splinters from becoming shrapnel.

She took the warm, melted butter off the stove and poured it into a bowl.

She then served the feast at the table.

"The butter is for dipping the lobsters. But also for later," she winked.

The food was incredible and the Rosé intoxicating. They didn't speak much. Katrina knew Ketch was leaving and Ketch knew he was leaving so there was not much to say to each other.

From time to time, they looked at each other and smiled.

Words were not necessary.

Ketch spent most of his life eating in restaurants or take-out joints, so he was extremely touched that Katrina came to his apartment and cooked something. In fact, there was so much loving care in this meal, that it was better than sex, he felt.

After a very satisfying dinner, Katrina grabbed his hand and led him into the bedroom.

"Come," she instructed. "This may be our last time before I see you in Riga."

She quickly undressed Ketch, pushed him down on the bed and undressed herself. Then she went back to the kitchen and came back with the warm bowl of butter that was left over from the lobster dinner.

She carefully poured some over Ketch's chest and loins, then poured some onto her own.

She then pressed her body onto his, massaging him with the warm butter on her body.

She glided her body along his, up and down, back and forth while kissing him full on the mouth.

She then pulled his hard shaft between her legs, but Ketch wanted to be on top. He gently turned her over so as not to lose his penetration and slowly started pumping her.

He then leaned over, supporting himself on his left arm, while his right arm massaged her buttered breasts. He played with her nipples and after they became hard, began massaging and rolling her breasts with the palm of his hand.

Throughout the exercise, they looked into each other's eyes. Lovingly. They didn't know what they were doing or where they were going. It was all about the moment.

Suddenly Katrina gasped and looked away while clutching her legs tightly around Ketch's waist. She came and Ketch came quickly thereafter, almost at the same time.

She then looked back at Ketch and smiled sweetly.

"Please kiss me," she said.

He bent over, but didn't kiss her immediately. Instead, he nibbled on her lips and her nose for a bit. Kissed her eyes, chest and breasts. He pressed his lips to hers and they embraced tightly as their mouths played with each other. Then they kissed each other hard like tomorrow would never come.

It was not about the sex. It was about the mutual spiritual and physical comfort and security they gave each other in the intimacy of the instant.

It was a short-term illusion. They both knew that. But they made the most of the moment.

Tomorrow came too quickly for both of them.

Katrina saw him to the airport and waited with him until he went through security to the boarding gate. There were no teary-eyed farewells and no regrets. One last big hug and a kiss on the forehead.

"See you in Riga," were her last words.

Her big blue eyes stayed on him as he went through security and passport control.

"Are you ok?" the immigration officer shouted at him.

"What do you mean?"

"You look very sad."

"My girlfriend," he responded.

"Don't worry," the officer replied. "There are as many pretty girls in the world as there are fish in the sea. And Egyptian women are very nice. You will find another girlfriend."

Ketch felt like punching out the guy for his cynicism but restrained himself. Katrina was not a one-night stand, but a loving, giving person that he wanted to get involved with. She exuded goodness in a very natural, caring way. Not for any purpose. It was just her nature. Ketch was in love with her.

The officer stamped his passport and Ketch walked through to the waiting area. He looked back, but Katrina was gone.

Chapter Sixteen

The flight to Cairo was short and uneventful.

A hotel car picked Ketch up at the airport and the Nile Hilton efficiently checked him in.

As the porter escorted him to the room, Ketch noted that some rooms had goat or lamb carcasses outside the doors.

"Is that on the room service menu?" Ketch asked jokingly.

"No. They are wealthy Arabs. And they have their customs. They buy live animals in the market, make a fire in their rooms from the furniture and cook the animals there.

"But they pay for all damages to the room. Cash. American dollars. They are wealthy Arabs. They do as they please."

"What are the damage costs to the room?" Ketch inquired.

"Typically, we need to replace the whole room," the porter replied. "So maybe about forty or fifty thousand American dollars.

"But they are wealthy Arabs and we respect their customs," he added.

Ketch got to his room and tipped the porter, declining the offer to provide him with a girl, a boy or hashish.

The phone rang as he put his suitcase onto the luggage rack.

"Be in the lobby in five minutes," said a sultry British-accented female voice.

"Ok. But how will I recognize you?" Ketch returned.

"From the crème de menthe."

Ketch's heart skipped a beat. He now recognized the voice. Elizabeth.

Elizabeth was the long-legged Eurasian woman who ex-filtrated him from Hong Kong after his cover was blown on a previous assignment. He wanted to bed her then and wanted to bed her now.

Crème de menthe was the drink in the Hong Kong bar he was instructed to put on the table that allowed her to identify him at the first meeting there. It was bright green and came in a unique glass and nobody had ordered it since the 1960s. So it was a good signal for meeting a stranger in a bar.

He jumped into the bathroom and took the fastest shower he ever had in his life. He dressed up as best as he could and proceeded to the lobby.

He instantly recognized her. No need for the crème de menthe anymore. She was drinking a gin and tonic but dressed far more conservatively. A Brooks Brothers suit worthy of an investment banker, flat shoes and very little makeup. But her charm still shone through.

He sat down across the table from her.

"Welcome to Cairo," Elizabeth said. "Nice you recognized me even without the lipstick, slit *cheongsam* and all."

"How could I forget?" Ketch replied. "You still have my gun."

"You'll get another one, but not here. I understand you somehow managed to get your new toy, a Browning Hi-Power pistol into Cairo."

"How would you know that?"

"Well, maybe you showed it off to someone in Cyprus. Likely a girl in your room, or she found it there, when you were drunk. Maybe she was our girl," Elizabeth said with a snicker.

Ketch's heart sank. He assumed everything with Katrina was sincere. He was certainly sincere about her, and it broke his heart to leave her in Cyprus. Worse, it now broke his heart even more to learn that she might actually have been working for the agency and was just minding him on his stay there.

He now started to get paranoid. Why did she spend the night with him? Why did she make dinner? Did she really like him or did she just use that as a ruse to get closer and win his trust?

Elizabeth interrupted his thoughts.

"I know paranoid agents such as yourself never give up their piece. And if you didn't successfully bring it to Cairo, you'd be detained at the airport right now and I'd have to come and rescue you. Thank you for saving me the trouble."

"Yes. I just put it in my check-in luggage. Nothing stealthy. Friends advised that would suffice."

She obviously didn't know about the pen gun, he noted to himself.

"However, if that's your new weapon of choice, we'll get you one in Beirut. But you'll have to give me the one you have. Can't take any airport risks. You think you'll still be with us for a few more assignments? I'm building up a collection of Eric Ketch guns."

"Yes. That's what I want. The Browning was one of my first training weapons. I feel very confident I can draw, point and shoot it in no time flat. But I want the double-action model, the BDA. The one I got in Pakistan was only single-action," he added.

"Well, if that's what makes you feel secure, we'll get you one. But Beirut is more about bombs, rockets and AK-47s. Your 9mm pistol is not going to help you with that."

"I don't care. I want one. With lots of ammo and magazines. Subsonic ammo. And a silencer."

"Done. So give me the weapon you have and then we can get on with the briefing. But as far as the ammo is concerned, don't expect more than three clips.

"Anyway, the Browning takes 9mm rounds which should be easy for you to buy in Beirut," Elizabeth said.

"The gun is in my room. We can continue the conversation there," Ketch replied flirtatiously.

"Very tempting. But as I told you in Hong Kong, I'm not just a crème de menthe girl who meets guys in bars, she coldly returned. "So here's what we're going to do. I'm going to give you my attaché case. You're going to go to your room, put the gun in it, along with any ammo and come back down. Then, I'm going to brief you.

"You're here for a few nights, while we get some things sorted out in Beirut regarding your arrival," she explained. "In the meantime, I'm sure you can make some nice friends at Jackie O's in the basement of the hotel or go sightseeing. See the Pyramids. Who knows when you'll be in Cairo again and you can find pretty girls anywhere in the world."

Ketch went to his room and reluctantly put the Browning and ammo inside Elizabeth's case. He then went back to the lobby.

"What brings you to Cairo?" Ketch asked when presenting the goods. "Just to see me?"

"What brings me anywhere?" Elizabeth replied, still stiffly professional. "Just following orders. The Mideast is where all the action is. I can't tell you where I live, but not really here. Anyway, the seniors thought things would go a lot more smoothly if you were contacted by a familiar face. Particularly, since you are being loaned to another agency."

"So, I've heard. Loaned to who?'

"Loaned," Elizabeth replied crisply. "That's all I know."

Elizabeth was ice-cold. Ketch was now out of love with her and no longer had any aspirations to bed her. He decided to get through the briefing quickly and see what was happening in Jackie O's. The cool conversation as well as the conservative look, though appropriate for the Middle East, snatched away any remaining fantasies he had about her.

Some men would consider her coolness a challenge and work to build up a relationship. After all, she was very desirable. Smart, sexy and international.

But Ketch was not one of those guys. There were already enough challenges in the world. If something didn't happen quickly with a woman, he let it go as a bad investment.

He started thinking again about his brief time in Cyprus with Katrina, when Elizabeth interrupted his thoughts.

"Right. Here's the brief," she announced.

"Your job is to find an American hostage in Beirut and bring him out alive. He was a chemical engineering professor at the American University there. You'll get a picture and profile of him, but it's not that relevant. Mostly academic. You'll get them in Beirut so nobody sees them at the airport and asks questions. Then you need to work your way around the militias to find out who has him and what they want.

"His name is Adam Smith."

"Like the famous economist?"

"Yes. Everyone thinks it's a cover name, but apparently it's not. That's really his name," Elizabeth returned. "We know because we've been in contact with the family."

"Your first priority is to strike a deal. The militias do these kidnappings mostly for money, not politics. However, the money can be very complicated because the militia that kidnapped him likely sold him to another militia who sold him to another militia and once they find out there is a foreign buyer out there, they will start squabbling among themselves about the price and who gets what in finders' fees.

"So, if the deal strategy becomes too complex, use the intelligence from that to plan a military option. As someone once said, diplomacy is useless without a military option.

"And if you have to kill a lot of these bastards in the process, you are authorized to do so. Everyone is fed up with their gangster politics posing as religion.

"If it's too big for you alone, we will team you up with the U.S. Marines there. Force Recon guys who have already been sneaking around on their own and know the backstreets and alleys better than a Beirut taxi driver. They claim they are better than the SEALs because they are Marines. I wouldn't know. Typical inter-service rivalry ego stuff best left for beers and bars back in the States. Anyway, the Marines are already on the ground. A SEAL team would have to be dropped in from a nearby navy ship. And that would complicate the logistics.

"The SEALs move fast, but they would also need someone to lead them on the ground to the target. They wouldn't know the ground. And neither will you.

"So the Marines would be your option. I know the SEALs get a lot of positive hype. But the Marines train as tough as the SEALs. They also go through the same advanced air, sea and land training schools as the SEALs.

"So, worst case scenario, we'll send in the Marines, as you Americans would say. But you would need to set up the target and give them enough intel so they can be smart about the op.

"Nobody wants to walk into a blind op. Except you, Ketch. Apparently you will walk into any op. It seems you consider it a personal challenge. Actually, that's why they specifically asked for you. Because they have nothing to go on. And you have the knack to drop into places, hit the ground running, figure out who you need to meet, find them and finish it.

"Also, your name was put forward by Smith's family in Detroit. They got it from some Lebanese friends there. Apparently, you have some creds with the most unlikely of communities. They think you are a journalist and that journalists have some power to make things happen. So that helps your cover.

"The agency contacted the Smiths to pre-empt the media. We didn't want them to go public and make a mess out of things. They were told that you'd be on the job and that calmed them down. But if you screw it up, you will answer to them, which will be worse than answering to Evans.

"Anyway, D.C. thinks you are a good choice for this. An expendable choice. Physically and politically. You already screwed up your last assignment in Pakistan, so nobody wants you.

"Also, your shaggy brown 1970s haircut, blue eyes and lean build don't type you as an operator. I can only tell from the sharp look in your eyes that you've been to the dark side and back. So I know better. I'd spot you in a crowd from fifty feet. Maybe, you should start wearing glasses, even fake ones, to tone down that soulless stare and the detached 'I don't give a shit whether I live or die look.'

"Unfortunately, we can't give you a transmitter, because if the militias find it on you, you'll be tagged and shot. So any communications will need to be done over a convenient phone."

"And if there's no convenient phone around, what do I do?"

"Find one.

"We will give you a Sony mini-shortwave receiver. It's about the size of a small paperback novel. At ten o'clock every night and six o'clock every morning, we will broadcast any intel updates we have in Morse code."

"Morse code?" Ketch asked, somewhat astonished. "That's a bit archaic."

"Yes. Morse code," Elizabeth returned. "According to your file, you are fluent in it up to twenty words per minute. I have no idea how that happened, since none of the agencies or the military train their people in it anymore. But it's in your file."

"Pretty impressive homework," Ketch replied.

"Actually, my father got me into ham radio when I was a kid," he explained. "The test for the Novice Class license was five words per minute. But the test for the General Class license was thirteen words per minute. I had to take it twice to pass.

"The Novice Class license only allowed you to communicate in code. You needed the General Class to use voice. Of course, that was the goal. It enabled you to talk to anyone, anywhere in the world.

"When you contacted someone, you exchanged QSL cards. A postcard with your call sign that acknowledged you two had met on the radio. It was better than collecting baseball cards.

"I think I got cards from around fifty countries at the time, including exotic places like Africa.

"However, on a practical note. Yes, I did get a certificate in twenty words per minute at one point to prove myself, especially since I failed the thirteen words per minute code test the first round. But I was a teenager at the time.

"What's interesting is that at the faster speeds, you don't hear the individual letters anymore, but complete words, like human speech.

"I still remember the code, but would suggest you send it at five words per minute.

"It's funny how you still remember languages you studied as a kid," Ketch said. "I just wish my father pushed me to study French instead. At least I'd be able to impress girls in restaurants."

"Thanks for the insightful, background," Elizabeth returned sarcastically, noting he was trying to impress her with all the technical details, but bored with all of it. "Ok. Five words per minute.

"The message will be broadcast on the frequency of 7.15 megahertz in the forty-meter band. It's one of the ham radio bands, so it will seem like normal chatter traffic to anyone listening in.

"I assume you understand what a megahertz is. In your day, that would have been megacycles, but they renamed it "Hertz" in honor of the guy who discovered radio waves.

"It's a good wavelength for transmissions. Very reliable day or night and through varied atmospheric conditions. I assume you know what I'm talking about."

"Yes," Ketch replied, now very irritated at being lectured on a subject he knew more about than some cold, crème de menthe briefing girl.

"Unfortunately, it's also popular with foreign commercial broadcasters. So, if you find yourself tuned into Radio Moscow, fish around a bit to find our signal. It will be strong enough to shout itself out, but not talk over them. So, the communications team would likely move it around a bit to the right or the left of the dial.

"Your handle will be very easy to remember. K-T-H. That's dash-dot-dash, dash, dot-dot-dot-dot."

"I know what it is," Ketch interjected.

"It will be sent four times, there will be a pause, then any message will follow. If there is no news, the letter "N" will be sent four times, so you can go back to bed. That's dash-dot."

"Yes, I know," Ketch responded, now even more annoyed.

"But, I'd like to suggest an easier handle," Ketch challenged."

"What's that?" Elizabeth replied coolly.

"Dit-dit-dit, dit, dah-dit-dit-dah," Ketch returned in the lingo Morse operators use when speaking the code.

"And what's that?" Elizabeth asked with some irritation.

"Apologies," Ketch answered with a snicker. "It sounded like you were fluent in Morse code. It's S-E-X."

"Cute," Elizabeth answered. "But if you want your toys to show up in Beirut on time, don't push it."

"Not pushing at all," Ketch replied, "I'm happy with K-T-H. But tell me again why you can't just give me a transceiver, so I can talk with someone directly and ask questions about the intel. Otherwise, I need to second-guess any bit of info they send me, which may be totally out of context by the time I get it.

"I promise to leave it in my hotel room."

"It would be a big mistake," Elizabeth responded.

"Beirut is probably one of the most monitored places in the world right now. The minute you push the transmit button, you will be picked up by every intelligence agency in the region. Lebanese, Israeli, British, French, Syrian, Iraqi, Iranian. And the bad guys will pass on your details to all their clients in Lebanon. Palestinians, Amal, Hezbollah.

"You will be made the minute you hit the 'On' switch. They will type you as an operator and you will likely be blown up, shot or kidnapped within a week.

"They will immediately know where you are. The tracking technology is pretty sophisticated these days. It's not like you see in World War II movies, where trucks with revolving antennas roam around the neighborhood. Then you grab a suitcase and run to the roof as the storm troopers break down the door.

"There will be no trucks or storm troopers. Just guys in suits that shoot you in the street as you leave your hotel.

"So consider this for your own good.

"If anyone asks why you have a shortwave radio receiver, you can just tell them that you're a journalist and need to listen to the BBC news to stay updated," she explained.

"So that's my cover?"

"Yes. Journalist, as before. Not one of the major dailies. A paper in Detroit. That's where the Smiths live so it makes sense the local press would want to follow it up. We made it up. I don't how they found out, but the *New York Times* gave us a lot of grief for using their name on your last op in Hong Kong. They claimed it compromised the integrity of their paper as well as the security of their correspondents and threatened legal action.

"The British press, or any British company for that matter, would not have issue with this. Journalistic or corporate cover is quite common for British agents. The companies cooperate because they see it to be in the national interest, hence in their own interests. And the bad guys haven't figured it out yet.

"But you Americans still seem to think that you are so above it all in these matters.

"Anyway, there are so many papers in Detroit, we were challenged to come up with an unused, neutral name. *Detroit City News*.

"As I said, we made it up. It doesn't exist and doesn't sound that impressive. But someone will answer the phone number on the card, just like your handler Jennifer did before when you were in Hong Kong and posing as a *New York Times* reporter.

"Your title is Foreign Editor.

"Apparently, Detroit has a huge population of Lebanese and others from the Middle East. So, it will provide a sympathetic angle for you to pursue as a journalist.

"The name cards, Browning, Smith bio and radio will be at the hotel desk when you check-in.

"Assuming you make it to the hotel. Don't take any chances from the airport. The militias take pot shots at the cars going back to the city, and foreigners are ripe fruit for kidnappings.

"Pay your driver extra to drive fast and don't pay him until you get to the hotel."

"And who do I call? You?"

"No. I don't even know who will be picking up the phone number on your business card.

"Your key contact in Beirut will be Major Collins. He is with the twenty-second MAU, the Marine Amphibious Unit. They replaced the twenty-fourth MAU which got blown up last October. He's a cynical but likeable guy, so you two should get on well. But, they are very sensitive about the bombing right now because politicians, who constrained their security, are looking to blame the bombing on the Marines to cover their own political asses. So, don't get into it with him."

"And the asset? Shouldn't he be dead by now?" Ketch asked.

"We know he's not dead yet, because there's still a price on his head. Currently half a million U.S. dollars," Elizabeth replied. "Importantly, despite what I said about sending in the Marines, we'd prefer you do this by yourself.

"International assets in Beirut are severely compromised.

"You know about the bombing of the U.S. Marines and French headquarters there, as well as the U.S. Embassy earlier in the year.

"The Italians are still intact, but mostly in defensive positions. They didn't get hit. Maybe because one of their officers stumbled into a street situation where he found some Christian militiamen thugs bullying some Muslims. He got out of his jeep, pistol drawn and told the Christians to back off. He was outnumbered three to one. However, he made it very clear to the Christians, that he'd have no problem shooting them. According to the story, they gave him the finger and apparently one of them raised his rifle at the officer. Without a second thought the Italian officer fired off a shot that tore off the guy's cap and they ran off. The Muslims respect that sort of thing."

"What about the Brits?" Ketch inquired.

"You can ask Major Collins for the contact," she replied dismissively.

"By the way, we're not giving you much of a budget. Only travel and incidentals. But that includes bribes of course. So you'll have to make do. We know you won't run up a big booze bill. But operators always find ways of spending other peoples' money.

"Evans decided we'll keep you on salary, despite your walkout in Pakistan, but the rest of the work is based on a success fee.

"Deliver the goods and you get a bonus."

"What's the bonus?" Ketch asked.

"One hundred thousand U.S. dollars. Before taxes, of course."

"So, only maybe seventy thousand dollars. Not to mention maybe ten thousand dollars in accountants' fees to file the tax return."

"Your government, not mine."

"Not something I can retire on."

"No. But like your fellow action agents, you got into the game for honor, truth and justice. Not a country estate. You want big money, get your MBA and become an investment banker or a so-called financial advisor and spend your life hustling people out of their life savings. If you're not smart enough to do that, then maybe you can become an insurance salesman. Anyway, seventy thousand net is not bad for only a couple of weeks' work," Elizabeth returned.

"If it's only a couple of weeks," Ketch replied.

"You chose this life, so live it or leave it," Elizabeth responded. "You can decide whether you want to be an action agent or a sales agent."

"Harsh," Ketch answered.

"Look, I'm not paid to be a counselor. So, let's stop there," Elizabeth continued.

"You now have a project. As I said, you don't have a lot of intel, but that's why they used you. As I said, you seem to have the ability to fly into the shit with nothing more than your own wits, figure it out and make something happen."

"Flattered," Ketch answered sarcastically.

"Don't be. I'm not sure how you do it, but I'm sure I don't want to know," Elizabeth continued. End of story. You've now been briefed. That's all we can give you. A picture and a bit of background.

"When you get to Beirut, first contact the U.S Marines. They got hurt pretty badly by the bombing, psychologically as well as physically, but they are still a strong functioning force on the ground. The Marines always seem to drive their way through the shit, despite the setbacks. That's what makes them Marines.

"As I said, your contact there is Major Collins.

"Here's his phone," Elizabeth stated, passing a cocktail napkin across the table with some numbers on it. "He is expecting your call."

"So, I should just call up the Marines and make an appointment?" Ketch asked.

"Exactly. If you just show up at the gate, they may shoot you. After the shit they've just been through, they're allowed. Don't worry about calling them from the hotel.

"All journalists are doing it. So you'll just blend in.

"Also, don't get arrogant and lord your mission over them. They don't work for you. They have their own mission. But they are your only friends on the ground. Trust no one else.

"And if the shit hits the fan, it will be the Marines who come get you. If they like you enough. So, be polite."

"Tell me about the money negotiations," Ketch asked. "I thought the U.S. government doesn't negotiate with terrorists. And what about other hostages? What makes Smith so special?"

"Technically, they are militias, not terrorists," Elizabeth explained. "So, the rule can be overlooked. Also, unlike other hostages in Beirut right now, Adam Smith knows stuff we want to know."

"What stuff?" Ketch asked out of more than curiosity.

"I don't know," Elizabeth replied. "All I know is that a number of big shots in D.C. want him back, whatever the reasons."

"And how do I get the money?" Ketch asked. "What's the upper limit?"

"Call your office," Elizabeth replied. "Number on the card. Discuss with them when you think you have a serious deal."

"Just one more question," Ketch persisted. "How do I get this guy out, if I find him?"

"That's up to you, based on what you learn on the ground.

"I'm not a field agent, only a crème de menthe girl, but if you want my advice, I'd get him to Christian-controlled East Beirut, then just hop on the ferry to Cyprus."

"But that means getting him across the Green Line," Ketch replied.

"Yes, but something you can figure out. I've done it a few times myself."

The Green Line was not an eco-friendly area, as its name suggested, but a battle-scarred war zone that separated Christian East Beirut from Muslim West Beirut. All the buildings were bombed out and the streets full of debris beyond imagination. Most of the fighting among the various militias happened there.

There was no life there, except various militias hiding out in the rubble and staking their turf, like street gangs.

"If you don't want to cross into East Beirut, another option would be to fly out of Beirut airport. But we don't know what documents he might have, so I'd suggest the airport option would not work.

"You could drive south into Israel through Sidon and Tyre. However, driving south into Israel would require you to have a lot of passes to get through the various militia checkpoints. A good driver could get these for you.

"If you got far enough south, you'll find that the militias there are managed by the Israelis. Specifically, the South Lebanon Army based in Sidon. However, to go south, you will have to cross checkpoints for Amal, Hezbollah and the Palestinians. So, even if you get the passes, it would be very risky.

"Every teenage boy manning a checkpoint, who wants to feel important, could decide to take you hostage regardless of your credentials.

"You could also drive to Damascus. The Syrian border is open right now and many journalists are doing it for the bragging rights. About a three or four hour drive from Beirut. Damascus is one of the most ancient cities in the world, so worth seeing. I'd do it alone but not with some asset in tow that you don't know.

"If it were up to me, I'd cross the Green Line and take a ferry from Jounieh, the port in Christian East Beirut. Better yet, I'd hire a speedboat. Just go down to the marina, find someone with a boat and negotiate the price."

"Last question," Ketch interjected. "You seem to have something against the SEALs. What's the story?"

"Ketch, I am not drunk enough to have this sort of conversation with you," Elizabeth replied. "But, I'll give you this. My ex-boyfriend was a SEAL. He was never home. But I understood. And the fantasy of dating James Bond kept me going. But I kept pushing him to get out of the game.

"So he got out, got an MBA and joined a top investment banking firm. That's where all the money was. He was a good salesman and they merchandized his SEALs credentials, which impressed a lot of customers. He brought in a lot of investors.

"Once he left the U.S. government, as an overseas American, he had to file lots of forms every year with your tax people. He got fed up and decided to move back to the U.S. to avoid all the paperwork and hassle.

"In the meantime, his banking firm kept flying him around the world to pull in international investors. He was good at it. And he talked with me about joining him in the States. He said he had already bought a house outside New York City. He hadn't proposed marriage but said it would be a great place to raise a family.

"That was enough of a hint for me to continue corresponding with him.

"He also noted that he was able to buy a small flat in Manhattan for fun on the weekends.

"So, we made plans to meet at his New York City flat.

"We exchanged dates and I took that horribly long flight to America in economy class no less.

"The flat was in a fashionable neighborhood on the Upper East Side and he left the key with the concierge.

"But when I got there, I found a note on the dining room table indicating that the bank had sent him out of town on something urgent, but he promised to be back in a couple of days.

"However, he never showed up.

"His firm got greedy, as all investment banks do. They pushed him to go after big money in the Middle East. He spoke Arabic, knew the land, and they hoped to exploit that.

"After waiting a week in New York, they informed me that he was found drowned in a hotel swimming pool with all his clothes on. They wouldn't tell me what hotel or what country.

"SEALs don't drown. They get killed or kill themselves.

"So I assumed someone had persuaded him to use his investment banking career as cover to help them with an op.

"He didn't need to do that. He had already proven himself professionally and personally, so I assume someone twisted his arm or it was payback from the bad guys, who probably tracked all his visits to the Middle East."

Ketch now assumed, based on that experience, she'd never get involved with another special ops guy like him and would now sell her soul to any wanker banker for the money and security. So he should stop thinking romantically about her.

"Sorry," he said.

"Me too," she replied.

Chapter Seventeen

Ketch left Elizabeth in the lobby and went back to his room.

He would get nothing more than a picture and a name, maybe a fake one. But he reveled in challenges and rose to the occasion. That was one of his biggest weaknesses.

When he was a young boy, his father typically gave him puzzles as presents. Ketch spent days figuring them out. He wasn't sure whether he did that to please his father or saw it as a way of training his brain to become one of the best and the brightest.

The only thing that stumped him was Rubik's cube. It was one of his Christmas stocking stuffers and a nightmare.

He became totally obsessed with it. He spent his entire Christmas vacation trying to get all the colored sides to match up but could not do it.

Then to add insult to injury, just after the New Year, a late night talk show featured a six-year-old boy who could do it in less than a minute.

Not only did Rubik's cube teach him he was not the genius he thought he was, but that he might be more suited to pursue his other interests such as the military.

His proudest moment was when he qualified for Special Forces. It suggested he might be one of the best. He still had to prove himself in the field, but at least he would get the chance.

Also, his Special Forces training was not just about shooting guns and sneaking behind enemy lines, but also about leadership, management and sales skills. Things he could transfer into the civilian sector if he wanted out.

As Elizabeth told him, the special ops commanders chose him for being instinctive, innovative and not bound by the rules.

It was a double-edged sword. His bosses preferred people they could control, but sometimes realized they needed to let them run loose to get the job done. It was a fine balancing act.

Ketch took a nap in his room, then refreshed himself with a shower and a room service meal from the hotel's international menu. French onion soup, a burger and a beer. Heineken.

Ketch always regretted ordering a burger overseas and this time was no exception. But he had a taste for one and took a chance. You might expect to get a tough, stringy steak, but not a tough, stringy burger, which was essentially ground-up meat. Unfortunately, he got a tough, stringy, dried-out burger.

The ketchup didn't help, so he made a meal out of the French fries and the onion soup, which he washed down with the Heineken.

After his room service meal, Ketch ventured down to the nightclub in the basement. Jackie O's.

It was only eight o'clock in the evening, but the place was already buzzing.

"Are you a member or staying with us?" asked the sexy, Egyptian hostess at the door, in a sultry British accent. She had big, cat-like, Pharaonic eyes and a trim, but full-figured body. She wore a sleek, black mini-dress and red high heels. A string of pearls around her neck and she'd be someone's date at the Oscars, Ketch thought to himself.

"Staying with you," Ketch responded suggestively, producing his room key.

"If you'd like a table, the minimum order is one bottle of champagne. Five hundred dollars, American. Cash."

"Thanks, but I'm just going to have a quick beer at the bar," Ketch replied.

"No problem, sir," she answered. "Let me help you find a seat."

She led Ketch to a corner seat at the bar that also gave him a view of the venue. He ordered a Heineken then settled back, expecting to be no more than a spectator for the evening.

As he surveyed the bar, he noted a nearby table of three young girls, maybe twenty-something who were looking at him, then giggling among themselves.

One was very cute. The others were not so cute and reminded him of Cinderella's evil, ugly sisters. Of course, he cynically assumed the cute one was a prostitute and the ugly ones her managers.

The cute one kept trying to catch Ketch's eye but he resisted. Finally, when their eyes met, she nodded her head suggesting he come over.

Ketch gave in and joined them.

"Hi ladies, nice to meet you. Can I get you a drink?" he said lamely, introducing himself.

"Thank you. That's very kind of you, but we already have a bottle of champagne," the cute one replied. "You are by yourself, so we thought you should come over and join us.

"You must be staying at the hotel," she continued.

"How would you know that?"

"Because this is a private membership club. But if you stay at the hotel, they let you in."

"What's your name?" Ketch asked.

"I am Lena," the cute one said with a smile.

The other two quickly introduced themselves, but Eric's focus was on the very cute, engaging one and he blotted out the others. The ugliest one was called Nesrine, the other name didn't even register.

"I'm Eric."

"Eric. Nice to meet you. What are you doing in Cairo?"

"I'm just in transit for a couple of days. What are you doing in Cairo?"

"We live here. We are TV actresses."

"Very cool," he responded genuinely. "I guess I'm lucky you are even talking to me."

The girls laughed and exchanged a few words in Arabic.

"You are really a TV star?" Ketch asked, redirecting the conversation back to Lena.

"Well, I'm just a soap opera actress. I play the crazy, secret girlfriend of a boy in a silly TV series, mostly watched by teenage girls. But the real star is the boy's main girlfriend. My role is to make her jealous and to cause them trouble."

"Unlike Hollywood, acting is not a good job in Cairo, but good fun," Lena explained.

"However, Nesrine is a very famous comedian."

"Really?"

"Really. Can't you tell by the way she likes to twist her face around when looking at you?"

They all laughed at this and toasted each other with their champagne glasses, again muttering something in Arabic.

Ketch couldn't believe his luck. He fell into a bar expecting to drink himself to sleep and three lovely Egyptian girls invite him to their table.

Lena was really cute. She had a bit of a baby face, but big almond eyes, long brown hair and rich, pouty lips that revealed beautiful teeth every time she slipped into a smile.

She was dressed in a tan two-piece outfit that was fit to kill. The bottom consisted of tight slacks that showed off a very hot figure. The top was a long-sleeved, form-fitting blouse that matched the bottom in color and fabric like a suit and merchandized her small, but firm breasts. It was buttoned up to her neck, but cut just below her breast line, maybe about six inches above her belly-button, and exposed a tight six-pack tummy worthy of an aerobics instructor.

Ketch hadn't seen a two-piece combination like that since the 1960s. And only on television. Egypt's secular elite, he noted to himself.

There was not much conversation after that.

Ketch couldn't stop staring at Lena, and they all noticed.

"Can I invite everyone to dinner?" Ketch proposed.

"Thank you, that is very kind of you. Unfortunately, we have another commitment tonight," Lena answered. "But if you are free tomorrow, I can invite you to the Pyramids. You cannot leave Cairo without seeing the Pyramids. I will pick you up at nine. We need to be early to miss the tourist traffic. Wait outside the hotel. Don't be late, or I will think you stayed here too long and have a girl in your room," she laughed.

Ketch was struck. Not just by her looks, but by her frankness, her friendliness and her offer to look after him as a stranger in a strange land.

"Yes, I'm definitely free tomorrow," he replied.

"Great. I will see you then," she answered."

Ketch took that as a cue to disengage gracefully, noting it was ladies' night out. He went back to the bar, ordered one last Heineken then left after they left.

He immediately went back to his room and ordered a seven a.m. wake-up call. He didn't know whether Lena was just playing with him or whether she would turn up. But he didn't want to miss out. Elizabeth advised him to see the Pyramids, so that's what he'd do in the morning. If Lena didn't show up, he'd do it on his own.

Chapter Eighteen

Ketch got little sleep that night. All he could do was think about Lena and her tight tummy.

He woke up before the wake-up call, got himself into the shower and called for breakfast. Scrambled eggs, bacon, toast, orange juice and a 7Up. He cut the bowl of cereal from his routine because he didn't trust the milk in this part of the world and couldn't envision eating cereal without milk. Some of his friends substituted yoghurt for the milk, but that made it a meal not a breakfast.

He also skipped his morning exercise of stretching, kicking, punching, push-ups and crunches.

Lena dominated his head.

Ketch finished his morning routine by eight. Another hour to go. Ketch couldn't stand waiting and didn't know what to do with himself. So he went down to the lobby, exited the hotel and went for a walk.

Old men were already out in neighborhood cafes sipping strong tea, the national drink of Egypt, eating bits of pastry and smoking hookah water pipes.

The tea was heavily sweetened with sugar and mint leaves.

The hookah pipe consisted of a glass vase with several tubes coming out of the top. The base was filled with water and the top held a bowl for the tobacco, which was not burned, but heated by charcoal. The tobacco was placed on a small mesh grill above the charcoal like a barbeque.

The tobacco was also very sticky and specially formulated for the hookah. It contained molasses and offered a selection of flavors, typically minty or fruity.

The tobacco smoke was drawn down into the water at the bottom of the vase through a pipe that was immersed in the water. As the user drew air out of the top of the vase, the smoke emerged, supposedly filtered by the water. Several customers sucked on the tubes, enjoying the smoke.

The assumption was that it was a healthy way to enjoy the pleasures of tobacco. Allegedly, the water filtered out all the toxins from the tobacco. Also, you didn't inhale the smoke, but only sucked it into your mouth.

But the reality was that the set-up with the water only cooled the smoke, so it contained the same bad chemicals as all other tobacco products. Additionally, you drew in the carbon monoxide from the burning charcoal. And all the customers sucking it in, also sucked in each other's germs.

Additionally, the smoke's tar content was extremely high. One hookah session was equivalent to smoking several packs of cigarettes.

In previous years, a number of Ketch's friends took up cigar smoking. It was very trendy in the U.S. at the time. Like wine, cigars were expensive and they merchandised your connoisseurship.

It was a very self-indulgent way to show off in front of your friends. Like burning a twenty-dollar bill in the ashtray, but with a bit more style.

One of Ketch's colleagues back in D.C. tried to recruit him into the cigar society.

"Hey Eric," he pitched. "It's not like cigarettes. You don't inhale. It's like sex with a condom."

Davidoffs were preferred among the yuppies, simply because they were expensive, but smuggled in Cubans were the rage and the height of prestige. The U.S. had an embargo against Cuban products, so the only way to get Cuban cigars was to buy them overseas or have a foreign friend ship them to you.

Typically, the friend would slip off the labels and send them separately.

You'd then slip the labels back on before you smoked them in front of your friends.

The most sought after were Cohibas, because allegedly that's what Fidel Castro smoked. They were long and of medium thickness, but a bit imposing.

Next on the list was Montecristo No. 4. rumored to be the preferred choice of Ernest Hemingway, journalists and spies in pre-Castro Cuba. It was shorter, thinner and less imposing than the standard Cohiba. And that presumably signaled style and refinement. It also had a mild, distinctive aroma and flavor. Ketch liked the Montecristo No. 4, but didn't enjoy the ritual enough to keep it going.

The reality was that each puff of a cigar, delivered a huge nicotine punch, much more than a cigarette. Hence the buzz sought after by cigar smokers. One cigar probably had more impact on your mouth, tongue and throat than an entire pack of cigarettes.

In fact, nicotine was a deadly poison. In special ops school, Ketch learned how to distill a concentrated amount of it from a pack of cigarettes to kill a man.

But, the hookah cafes were a very pleasant, social experience. The air was sweet and fruity and all parties took no mind of the risks.

They were a gathering place for old men to be with old friends. They'd spend the morning sharing gossip and debating the doings of the world, then have a nice shared lunch.

Lunch was typically followed by a nap back at the apartment, most likely the apartment of a son, daughter, son-in-law or daughter-in-law.

Then back to the cafes for late afternoon challenges across the backgammon board fueled by more strong tea. Finally, they were picked up by their wives, sons, daughters or other relatives for a big family meal in a nearby restaurant.

Much better than the American and European systems Ketch noted, which dumped their elderly into prison-like nursing homes where they were treated like inmates in cells with no connection to family or friends. The family never bothered to visit because they were too busy with their own lives, taking the kids to music lessons or sports, or just going to the shopping mall, checking out a new restaurant or watching a movie. Meanwhile, the elderly in America were trapped in their nursing homes and the best they could hope for was cafeteria-style food and maybe a bingo game in the evening.

Ketch was afraid he'd get lost in the maze of Cairo streets, so he made a point of getting back to the hotel quickly. He was now ten minutes early but waiting out that ten minutes was agonizing.

Finally, Lena showed up exactly at nine. Unlikely for an Egyptian to be on time, but it pleased Ketch, who hated waiting for people.

She greeted Ketch with a handshake and invited him into the back seat of a current model air-conditioned Mercedes. Ketch was beginning to feel a bit vulnerable without a weapon and started thinking about being kidnapped before he even got to Beirut.

However, when they got into the car, Lena introduced the driver as her father.

Now Ketch was feeling this would not lead to the conclusion he had hoped for.

"What is your business?" the father inquired, as they drove away.

"I'm a journalist," Ketch lied.

"Where are you going?"

"Beirut."

"That is very stupid," the father remarked. "Beirut is only chaos. It always was and always will be."

"Well, that's my job."

"Sorry for your job. At least enjoy the Pyramids while you are in Cairo. After Beirut, maybe you will think about a new job. A job that will let you have a family."

Ketch noted the father's slight. Obviously, he was not worthy of Lena because he was not offering enough stability to raise a family.

They wound themselves around downtown Cairo traffic, then entered a main road named Avenue des Pyramides. Ketch assumed it was named by Napoleon's *Grande Armée*, the "Great Army," during its campaign in Egypt some hundred-plus years before.

The street was already clogged by double-decker tour buses with dark, tinted windows. One side of the road was filled with back-to-back trinket shops. The other side was lined with restaurants offering belly dancing shows.

"Belly Dancers from Arabia," one sign read.

"1001 Nights Dinner Show," another offered.

"What do you do?" Ketch inquired of the father.

"I do business."

"What kind of business?" Ketch pursued.

"Whatever business is necessary to take care of my family."

Ketch let it go at that.

After stop-and-go traffic behind the tour buses, they finally arrived at the Pyramids. The parking lot was full of trash. Mostly KFC box lunches that the tour companies provided for their clients.

As he walked towards the Great Pyramid, he was accosted by touts left and right, each pulling on his sleeve to buy trinkets, take pictures of him sitting on a camel or in Arab robes and everything else. Lena did her best to shoo them off, and Ketch was beginning to think this was a total waste of his day until he confronted the Great Pyramid.

It was in bad shape. Its sides were crumbling and the base was flooded with tourists, touts and trash. But despite the buses, the hustlers, the KFC boxes, the camels and the hundreds of tourists, he was awestruck by it.

There was something cosmic, even spiritual about its presence that touched his soul. It exuded energy. Despite all the theories about how humans did the engineering, using ramps or pulleys, in his mind, it could not have been man-made.

He had never been touched like this before by a monument, not even by the famous Angkor Wat in Cambodia, which allegedly mapped out the history of time along its walls back to the beginning of the universe.

"There is something here that is sacred," he said to Lena.

"Yes," she replied. "We all feel it, but we don't know what it is."

He made a token visit to the Sphinx, which was much smaller than he had expected and did not impress him in any way, as he had assumed it would. There were also rows of folding chairs set up in front of it for a much-promoted laser light show after dark.

They made their way back to the car.

After they got in, Ketch invited Lena and her father to lunch. But the father declined on behalf of both of them.

"I am sorry Mr. Eric, but I can see that you are not a family man, so not good for my daughter. It is better that you do not get too familiar with her or with me and my family. I will take you back to your hotel.

"You have seen the Pyramids, so you have no more reason to stay in Cairo."

Ketch was stunned. Lena was silent and just looked down at the floor of the car.

Once again, Ketch was heartbroken. He started having thoughts about becoming a banker or insurance salesman, just so he could get the woman of his dreams. In the movies, all the hot women fell in love with the rebel, the rogue adventurer, or the secret agent, but in the real world, they married stability and security.

Lena and her father dropped Ketch back at his hotel. They departed with a handshake.

Maybe this was good, Ketch reasoned to himself. He no longer cared about love, life or death anymore. He was now focused on the mission in Beirut.

Chapter Nineteen

The next morning, Ketch took a hotel car to the Cairo airport.

He thought check-in would be simple.

He went to the counter of the Lebanese carrier, Middle East Airlines, aka MEA, and was attended to by some very professional looking uniformed staff.

He thought that was it.

But after checking him in, the airline staff held onto his passport and boarding pass, then told him to proceed to the baggage handler at the end of the counter.

They gave his documents to a one eyed-man with missing teeth who shook them in front of him, saying, "You must give me some *baksheesh*."

Baksheesh was the Arabic word for tip, kickback, or bribe. Whatever you wanted to call it.

Ketch had been through this before and knew he couldn't fight it.

"How much?" he asked the one-eyed man.

"Five dollars, American," was the reply.

Ketch reached for his wallet, pulled out a fiver and handed it over.

The man gratefully accepted, gave him back his passport and boarding pass, then put his suitcase on the luggage belt.

Ketch moved on.

Immigration was easy in comparison. The official simply stamped his passport without even checking the picture and did not demand any *baksheesh*.

The security check was non-existent. He walked through a metal detector that was obviously not turned on, because just the loose change in his pockets would have set it off.

He wandered around the gate area a bit, then stumbled into a bar near one of the lounges.

Coincidences of coincidences, at the bar, he ran into an old friend from Hong Kong, a Canadian TV news cameraman named Liam Williams.

Liam was there with a few other international news types sporting large shoulder-held TV cameras and their local "TV producers."

"TV producers" in this part of the world were basically "fixers" who bribed the way in, and bribed the way out for their news teams.

"Liam, what the fuck are you doing in Cairo?"

"We were on the boat from Tripoli that pulled out Yasser Arafat and his guys. We're waiting for a flight back to Beirut. But someone's bombing the airport right now, so it could be a long wait."

"That's intense," Ketch replied respectfully.

"Actually, the most intense part of it was sitting on the deck across from one of his troops, and the guy started unlacing his boots," Liam explained. "I knew that boot hadn't been off in a month and his feet would stink to high heaven. Fortunately, he kept them on."

They both laughed hysterically.

"So where are you based these days?" Ketch asked.

"Cyprus. Easy access to Beirut and a better place for the wife."

"Where in Cyprus?" Ketch enquired. "I just flew in from Cyprus."

"We have a flat in Larnaca along the beach front," Liam answered. "It's a bit crowded there, but I need to be close to the airport and the ferry service to Lebanon."

"And how's the wife?"

"A difficult question right now."

"Sorry," Ketch replied gently, assuming that divorce proceedings were in the works. Standard for journalists. The wives liked the idea of being married to a man in the middle of the action with impressive passes and credentials, but couldn't deal with the reality of his constant travel and never being at home. And when he was home, he was always writing or re-writing a story, ignoring the wife and kids to meet his deadline, just when they thought they might get some attention.

It was exciting at first, but then the wife got bored being alone or worse, managing the kids by herself.

Also, unlike army wives who lived on a military base and had the support network of other army wives to lean on, there was no such thing as a club for the wives of newsmen who were never home.

Ketch and Liam caught up on old times for a while, but then got hungry and the bar didn't serve any food.

"Fuck it," Liam said. "We're going to the first class lounge."

"But we don't have first class tickets," Ketch replied.

"Fuck it. Pretend that you're British and just walk on through."

Ketch followed Liam into the lounge where they both put on their best, pompous, arrogant, British accents.

But it was more likely the TV cameras rather than the pomp and circumstance that got them through.

At least the lounge offered finger food snacks of egg mayo and tuna-fish sandwiches. It was filled with other journalists, mostly Europeans who were either flying first class or pretending to be British.

It was a long, agonizing wait.

"What is the latest takeoff time?" Ketch inquired of the clerk after an hour.

"We can't say. They are shelling the airport."

"Who is shelling the airport?"

"We don't know. Anyone could be shelling. This is Beirut.

"We are talking with Beirut on the telephone. They are talking with the people who are doing the shelling. But I don't know who they are. Once they say the shelling will stop, we can take off."

"So what will make the shelling stop?"

"Money. They are negotiating the amount. This is typical, so don't worry."

After a three-hour wait, they finally got permission to board the aircraft. The wait was grueling for Ketch. Everyone else in the lounge was drinking their way through it, but Ketch never drank on assignment.

The flight to Beirut should have been short.

However, as the aircraft banked in a low circle around the airport, Ketch noticed that bombs were still going off, not on the runway but along the perimeter. The plane circled the airport for another hour as Ketch watched the explosions below.

The other passengers kept demanding more champagne.

Ketch focused on his breathing exercises.

Finally, the plane landed.

Immediately after touchdown, all the passengers were scrambled off into a concrete bunker close to the runway.

Everyone was packed in like sheep. As soon as the last passenger left the cabin, the stairs were pulled away and the plane immediately took off again. Presumably, somewhere safe. Maybe back to Cairo. Maybe Amman, Jordan.

In the bunker, the crowd was screaming, pushing and shoving towards the immigration counters.

Luckily, Liam's "producer" somehow got them to the head of the line.

"You go first," he said to Ketch.

Ketch approached the immigration desk and presented his passport.

The officer scowled at him.

"Baksheesh," he shouted at Ketch.

"How much?"

"Baksheesh," the officer just shouted back at him.

"Ok. How much?" Ketch replied, trying to be cooperative.

"Baksheesh," the officer returned more aggressively.

At that point, Liam's producer stepped forward and said something in Arabic. The officer screamed something back angrily at him in Arabic, but stamped Ketch's passport and sent him through.

"Wait for me," Liam shouted after him.

There was no customs to speak of and Ketch found a man holding up a signboard with his name. He assumed it was his hotel pickup, but waited for Liam.

When Liam got through the process he grabbed Ketch. "Where are you staying?"

"The Commodore Hotel."

"Great. We're all staying there. I'll give you a ride."

"Thanks, but I already got a hotel car pickup," Ketch noted, pointing to the guy with the sign.

"Forget it. That's the easiest way to get yourself kidnapped. A pickup from the airport. Give the guy some money and come with me."

Ketch paid off the driver and followed Liam into a beat-up Chevrolet, driven by another one of Liam's "producers."

When everyone was packed in, they screeched out of the airport and down the street.

"This is Sniper's Alley," Liam noted. "They like to take pot shots at the cars from the airport."

"Why?"

"There is no 'why' in Beirut, Eric. Only Beirut. Get used to it. Quickly. If you want to survive here."

Chapter Twenty

Thanks to Liam, Ketch made it to the Commodore Hotel without incident.

The Commodore was a nice property in the once-fashionable Hamra district of predominantly Muslim West Beirut. All the journalists were staying there and it apparently had some halo of protection. Allegedly, it was owned and operated by Palestinians who negotiated good deals with the militias. Most of the other hotels in the area had been shattered in the fighting.

Ketch asked for a room on the first floor and in the back of the hotel if possible. He wanted to be able to walk to his room and didn't want to be in the front, where it was more likely he'd experience any bomb blasts.

"There is also a small package for you, Mr. Kelly," said the desk clerk. "Were you expecting one?"

"Yes, a colleague said it would be waiting for me," Ketch replied.

"Well, I should tell you that it is against the policy of the hotel to accept packages for guests because of the bombs," he explained. "We only took this one because it was brought by a man in a suit who said he was an American diplomat and showed his official passport.

"But, we cannot do it for you in the future," he explained.

"Thank you," Ketch replied. "Sorry, I troubled you."

Ketch presented an American Express card, the only credit card accepted by the Commodore.

Ketch finished the check-in process which required him to pay for his room in advance. He was also required to advance the hotel another thousand dollars to cover his food and drink incidentals. After all, in Beirut, he could get shot at any time and the hotel didn't want to foot the bill.

Then, he grabbed the parcel and made for the stairs next to the elevator.

The room was small but comfortable. Unfortunately, it was only about twenty feet across from the apartment on the other side of the alley. He could see families going about their business, cooking or watching television. He figured that meant they could also see him, so he quickly drew the curtains. When he went to bed at night, he also pulled the mattress onto the floor to the far side of the bed, away from the window, and sleep there, so he'd have additional protection.

He then opened the parcel left with the hotel.

It contained a box of business cards naming him Eric Kelly, Foreign Editor of the *Detroit City News,* as well as a Browning Hi-Power double-action pistol but only two clips of ammo. He expected at least three. And no silencer. The gun didn't even have a threaded barrel extension to accommodate one.

"Damn you Elizabeth," he said out loud. The box also included a table of the Morse code alphabet, which he found especially insulting.

There was also a manila envelope marked "Adam Smith," and a Sony pocket shortwave radio. As Elizabeth noted, it was the size of a small paperback novel. A telescoping antenna pulled out from the back and extended about two feet upwards.

Ketch opened the envelope. It contained a black and white photo and a brief profile of Adam Smith.

The photo appeared to be from a school yearbook and showed a young, chubby, student with straight, blond hair. The hair was short on the sides, but long in front and flopped over the forehead. The background info read:

> *"Adam Smith. Born and raised, Dearborn, Michigan. Father autoworker. Mother waitress. Educational aptitude enabled him to skip grades in elementary school and enter high school early, which he finished in three years. Nicknamed 'Twinkie', presumably for all the cakes he ate. Won first place at inter-city science fair, but project unknown. Completed university in fours years with a PhD in chemistry. Genius material. Married Lebanese girlfriend from school. Neither family approved of the marriage, so the couple moved to Chicago where he got a job as a university lecturer. In 1976, the couple moved to Lebanon during the height of the civil war there, where he took a teaching position at the American University of Beirut. Wife killed by unknown sniper in 1980. No known political affiliations or police record, but was suspended a week during elementary school for catching ants and setting them on fire on school playground during recess."*

"Boys will be boys," Ketch laughed to himself. Ketch noted that the brief didn't provide his age. Given that the boy genius was skipping of lot a grades in school, they probably lost track of it, he mused.

He locked up the goods in his luggage then went down to the restaurant for dinner.

The restaurant was filled mostly with journalists. They were all drinking heavily or zonked-out on other substances. He didn't try to meet anyone, but they all tried to meet him. He was the new boy in town and might lead them to a fresh story.

"Hey man," one said approaching his table. "I'm a combat photographer and always looking for good *bang bang*, so if you hear of any, let me know and I'll make it worth your while. Here's my card."

Bang bang was journalist slang for gunfire. Any gunfire by anyone or anything. Rifles, rockets, artillery. More guns going off or bigger blasts meant better *bang bang*.

Ketch noted that the card sported the name of a major international news organization.

He didn't invite the photographer to join him and ordered his dinner. Lamb chops which came with pita bread, rice and salad. He washed it down with a 7Up. Ketch never drank on assignment, even something caffeinated. He wanted all his senses in check and didn't want to be dulled or hyped on anything, be it alcohol or caffeine.

He passed on the salad. He never ate salads outside of the U.S. Too easy to pick up some water-borne disease, either from the water in the greens or the water they washed it with. Years ago, a friend was on vacation in Bali, Indonesia, taking meditation classes and getting back to basics. She thought she would follow a healthy routine by eating salad and raw vegetables. She was hospitalized for six weeks with typhus and nearly died.

Shortly after his meal arrived, a young kid showed up at his table.

"Hey, man. I hear you're new in town. You need a guide? I've been here a month and can take you anywhere."

"Where you from?" Ketch asked, noting the American accent.

"Connecticut. I'm a college student. I'm taking time off to pursue my studies here."

"What are you studying?"

"International politics."

"So you're at university here?"

"No. Just freelancing as a photographer. A combat photographer."

"Combat photographer? Where? The Shouf, the Green Line?"

"No. Those places are too hairy. I took pictures of the Marine barracks after they were blown up."

"Ok, I'll let you know."

"Hey, man. Look, I need a place to stay. I was staying with a journalist friend here, but he's kicking me out cause his girlfriend is showing up. Happy to sleep on your floor and I can show you around town."

"You came out here with no money for a hotel room?"

"No, my dad gave me enough cash for a month and his American Express card. But I've already run through the cash and I don't want to take advantage of him by using the Amex card."

"Sorry, I don't want a roommate. You should talk to your dad or go home."

"Fuck you, man, I'm just trying to help you."

Ketch finished his dinner quickly, and signed the bill.

Then he left and went to the reception desk.

"I'm looking for a translator and guide," he told the two clerks standing behind the counter.

The clerks looked at each other and smiled.

"Nikki Hassani is the best, but very expensive," one clerk replied.

"How expensive?"

"American dollars five hundred a day. Cash."

"If she's the best, why hasn't she been hired by the other news guys here?"

"They claim she is difficult to work with."

"How so?"

"She won't take you someplace if she thinks you will be killed. The other newsmen here want to be killed. So they don't want her. She is too careful."

Ketch decided that careful was a good place to start and decided to hire her.

"When can she be here?"

"We can call her now," the clerk replied. "Maybe one hour. We will call you in your room."

Ketch left the counter and went outside onto the street. He needed a driver. As soon as he stepped out of the hotel, he was swarmed by drivers offering taxi services, *bang bang* tours and militia passes. He was actually taken in by one old man who didn't appear to be on the hustle and just asked him where he wanted to go.

He had a rugged face, ragged hands and missing teeth, which didn't seem to bother him when he smiled. He wore a traditional *thawb* or *dishdasha*, a white, long-sleeved, ankle-length tunic with a few buttons up the chest. Foreigners often referred to it as a "dishdash." It was worn throughout the Middle East and a symbol of Arab culture. He also wore the black and white checkered *keffiyeh* head scarf made famous by Yasser

Arafat, which had since become a symbol of Palestinian nationalism.

Ketch thought his dress might give him credibility and help him blend in.

"Where you go?" he enquired good-naturedly.

"Nowhere special, just a quick tour of Beirut," Ketch replied.

"Ok, can go now."

"No. I want to go tomorrow morning. Seven o'clock," Ketch responded. "How much?"

"One hour, one hundred dollars American," the old man replied. "If you promise me two days, I can give a special price. Eighty dollars American."

"Ok. Two days. We start tomorrow. Seven o'clock."

They shook hands and went back inside the hotel.

"Cash dollars!" the old man shouted after him as he was leaving.

"Cash!" Ketch affirmed with a smile.

He went back to his room, pulled a 7Up from the mini-bar and started to outline his plans for the next day. He unfolded a map of the city, but it meant nothing to him. He found the hotel, but he couldn't figure out anything else. So tomorrow's tour would be a good orientation, he noted to himself.

After half an hour, there was a gentle knock on the door.

Ketch braced the door with his foot and opened it slowly.

A woman stood in the hall. She wore a white, cotton blouse, with a blue skirt, and flat shoes. Only a hint of lipstick. Pink. A lace bra was visible under the thin cotton blouse. But what first grabbed Ketch's attention were her big, dark, mysterious eyes, and generous smile.

"Nikki?" he asked as he opened the door.

"Mr. Kelly?"

"Yes."

"May I come in?"

"Of course, please have a seat."

There was only the desk chair or the bed. Nikki chose the chair, while Ketch sat at the foot of the bed.

The minute Ketch saw her, he knew he would have sex with her. The moment she saw Ketch, she knew she would have sex with him.

Nikki Hassani. Ketch learned later that her father was Muslim, but her mother French Catholic. She spoke English, Arabic, French, Spanish and Portuguese.

Nikki's father was in the construction business. Buildings were always being blown up in Beirut, so they constantly needed to be rebuilt. It was a good business to be in. She came from money, but didn't like asking daddy for it because he would always ask for something in return. So, she preferred to make it on her own.

Nikki was stunning. Her incredibly big, Pharaonic, cat-like eyes were worthy of an Egyptian queen. Her body was tight, toned and tanned. The benefit of living along the Mediterranean seaside. Her hair was light brown, but with random natural blonde streaks from the sun. She had firm, medium-sized, breasts that seemed to stand up and stare back at Ketch whenever he looked their way.

Ketch explained that tomorrow would be very easy. He just wanted someone to take him around the city for a couple of hours, so he could get oriented. But he wanted to start early in the morning. Seven.

"Mr. Kelly," she said. "Can I make a recommendation?"

"What's that?"

"I know you want to fuck me. And I want to fuck you," she announced unabashedly.

"So, it's better if we get it out of the way right now. Otherwise, we will be very distracted and that will make it difficult to work together."

Ketch took a moment to recover from her directness, then laughed to himself.

"How much for that?" he returned somewhat cynically.

"No charge," Nikki replied. "I'm a translator, not a prostitute. It will be better for our working relationship."

"How so?' Ketch asked sheepishly.

"Come on. What kind of little boy are you?" she challenged. "I'm sure there are many women in your office back home that you want to fuck, but can't, so there is always tension with the work. But if you fucked them, the tension would go away because, you'd no longer be interested in them once you fucked them," she answered.

Ketch loved the way she nonchalantly used the word "fuck."

"How do you know? Maybe after the first time, I would want to fuck them even more," he replied. He couldn't believe he was having this conversation.

"Because, you are a man. And once a man fucks a woman, he loses interest in her," Nikki explained. "Men are programmed to propagate the species. So, you need to fuck everything in sight, then go on to fuck the next one. It's in your genes.

"So, better you fuck me now, and get it out of your system, so we can work together as professionals. Otherwise, tomorrow, all you are going to do is stare at my breasts," she said with a laugh.

Ketch smiled. He was caught.

At that point, Nikki went over to the bed, pulled Ketch up by his shirt collar and began searching his body with her hands. She started by caressing his cheeks, then put her arms around his neck. Her hands slid down his back to his butt, which she squeezed as if testing ripe fruit in the grocery store.

"Nice butt," she noted.

"Thanks," Ketch replied with a laugh.

She drew her hands back to the front, gently stroking his groin, just enough to tease him a bit. Then both hands went to his shirt collar, and started undoing his buttons one by one from top to bottom.

She pulled back the sleeves and let the shirt drop to the floor. She then yanked off his T-shirt and tossed it onto the chair.

"Why are you wearing a T-shirt? Are you cold?" She inquired.

"It keeps my shirt from getting sweaty," he answered.

"Your shirt is off," she announced. "So now you must take off my shirt and we will both get sweaty."

She directed Ketch to the buttons on her blouse, which he undid then slipped off the thin cotton blouse, dropping it onto the floor. There was no kissing or hugging, only undressing.

"You know how to take off a girl's bra, little boy?" she said teasingly.

"I've had some experience," Ketch replied and reached around her back.

She grabbed his hands from behind and brought them back to the front and placed them on her chest in between the cleavage.

"This one is attached in the front," she noted.

"You are right-handed, or left?" she asked.

"Right."

She grabbed his right middle finger, slipped it under the front of her bra and pinched his thumb and index finger across the clasp.

The bra sprang open and her firm, round breasts blossomed like flowers as the halter fell away onto the floor. Two ripe grapefruits, Ketch mentally noted.

"Get down on the bed," she instructed and he did as told.

She removed his shoes and socks, then undid his belt and pulled his pants off.

"Looks like you like me," she said, noting the shaft bulging through his briefs.

She let her skirt slip to the floor, then looked deeply into his eyes while peeling off her g-string. It revealed tightly trimmed pubic hair shaped like the leaf of a palm tree.

Ketch was without words.

She then carefully pulled off Ketch's briefs, making sure not to catch him on the tight waistband. When she did, his shaft snapped upright like it was on a tightly wound spring.

"I thought all older men wear boxer shorts," she teased. "Only little boys wear panties.

"Well, this little boy doesn't like having his balls bounce around, when he's running down the street with his cameras," he replied.

"Circumcised," she noted. "Are you Jewish?"

"Roman Catholic."

"Of course, a Jewish one would be much bigger," she teased again.

"Funny," Eric answered back.

"Well, I'm not going to kiss that one," she said. "It needs a big haircut. I don't like to get hair in my mouth.

"Don't you know that girls don't like going into the jungle anymore than men like going into the bush?"

She then mounted him and announced, "I'm on top. As I said, we are just fucking, not making love."

While Nikki worked on Ketch, she leaned forward and caressed his face with her breasts. Ketch tried to kiss them, but every time he did, she pulled them back, then danced them around his face teasingly.

"Ok, this is enough for the first time," Nikki said sitting up but still straddling him. "I want to come now."

She then placed Ketch's hands on her breasts and instructed him to grab them gently. Meanwhile, she kept rubbing her groin against his, front to back, then up and down.

Nikki took a deep breath, held it a moment, squeezed her legs tight, then collapsed on top of him, kissing him gently on the cheek, forehead and mouth.

"You have a lot of stamina, Mr. Kelly," she noted. "Why didn't you come?"

"I guess I'm nervous," Ketch answered jokingly.

"Well, I'm not going to explore that jungle down there, just to please you," she laughed. "You should shave it."

"I couldn't do that. What would the guys at the gym say?" Ketch laughed.

"Tell them you did it for the woman you love."

"Would that be you?"

"No. This is about pleasure, not love.

"Many men and women in this part of the world shave their private parts. It is skin to skin. Wet and oily. The sensation is incredible. You should try it.

"You can always tell if a man is shaved, because he is scratching his groin all the time. After shaving, you need to put on some lotion, but men are too proud to do that. They think it's only for girls.

"Never mind, I know how to finish this. She stayed mounted on top of him, but drew her knees together, squatting over him and making herself tighter. She then put her arms behind her and slowly leaned back on them.

As she did, she carefully raised his shaft to a more vertical position for heightened sensitivity, then began pumping Ketch like a porn star.

He came in less than a minute.

"Ok. Stop! Stop now!" he shouted, breathing heavily.

Nikki laughed a bit, climbed off of him and popped into the bathroom. She removed the shower head from its European style sliding fixture and washed herself from the waist down.

Ketch had been with a lot of beautiful and sensual women in his time, but not like Nikki.

Nikki was confident and smart. She was more than smart. She was really smart. Ketch learned that she was an associate professor at the American University of Beirut. She had a PhD in physics and could explain quantum mechanics in five minutes, in a way that even Ketch could understand.

On their first day out, Ketch learned that she was also street smart and most importantly, she was passionate and stood by her man and friends in the way that only a Mediterranean woman would.

"Ok. I must leave. I will see you in the morning for your tour of Beirut. Seven is it?"

"Seven."

"Don't dream about me," she said with a wink and left.

Chapter Twenty-One

Ketch woke up at four in the morning to the sound and reverberation of a bomb blast.

In fact, there were two bomb blasts. Only minutes apart. Ketch noted the tactic from his Vietnam experience.

The first one was to do immediate devastation. The second was intentionally delayed to injure people and rescue workers who rushed in to assist the victims. It was set to maximize innocent casualties and demoralize the rescue teams.

Ketch ran down the stairs to see what the commotion was about. When he got outside, he found that the apartment building next door had been the target. It was now an ugly black, oily color, and women on the upper floors were hanging out the windows screaming for help as smoke poured from the building.

The women all had covered heads. They either wore the *hijab* or the *niqab*. He didn't see any men in the windows.

Big chunks of concrete and twisted metal littered the street.

A Caterpillar bulldozer was already scooping up the debris.

Ketch pressed the bystanders for details.

He got two different stories.

"The downstairs shop was selling alcohol. It is against Islam. So they needed to be punished," said one.

Another had a more practical story. "The building owners were pushed for a twenty percent increase in protection money from the militias and refused to pay."

"Were they Muslim or Christian militias?" Ketch asked naively.

"Who knows? This is Beirut," the man replied. "It doesn't matter."

Chapter Twenty-Two

Ketch went back to his room, hoping to catch at least another few minutes of sleep.

He set his alarm clock for 5:45 a.m. so he could check the shortwave radio broadcast from his handlers to see if there was any news.

He tuned to the forty-meter wavelength band and looked for 7.15 MHz. Of course the dial was not that finely calibrated because of the small screen. The best he could do was position the needle on the dial between 7.1MHz and 7.2MHz and wiggle it around. But the spacing was only the width of the needle, maybe a sixteenth of an inch, so there was not a lot of wiggle room.

He plugged in the earphones and waited for the clock to strike six a.m. and listened for "K-T-H" in Morse code.

At exactly six a.m. to the second a very strong signal presented itself on the frequency. It sent *"dah-dit-dah-dit, dah-dah-dit-dah,"* repeated over and over again.

"C-Q".

It was Morse code shorthand, initially sent out by a ham radio operator and meant calling all stations, looking for someone to chat with. If the operator wanted to contact someone specifically, he'd enter their call sign after the sequence followed by "D-E" or *"dah-dit-dit, dit"* followed by his own call sign. "D-E" meant "from" and was presumably borrowed from the

French, like "Mayday" allegedly came from the French *M'aider,* which meant "Help me."

The C-Q string continued for a good thirty seconds. There was a noticeable break of a few seconds, then it started up "C-Q-K-T-H," "*dah-dit-dah-dit, dah-dah-dit-dah, dah-dit-dah, dah, dit-dit-dit-dit.*" Ketch's handle.

Ketch was pleased that he was able to lock onto the right signal and anxiously waited for the update. He could tell by the uneven rhythm of the message that someone was keying it manually and tapping on a brass code key, not unlike the ones used in old telegraph offices.

He laughed to himself. Even as a teenager, he had graduated to a "bug." It had a rod that you rocked side to side. At the end was a sort of handle. The left side of the handle was a paddle and the right side a knob. You pushed the knob to the left to manually enter dashes and the paddle to the right to automatically enter dots.

Physically, it was harder to enter dots so the "bug" created them, by mechanically bouncing off a steel spring. You adjusted the speed by sliding a weight along the end of the rod, which was fastened with a screw.

At fast speeds such as fifteen-to-twenty words per minute, you didn't push the handles back and forth so much as you rolled your fingers off them.

At even faster speeds, you needed an "electronic keyer." It consisted of two paddles connected to a short lever that had electrical contacts on either side. Contact in one direction electronically produced dashes. Contact in the other generated dots.

It required a very light, sensitive touch and was probably good up to thirty-five words per minute. At those speeds the dots and dashes melded into words and the radio operator on the other side didn't bother to write them down, because he'd never be able to keep up.

At that point, the dots and dashes became speech and it was like having a conversation.

Ketch waited impatiently.

After the station repeated his handle three times, there was another noticeable pause, then the letter "N" was sent three times.

"No news".

"Fuck you!" Ketch shouted at the radio. "What a bunch of bullshit."

He resolved not to bother with it again.

Chapter Twenty-Three

Ketch took a quick shower, stretched out on the floor, then went downstairs to the dining room for an early breakfast.

He ordered scrambled eggs, bacon, toast and a 7Up.

"Would that be 7Up or Sprite?" the waiter asked.

"7Up," Ketch returned. "Sprite is too sweet."

"Would you like a slice of lemon or lime with your drink?" the waiter continued.

Ketch wasn't sure why you'd put a lemon or lime in a lemon-lime soft drink, but acquiesced.

"Sure," he replied. "A lime."

"Very good," the waiter responded. "It will only be a moment."

Ketch gobbled down the meal, then climbed the stairs back to his room, deciding how to equip himself for the day.

He thought about the Browning for a moment, then decided to leave it locked up in his suitcase. Today was only a quick orientation tour, he told himself.

He pulled open the mini-bar and grabbed a few bottles of water as well as all the nuts and crackers from the rack. He hoped they would sustain him through the day if he couldn't grab food somewhere. Based on his experience, he found that he could live off nuts and water for a week.

More importantly, he checked out the Canon 35mm single-lens reflex camera he brought with him. This was not just to give him credibility as a journalist, but also to snap some intel shots he thought could be useful.

He opened the back, checked the feeds and loaded a can of Kodak Ektachrome 400 ASA color transparency film into it almost as carefully as he'd load rounds into a pistol magazine. The ASA number indicated the light detection sensitivity of the film. The higher the number, the less light you needed, but the lower the resolution.

Most journalists shot 200 ASA or lower for fine-grained resolution but they took time to pose their shots, and get the light right so they could send perfect, high-resolution color shots back to the magazines. For large format color magazine covers, they typically shot 64 ASA.

Ketch didn't need beautiful color shots. That was not his mission. He was there to capture a moment of history and get usable intel, not win an art award. He didn't care about the grain or the standards of news magazines.

Also, Ektachrome could be processed anywhere in the world within a day, even in Beirut. In addition, the more high-resolution films needed to be kept in a refrigerator and had to be shipped out to a lab in Europe or the U.S. for processing. Too much valuable time lost.

Ketch snapped the back of the camera shut, shot off two frames to start the roll then went downstairs.

Chapter Twenty-Four

Ketch packed a small backpack with his gear and walked down the stairs to the lobby.

He didn't see anyone there, so went outside. Nikki was waiting for him in front of the hotel.

"Where is this driver you hired?" she demanded.

Ketch pointed out the old man across the street squatting on the curb.

"That guy? He is crazy. Never hire these guys again before you talk to me. Or find yourself another tour guide."

"I promised him two days of work."

"We will see if we are not dead by then," Nikki replied angrily.

The old man recognized him, ran to his car and brought it round to the front of the hotel. It was white, beat up and with no air conditioning. Ketch couldn't place the brand, but it reminded him of a box-like Russian *Lada*. Maybe imported from Syria.

It was a fine, mild Mediterranean day. So they didn't require air conditioning to cool themselves off, but they did require air conditioning so they could close the windows to prevent the dust blowing in from the dirty roads outside the car.

Anyway, it would be a very brief tour, Ketch consoled himself.

"We will go over to the coast road to see the wonderful beaches. But not too far south, otherwise, we will need to pass through militia territory," Nikki explained. I will show you the Marines bombed headquarters at the airport and the bombed French headquarters. Some photographer took a very famous picture there showing a French officer holding the hand of a soldier buried under the rubble.

"Then I will show you the other multinational forces. The Italians. They have colorful uniforms. That will make a nice picture. The Italians are between the Americans in the south and the French in the north but better if we see the French first. The Italian area is more dangerous.

"Then I will show you the bombed American Embassy and we can stop on the Corniche for a quick sandwich."

"The Corniche?"

"Yes. It is a place in the northwest section of West Beirut. It has a nice view of the sea. It will make you appreciate what a beautiful city this was before the foreigners came here. Maybe it could be beautiful again some day."

"I thought the foreigners came here to stop the Christians and the Muslims from shooting each other," Ketch remarked, resenting the self-serving blame that locals from all over the world put on foreigners.

"Who do you think gives them guns?" she replied. "War is expensive. One rifle bullet costs one dollar American. A little bit of fighting between a few men and you spend enough money to buy a decent car.

"The foreigners pick their favorite militia to fight with the other ones. Then the other ones get paid by another foreigner to fight them back. It is a sport. Each bets on his team to win.

"Then we have the Palestinians. They were pushed out of Jordan because they were becoming too strong and started a war with the government to take over.

"Then, they tried to take over Lebanon, so the president made a deal with the Israelis to kick them out.

"Nobody wants them here.

"Wherever they go, the Israelis will go to bomb them. I feel very sad for them. They live in dirty camps south of here with no water or toilets.

"Israel was their country. Even the British called it Palestine. Then after Hitler killed so many Jews, everyone felt sorry for them and the British gave them Palestine without asking anyone's permission.

"Nobody tells you about all the other people that Hitler killed in Poland, including many Catholics.

"He wanted to replace everyone with Germans. I am Catholic and my mother has Catholic relatives who were in the famous Auschwitz concentration camp. Five of them. Four men and one woman. All the men were tailors, except one who was a cadet in the Polish army.

"The funny thing is that all the tailors and the woman were killed, but the army cadet was released.

"But, his life was very difficult after that. He went crazy and killed himself.

"And while Hitler was killing Catholics in concentration camps, he was dancing with Catholic, fascist Italy for an alliance.

"My own theory is that the British plan was to get rid of the Jews in Britain. The British also don't like the Jews. They are very racist about it. At one point, they even suggested that the Jews make their home in Africa. How ridiculous is that?

"But the Jews went to Israel in the thousands and started to push out the Palestinians, so the two started fighting. The British tried to control immigration because they didn't want the Jews to overwhelm the local Palestinians, so the Jews started attacking the British demanding unlimited Jewish immigration. Then the Jews started the bombings. They even bombed a big hotel in Jerusalem, killing many innocent people, because there were British soldiers there.

"The Jews were the first terrorists in the Middle East.

"Look at the history. The first Jewish organizations there, Haganah and Irgun, were declared terrorists by the British. The British were trying to make peace.

"But the Jews didn't care about peace. They only cared about getting what they wanted. And one of their terrorist leaders later became prime minister to Israel.

"Unfortunately, the Palestinians tried to adopt their strategy, but didn't have Hitler's death camps to create sympathy. So they got branded as terrorist enemies of the entire world.

"That is why everyone is fighting in Lebanon right now."

Quite a speech, Ketch thought to himself. He couldn't tell whether she was being anti-Semitic or just venting a lot of frustration and anger over the situation in Lebanon. He didn't want to engage her and fuel the rant, but felt he needed to say something.

"If the British wanted to get rid of the Jews in England, why did they control immigration to Palestine? They would have let all of them go," Ketch challenged. "Also, the British didn't control Lebanon," Ketch responded. "The French did. When the Ottoman Turkish Empire was carved up after World War I, the French were given the mandate to manage Lebanon and Syria, just as the British were given the mandate for Palestine.

"And there were not many Jews in Lebanon," he added. "So, I don't think it's their fault."

"Yes," Nikki replied dismissively. "It is a long, sad story."

Chapter Twenty-Five

Ketch left it at that.

He decided not to continue the debate, but enjoy the ride and focus on getting oriented.

He pulled out his city map of Beirut and tried to figure out where they were.

"Give it to me," Nikki shouted from the back seat. She grabbed it impatiently and said, "We are here. Soon, we will turn onto the road along the sea."

They passed some attractive beaches overlooking the Mediterranean and a clear, blue sky. After a short while, the driver turned inland.

Nikki shouted something in Arabic at him, but he ignored it.

"I told you this guy is crazy," she screamed. "He doesn't know where he is going."

After a few blocks, they were stopped at a militia checkpoint. Ketch didn't know whose militia, only that they weren't friendly.

"They want to see your pass," Nikki said.

"What pass? I don't have a pass," Ketch returned.

Beirut was controlled by a variety of gangs, sects, militias, whatever you wanted to call them. Crossing town meant having a "pass" for each of them. You might need six different passes just to go a few miles, depending on which direction you were traveling.

"You don't have any passes?" Nikki returned angrily. "That is the job of the driver. I told you not to hire a driver without me."

The boy on duty kept demanding a pass, but Ketch didn't have one. Meanwhile, the old man kept smiling at him, waving his hands about and dismissing the whole affair.

The boy was not impressed. He pushed an AK-47 assault rifle through the window and into Ketch's face. He then started shouting at him in Arabic.

Ketch responded with the only two Arabic words he remembered, *habib*, "friend" and *sahafi*, "journalist." The latter was not always the best response because many journalists were considered good hostages and their news organization would pay a big bounty for their release.

However, Ketch thought, at best it would only get him kidnapped as opposed to shot on the spot. And, based on his training, he figured he could escape.

Ketch noted that the boy's finger was not on the trigger and that might give him an opportunity to react. Ketch visualized that he could force open the door, hitting the boy in the knees, then jam the gun in the window, slide himself inside of the barrel and neutralize his ability to shoot just by cupping his hand over the bolt and jamming the gun's ability to engage.

However, before he executed that plan, a little voice told him to wait. The minute Ketch opened the car door, the barrel through the window would be leveraged in a game of push and pull that somebody would lose. Most likely, Mustapha or Nikki.

In the meantime, Nikki calmly got out of the car from the back seat, grabbed the barrel of the boy's rifle, pulled it out of the window and pushed it into her cleavage. Then, she did her own shouting in Arabic, meanwhile pressing her chest up against the muzzle and daring the boy to shoot her.

The boy was now visibly scared and didn't know what to do. He lowered his weapon, apologized to Nikki and waved them through.

Ketch didn't know what she said and didn't want to ask. But he was now in love with Nikki.

Ketch asked her what a university professor such as herself was doing wasting her time as a translator. What she said unnerved him.

"I make more money in a week as a hard-currency translator, than I would in a month at the university," she replied. "I'd make more in a day as a hard-currency prostitute."

Ketch shuddered that such a beautiful, smart, educated woman could be selling her body for pounds, deutschmarks or dollars. But maybe that's exactly what Nikki was doing right now. He started to wonder whether she slept with him because she wanted to, or if it was just part of the service he was paying for.

After the incident at the checkpoint, Nikki decided to cut the sightseeing short.

They quickly drove past the walls of the U.S. Marine compound.

"U.S. Marines," Nikki announced, pointing at the walls.

They drove by the perimeter, then started for the French headquarters.

Well in advance of the French compound, they were stopped by a French trooper, wearing a red beret, cammies and what appeared to be a Heckler & Koch submachine gun.

He just stepped right out in front of the car and pointed the gun at the driver through the windshield. The old man screeched the car to a jolting halt, but laughing in the process. Then the soldier got on a walkie-talkie handheld radio and two other French soldiers quickly appeared out of nowhere and surrounded the car. They motioned for everyone to get out.

The old man jumped out of the car, smiling, laughing and waving his arms about, causing one of the soldiers to flinch, take a step back and raise his rifle at him.

Nikki immediately intervened in French and calmed things down.

One soldier motioned them to the side of the road, while the other two searched the car. They opened the engine hood, the trunk, slid a mirror underneath, then rifled through their belongings. Ketch was grateful that he had left the Browning back in his hotel room.

After a brief exchange between Nikki and the soldiers, they were motioned back into the car and waved away.

"I told you this old man was stupid," she said angrily.

"Where next?" Ketch inquired innocently, trying to appear unfazed by the incident.

"Back to the hotel," Nikki said abruptly.

"But what about the Italians and the Corniche?"

"I will think about it," she replied curtly. "The Italians are on the way back to the Marines, but the Corniche is nearby the hotel.

"But this old man will get us killed. You were stupid to hire him."

Nikki then started a heated discussion in Arabic with the driver.

The driver just responded by smiling and nodding.

After a short drive, she instructed him to pull over and park on the street.

"The Italians are over there," she said. "We will leave the car and the driver here. I will walk with you."

Ketch left everything in the car except his Canon camera.

As they walked further down the street, Ketch spotted a white armored personnel carrier, also known as an APC, sandwiched between two mounds of dirt, each about eight feet high. Coiled razor wire topped the mounds.

Three soldiers poked themselves out of the top. One manned a mounted .50 caliber machine gun. The other two had what appeared to be M-16 rifles pointed forward.

They all wore dark green cammies but different headgear. One wore a blue beret, another a red beret with a cravat around his neck, and the third a dark red woolen ski sock.

A brightly colored flag of red, white and blue vertical stripes was posted on a thin, metal antenna at the back of the APC. The French flag. All the guns on the APC were pointing in their direction, though didn't seem to be aiming at them.

Ketch was confused.

"That looks like a French flag," he noted to Nikki. "Shouldn't they be flying the Italian flag of red, white and green?"

"I don't know," she responded. "This is Beirut."

Ketch didn't press the point. Nikki was right. It would make a colorful picture.

Before they got within fifty yards, the soldier behind the machine gun shouted into a handheld radio and another solider emerged from behind the vehicle. He was also dressed in dark green cammies, but with a baseball cap on his head and armed only with a pistol at his side. The pistol's holster was canvas and had a flap covering the gun, so the solider was obviously not planning to draw it on them.

"Good morning, folks," he shouted with a touch of American in his voice, as he walked towards them. "How can I help you?"

"I'm an American journalist and just wanted to take a quick picture of the vehicle." Ketch shouted back.

"Why?" the soldier yelled, still approaching them, but not drawing his sidearm or releasing the flap on the holster.

"I want a picture of America's allies out here. And it's a colorful shot."

There were no signs of rank on his sleeves or collar.

The soldier met up with them, then asked to see the camera. He then pointed it at Ketch and Nikki, advanced the film and pushed the shutter button. Ketch wondered whether he had seen the camera guns in Darra, Pakistan.

"Maybe, you need to take another one," Ketch said cheerfully. "We forgot to say cheese."

The soldier laughed and shouted into his walkie-talkie in what seemed to be perfect Italian. The soldier on the top of the vehicle shrugged his shoulders and made a gesture with his hands.

"Ok. One picture. From here."

"Can I take three?" Ketch negotiated. "I need to bracket the exposure, to make sure I get the lighting right."

"What do you mean bracket the exposure," the soldier asked, a bit confused.

"I take one picture at a normal setting, then open the lens in one direction, then close it in the other direction to let in more light or less light with separate shots, to make sure I get the exposure right," Ketch explained. "That will insure that the picture turns out."

"Ok," the soldier responded. "Take your shots. But only from here."

Ketch pointed his camera at the vehicle and zoomed in as much as he could, then pressed the shutter button. The shutter was set on "motor drive," so with each press of the button, he actually zipped off a few shots for each setting. The soldier didn't notice.

"Thank you," he said, and turned away back towards their car.

"I hope you are happy now," Nikki said sarcastically as they walked back.

But when they got back to the car, the driver was not there.

"I told you," Nikki exclaimed disgustedly. "I told you this guy is crazy. Now, what do we do?"

"Wait," Ketch suggested.

After a few minutes, the driver emerged from a nearby building, laughing and waving his arms about.

"Pee-Pee," he said pointing to his groin.

They all got back into the car and drove off.

Ketch laughed.

Nikki did not.

Instead, she muttered something in French to herself that Ketch took to mean "asshole," but he couldn't tell whether she meant it for him or the driver.

"Ok, I will show you the Corniche, but that is the last stop," she admonished. "You can see the American embassy from there."

Ketch sensed that they were driving north, but didn't recognize any discernible landmarks from the previous drive.

He knew they were close when he picked up the salty smell of the sea air.

The driver made a turn and came out onto a promenade along the waterfront. Avenue de Paris. It was landscaped with a variety of flowers.

Old men sat on stools hunched over backgammon boards while sipping thick brown coffee from thimble-like cups. Meanwhile, young boys cast baited hooks with long fishing rods over a low railing out into the sea.

"Normally, I am afraid to go into an open space like this," Nikki explained. "But the buildings are far away. So, I don't think the snipers can shoot us."

"Why would snipers want to shoot us?" Ketch asked naively.

"Just for fun. They are bored sitting behind their guns all day long and need to do something," she explained. "You would do the same.

"I will show you the embassy and you can take a quick picture, then we will leave," she added sternly.

They walked west along the seafront a bit toward the American University of Beirut. All seemed relaxed and at peace. Ketch breathed in the salty air, the cloudless sky and the blue sea. He looked up and the sun bounced gentle rays off his face. He surveyed the promenade again with its young boys fishing and old men sipping coffee, chatting, laughing and struggling over their backgammon boards.

They passed the University and spotted the U.S. Embassy in the distance.

"Eric," she shouted and pointed across the way at a tall building, back towards the city.

"American Embassy," she said.

It was not blown up into a pile of rubble as Ketch had expected. Instead, it looked like someone had taken a dull razor and scratched off its face.

The front of the building had been ripped away, exposing offices and rooms inside.

Some furniture was still in place. But overall, the building was lifeless.

"Quick. Take your picture," she urged. He snapped off a few shots and she hurried him back along the promenade to the car.

He lost himself in his thoughts for a moment, but was interrupted by four young children, maybe five or six years old. The boys wore shorts and T-shirts, while the girls wore pretty white and pink fluffy dresses. All of them wore leather sandals.

"Take picture, take picture," one of the boys shouted as they ran up to Ketch grabbing his trouser belt laughing.

Fortunately, the contact didn't trigger the reflexes that would typically have caused Ketch to flinch and react physically. Normally, if someone entered his space quickly, he went into attack mode. But the sun and the sea had put him at rest.

Ketch looked down at the tiny figures below him. They were well-dressed, especially for children on the street, but their faces were smudged by streaks of vanilla and chocolate ice cream.

"Take picture," they pleaded in unison.

"These are our girlfriends," one of the boys explained. "We are having a date."

"Ok," Ketch replied. "But how do I send the pictures to you?"

"No problem," the other boy interjected. "Put in your magazine and make us famous."

Ketch smiled and instructed them to line up. He was glad he had the camera to hide behind, because their joyful innocence, in the heart of this entire tragedy, got him all choked up.

He glanced over at Nikki and noted that she was wiping her eyes.

The children climbed onto the railing overlooking the sea and sat boy-girl, boy-girl.

They all had big eyes, cheerful faces and tanned skin. The boys had short, cropped hair, while the girls wore their thick brown hair in pony tails. The kind that rides high on the head and bounces up and down as you skip down the street. A "high" pony tail.

They got themselves seated amidst lots of giggles. Then, the boys put their arms around the little girls' waists and the girls bent their small fragile heads onto the boys' shoulders.

Their smiles were devastating.

Ketch spun off a string of shots, adjusted the lens aperture for lighting, and whirred off a few more.

"Ok. Got it," he shouted.

They laughed, slid off the railing and shouted again in unison, "Thank you, Mister!"

Then they went running down the promenade holding hands.

Ketch shared a quick smile with Nikki, but hers quickly melted, almost as if she was embarrassed to be touched by her feelings.

Their feelings were interrupted by the high-pitched whining of a vehicle in low gear. Ketch looked towards the city and saw a blue pick-up truck driving along one of the streets that ran parallel to the Corniche.

In the back of the truck bed, there appeared to be a man dropping rocks into a long tube.

"Whump! Then *"Boom!"* And the crackle of shattering concrete in the distance.

An 81mm mortar.

As the truck drove along the street, the man fed the tube with mortar rounds. Essentially, mini-artillery shells. The mortar was positioned towards the city but didn't seem to be aiming at anything in particular. The rounds were lobbed over the buildings in front of him. The shooter couldn't possibly know where they landed or what he was aiming at.

"Hurry," Nikki shouted as they jogged the remaining way back to the car. "He could change his mind and start bombing the Corniche."

The driver was outside the car, waving his hands at the truck and laughing.

Nikki shouted at him in Arabic. He climbed into the car, brought the engine to a stuttered start and they made their way back to the Commodore. The driver kept laughing and seemed unconcerned about this event or any other incidents that had happened during the day.

"I will leave you now," she said. "I will come later to see if you want anything."

She got out of the car, said something angrily at the old man and strutted off.

Chapter Twenty-Six

Ketch decided to take lunch in his room.

He ordered a grilled ham and cheese sandwich with fries and a 7Up.

He then unfolded the map he had of Beirut and tried to figure out where he went and what happened that morning.

After twenty minutes, there was a light tap on the door.

"Room service," a young man's voice echoed from the hall.

Ketch positioned his foot near the door as a brake and opened it slowly.

A young waiter stood outside, balancing a tray on an upturned hand that appeared to have Ketch's lunch.

Ketch let him in and directed the tray to the desk.

He was starving. All the tension of the morning had already burned off the big breakfast he fueled up on.

He almost finished his lunch, then there was another knock on the door.

"Who is it?

"Room service," Nikki answered.

Ketch opened the door and Nikki pushed her way past him into the room.

"You need to fuck me," she demanded.

"You mean, right now?" Ketch responded.

"Yes. Right now."

"But I just fucked you last night," Ketch protested.

"I know. But I it was a bad day," she responded. "And it was all your fault."

"How was it my fault?"

"Because you hired that crazy old man," she shouted in a voice that was very agitated.

"He almost got us killed.

"So you need to fuck me again. Right now," she insisted.

"I am eating lunch," Ketch replied lamely.

"Too bad. You could have eaten me for lunch," she said teasingly. "But you seem to be finished, so you can have me for dessert."

She then walked straight to the bed, and took off all her all clothes except for a bit of g-string lingerie. She then slipped in under the crisp white sheets of the double bed. She eyed Ketch while she undressed to see if he noticed. He noticed, but didn't eye her back.

That surely irritated her, he thought. But Ketch was tired and just wanted to be by himself and figure out his plans for the next day.

She then reached down under the sheets, slipped off her g-string lingerie and threw it at Ketch, hitting him squarely in the back of the head.

"Are you going to fuck me or not?" Nikki asked after only a few moments.

"I'm thinking about it," Ketch replied.

"Don't think too long," she countered. "Otherwise you will be in trouble."

"Why will I be in trouble?"

"Because I am playing with myself right now and may like it more than you," she responded teasingly. "Then I won't need you anymore and you will be in Beirut by yourself without a girl that lets soldiers stick guns in her chest."

Ketch had no reply.

"You need to fuck me now, or I am leaving," she threatened.

Ketch relented.

After they were both satisfied, she got dressed and abruptly left.

"See you tomorrow," she said with a wink.

Chapter Twenty-Seven

Ketch took a six o'clock wake-up call and went down to the dining room for breakfast.

He didn't bother with the radio transmission.

He then went back to his room, took a quick shower and called the number for the U.S. Marines that Elizabeth gave him. The call quickly went through.

"U.S. Marines," the voice answered.

"Eric Kelly for Major Collins."

"One moment."

"Major Collins," the phone responded.

"Apologies, Major for calling you so early. This is Eric Kelly. I hope you expected my call."

"Bullshit. I've been up since five. Yes, I got the signal. Come by this morning and we can talk."

"What time?"

"Any time. We're going nowhere. Just make sure you leave your car in the parking lot and walk up to the gate. I'm sure you understand our concerns about cars given the bombing."

"Absolutely. Thank you for your time."

"Thank you for your interest," the Major replied and hung up.

Nikki and the old man were waiting for him in the lobby.

"I don't like this guy you picked to drive us," she reminded him. "You should have talked to me first."

"Well, today is his last day, then we can find somebody you like," he countered.

The previous day, their tour of Beirut should have been a wake-up call for Ketch after they got stopped by one of the militias at a checkpoint. Nevertheless, Ketch was committed to honor his two-day commitment to the old man.

"I promised him two days of work," Ketch explained.

"That was stupid," she replied. "This is Beirut. There are no promises in Beirut, only betrayals."

But Nikki was right. The old man drove like a speed demon and every time they got to a checkpoint, he didn't stop. He just waved and smiled. At one checkpoint, the boys on duty unleashed AK-47s in their direction.

"No problem," the driver laughed.

When they got to the Marine compound in the airport, the old man drove right up to the gate and insisted that the guards let them through. M-16s were trained on them from multiple points inside and outside the compound.

Meanwhile, two marines came out from behind the barricades, maneuvered their way around the car and pointed their rifles at them.

But the driver's response was just to shout at them in Arabic, wave his hands and laugh.

At that point, Ketch slowly got out of the car, put his hands up and told Nikki to get the car and driver out of there. The old man backed off and the marines backed off.

"I'll stay with the driver, to make sure he waits for us," Nikki shouted back.

Ketch then approached the gate in a more polite fashion, and told them he had an appointment with

Major Collins. He then stood patiently, arms and hands still up in the air, while the marines made calls from their phone boxes.

After, a short while, Ketch dropped his hands to the top of his head, not sure how much longer he could hold them up. But nobody seemed to mind.

After a few shouts back and forth into the field telephones, the guard approached Ketch.

"Sorry about the confusion, sir," he said politely. "Major Collins is expecting you."

"No problem," Ketch returned. "Sorry about the driver."

Chapter Twenty-Eight

As Ketch approached the gate, he noted that the kid from Connecticut was outside the compound shooting pictures without permission. The marines told him to back off, but when he saw Ketch, he shouted, "I'm with him."

"He's not with me," Ketch replied immediately, insulted by the kid's arrogance.

"Fuck you, asshole," the kid shouted back.

As Ketch entered the compound, he noted the carnage from the bombing. No way in his wildest imagination could he have believed that one guy in a small truck could have caused that.

Not only were all the structures a pile of rubble, but there was a deep crater in the ground that was filled with broken up pieces of concrete and twisted steel that were once the floors and walls of a building.

This didn't have to happen, he noted to himself.

But the Marines were under strict Rules of Engagement set by bureaucratic politicians back in the U.S. as well as State Department officers in Beirut. They pledged to the American public that there would be no collateral damage or civilian causalities in Beirut by sending in the Marines to help restore some measure of peace there. That was totally unrealistic but made them and their constituencies feel good.

Under the Rules of Engagement, the marine sentries at the airport compound could not have even one bullet chambered in their rifles unless instructed by an officer. In fact, they could not even have loaded magazines in their rifles and they could not fire on someone unless fired upon first. And only in equal proportion.

In addition, the diplomats didn't even want the marines at the airport to fortify their compound on the grounds that it would look too intimidating to the locals. Bad PR for the local press and public. However, what local would even approach the marines compound unless he was up to no good.

But being marines, they followed orders.

After the U.S. Embassy bombing earlier in the year, the Marines there could fire on vehicles attacking the building. They called it the Blue Card/White Card rules. The Blue Card only applied to the embassy marines and allowed them to aggressively engage an intruder. The White Card said you had to be polite. The marines at the airport were given White Cards and required to be polite.

The absurdity was obvious to all except the politicians that set the rules back in their safe American suburbs. But imagine you are not a privileged politician or diplomat and don't live in an upscale, safe suburb. You are working class, middle class and live in a neighborhood you can afford. You are a law abiding citizen and pay your taxes.

You are at home with your wife. It is late at night and you are in bed, but woken up by the sound of breaking glass.

You go to the closet and pull out your shotgun. You are not a gun enthusiast and bought the shotgun strictly for home defense. You grab several shells but don't load them into the gun for fear of being charged by the police for assault with a deadly weapon. But as you hear someone coming up the stairs, you take a chance against some court judgment and load the shells into the shotgun, but are still concerned about the legal issues, so don't chamber a round.

The intruder enters the bedroom and points a gun at you and your wife. But you are not allowed to shoot him until he fires first. Also, in court, he might claim unequal force was used because he only had a pistol whereas you had a shotgun.

He threatens to shoot your wife if you don't drop the gun. Your mind is racing, you don't know what you should do or are allowed to do under the law. He is angered by your hesitation and shoots your wife, killing her.

Finally, you feel you are allowed to shoot back. You pump a round into the chamber, but he has already run off.

So, the marines were totally compromised when the suicide truck bomber charged their gates. He actually circled the parking lot to build up speed. It was obvious that something was happening, but the marines were constrained by American politicians so many died.

They could have shot that bastard before he got anywhere near the gate with his truck bomb. But again, they were not allowed to keep loaded magazines in their rifles or a bullet in the chamber without the permission of an officer, let alone shoot at someone not shooting first.

As the suicide truck bomber charged the gates, the marines on guard duty fumbled for the magazines in their belts. They loaded their rifles, but still could not fire upon him because of the Rules of Engagement set by American politicians. Politicians who had probably never seen battle in their lives or even been in a street fight. The Marines weren't fired upon, so they weren't allowed to fire back. They were under the "be polite" rules.

The truck bomber crashed through the sentries and wreaked havoc. Allegedly, the blast was heard all the way to Tripoli in the north, Sidon in the south and Damascus, Syria in the east.

It was reported in the press as the biggest non-nuclear blast in the history of war.

Meanwhile, none of the local armies or militias in Beirut had Rules of Engagement and couldn't care less about civilian casualties. They directly targeted and slaughtered unarmed civilian communities whenever it suited their purpose. Muslims, Christians, whatever.

Beirut was anarchy at its best. Everyone was shooting each other and forming and un-forming alliances on a daily basis, based on what real estate or business they wanted to control or what their paymasters wanted.

The international press reported it as a Christian versus Muslim affair. However, Christians were shooting Christians, the Muslims the Muslims and the Israelis and Syrians were shooting a bit of both as well as each other.

The press overlooked the significant sectarian conflict within the Christian and Muslim communities themselves. Alliances depended on your family background or your clan background or what village you came from. That was your first loyalty. The rest was business. There was no sense of nationhood.

So it seemed there would never be a solution to make Lebanon a modern state.

The only so-called modern states in the Middle East were controlled by political strongmen who crushed all opposition. Despite their oppression, they gave their countries stability and that was more cherished by most of their people than democracy.

Westerners, with their notions of one-man, one-vote democracies never could understand that because they had never lived in the chaos of anarchy. Fundamentally, people want order in their lives, so they can work, raise families and enjoy the company of friends. Many populations sold out any sense of democracy for communism, socialism, fascism or petty dictatorships of one sort or another, for the sake of order and stability.

All these systems had their game boards, and the populations learned the games. As long as the families could put food on the table, they played along. It was pure animal survival. The Lebanese learned to live within the chaos.

If you accepted chaos as the normal state of affairs, that offered some form of stability.

As they say, the devil you know is better than the one you don't.

Chapter Twenty-Nine

Ketch was taken into a low-rise concrete building, and up a couple flights of stairs. His escort knocked on a door and introduced him.

"Eric Kelly. Major Collins."

The room was not much more than one would expect based on the concrete block architecture you saw from the outside. A metal desk, filing cabinet and a sleeping cot with a coarse wool blanket and plastic pillow.

Major Collins was dressed in dark green fatigues and Ketch noted his marine "high-and-tight" haircut. It was razor-short on the sides with a patch of hair on the top, like a pelt ready to be scalped by the American Indians. Ketch never understood the haircut. It typed marines as marines and made them walking targets wherever they went.

Major Collins greeted him with a handshake and gave him a seat.

"So they tell me you're a journalist," Major Collins said after introductions.

"That's right," Ketch lied.

"Well, I know you're not a journalist," Collins replied with a smile. "Cause if you were, I wouldn't be seeing you. I've had enough of their bullshit. They may get the facts right, but never the story.

"I'm not even going to ask who sent you here, cause I know you can't tell me," the Major continued.

"Actually, I don't know myself," Ketch replied truthfully. "I used to work narcotics, but something came up. They loaned me to somebody else and here I am. I don't even know who they loaned me to, but someone is paying the bills," Ketch explained.

"So, what do you want with the Marines?" the Major asked.

"I'm here to find Adam Smith, the American engineering professor who was abducted from the American University."

"Then what?" the Major inquired.

"Get him back home," Ketch replied.

"What if he doesn't want to go back home?" the Major asked, throwing Ketch off balance.

"What do you mean?" Ketch probed.

"Obviously your intelligence people don't know jack shit," the Major continued. "It always amazes me why they call it *intelligence*. They all think that we marines just sit around with our rifles up our butts, waiting to get shot at.

"But we've had our own people out and about since we landed. And not guys with funny haircuts like me and the other 'boots.'

"Guys who look the look, talk the talk and walk the walk. Fluent Arabic speakers who live in town, hang out in the neighborhood coffee shops, and buy their shit in grocery stores just like the locals. Mostly Arab-Americans.

"The Marines have been on the ground for some time and we know better.

"Obviously, nobody reads our intel reports back in Washington or anywhere out here for that matter.

"Adam Smith was a professor at the American University of Beirut and noted for his very radical, anti-

American points of view. Even before the U.S. got involved in the conflict or the Marines landed.

"His thing was that America is responsible for all the problems of the Middle East. Obviously, he never looked at a map of the British Empire.

"The map of the British Empire is all the trouble spots of the world. Over the last hundred years or so, their bureaucrats neatly sliced up everything with straight lines in the sand that made good presentations back in London, but had no reality on the ground.

"Anyway, initially, the locals loved Adam Smith and he got a lot of sympathy because he typically blamed all their troubles on foreigners. Locals anywhere in the world always love to blame their problems on foreigners, and particularly love to hear foreigners doing it. So, he connected with them and reinforced their point-of-view.

"But then, he overplayed his hand and started criticizing everyone.

"We asked the CIA about him, but some chickenshit, pencil-pusher in a suit told me that they are not allowed to spy on American citizens and claimed he couldn't give me squat.

"What a crock of shit. My two cents is that Smith was not kidnapped, but disappeared and is in cahoots with some militia. I've got good men in the field, checkin' out this shit. But if he's not been kidnapped, then he's in hiding somewhere. Maybe not even in Lebanon. Syria would be a good place to hide. But that's beyond my jurisdiction."

"So, what I am doing here?" Ketch asked.

"Hey Kelly, you know the game. Your bosses have an agenda but haven't filled you in. It's just like those guys.

"Sorry to say, but you are a tool, just like me. We all got into this for honor, truth and justice, but now we're just in it for our pensions so we can afford to send our kids to college. I'm already long overdue for retirement. But I couldn't stay away from the Corps. We have a lot of history and, as a Marine, you get to see a lot of shit you'd never get to see as a civilian.

"I have a small house in Cocoa Beach, Florida. Once my rotation is over here, that's where I'll be, focusing on my wife and daughter. But I wouldn't have given up my life in the Corps for anything.

"At least as a soldier, I know who my boss is," he noted. "As an operator, you do not. You are just a pawn on the chessboard and don't know who is moving the pieces."

"Ok. Thanks for the reality check. But what about my mission?" Ketch interjected.

"Well. You want to find this guy. Fine. But I warned you.

"You should touch base with all the players in town and make friends.

"First go see the head of intelligence at the Lebanese Armed Forces.

"The Lebanese Forces were supposed to be the national army of Lebanon, embracing all the sectarian groups. But, it is still dominated by Christians and used by the current president as his personal militia. The U.S. has been supporting them and trying to inspire them with Lebanese nationalism. But the individual soldiers don't buy into it. At the end of the day, they are loyal to their clans, be they Christian, Muslim or whatever.

"If you know anything about the Middle East, you know it will never work. Lebanon is all about tribal ties, sectarian allegiances and family politics. I've only been in Lebanon a few weeks since we replaced the twenty-fourth MAU, but I've been in the Middle East for several years. And it was obvious to me from the get go.

"Sectarian and family ties prevail here.

"As I said, the Lebanese Forces are essentially the tool of the current president who has strong ties to the Phalange. We're supposed to be training them, but we're not supposed to support them in combat, because that would violate our neutral "peacekeeping" status. And, if we get shot at, we're supposed to stand down and call them for help. You tell me how that's supposed to work. At the same time, our training support for them, is seen as support for the president. So, the various other militias don't see us as peace keepers but as king makers.

"Anyway, after you talk to the Lebanese Forces, you need to talk to the Phalange in Christian East Beirut. That's where the current president has his roots. They are nominally non-sectarian, but in fact, they are the most powerful Christian militia around, very independent and very aggressive.

"You hear about the massacre in the Sabra and Shatila Palestinian refugee camps?" the Major continued. "Based on all intel, the massacre was passively supported by the IDF, the Israeli Defense Forces. The Israelis surrounded it during their occupation of Beirut. Phalange forces were allowed in under Israeli cover, supposedly to dig out terrorists but a lot of women and children were put up against a wall and shot.

"After an international inquiry, the Israeli defense minister at the time was compelled to resign from his defense post, but the government kept him on as a minister.

"The Phalange later claimed it was retribution for the assassination of their previous president. However, according to our intel, the Palestinians didn't assassinate him, but the Syrians did it. They killed him for getting too cozy with Israel. Yet, just a few years earlier, the Syrians supported his fight against the Palestinians. This is Beirut.

"The standard military tactic out here is the massacre. Instead of troops attacking other troops, they go into unarmed villages, squatter settlements, refugee camps and wipe out their civilians."

"And the civilians don't fight back?" Ketch asked.

"They typically aren't armed," the Major explained. "Their leaders obviously believe in gun control.

"However, I love this story," the Major continued. "In Christian East Beirut, there was an incident last month when some guy in a ski mask tried to rob an upscale grocery store where all the rich housewives shop for their imported food and wine. The guy was only trying to hold up the cashier, not take hostages or do anything political. However, three upset women shoppers just pulled 9mm pistols out of their purses and shot the fucker dead. They didn't even give the guy a chance to surrender. Just blasted away. Miraculously, the cashier was not shot."

"Never underestimate the wrath of a frustrated, suburban housewife," Ketch laughed.

"Unfortunately, to meet the Phalange, you'll need to cross the Green Line between East and West Beirut." the Major continued. "It's the dark side of the moon. Nothing but gutted, bombed-out buildings and rubble.

"At night, the various militias shoot at each other to protect their turf, like the South Bronx in New York City.

"Get a good driver and he'll get you through. They actually have a call center indicating when the fighting will start. But don't try anything after four in the afternoon, in either direction.

"It's also a good exit strategy. If you can get to East Beirut, then you can catch a ferry or hire a private speedboat from the marina to get you to Cyprus.

"Lastly, I know your handler said that if you get into trouble, they'd send in the Marines. Good motivational speech. But quite frankly, given the low profile we've been put under by the politicians, don't count on it. So, assume you're on your own.

"You get into trouble, get out fast and rely on your local assets.

"Nobody will disrespect you for running if you have to.

"Give me a call, and let me know where you're going. But I can't promise anything if you step into the shit."

"Tell me more about the Phalange," Ketch said.

"They actually go back to the 1930s and were inspired by events in Europe at the time. Some of the athletes and political powers here went to Berlin for the Olympic Games and were mesmerized by the Nazi order and discipline they found there.

"They came back, hoping to impress that same order and discipline on Lebanon.

"They were Christians, specifically Maronite Christians, so got a lot of sympathy from the West. As I said, the Phalange forces are nominally secular, but dominated by the Maronites."

"And who are the Maronites?" Ketch asked.

"They go back centuries. Maybe back to the Crusades.

"They were Christians led by a guy named Maron. He brought his followers to the hills of Lebanon to escape all the turmoil around them. He got sainthood out of it. The West ate it up because they were Christians in the Middle East. Danny Thomas, the famous TV guy, was a Maronite. He was great PR for them.

"Over the years, they bred to become over fifty percent of the Lebanese population.

"They also resisted French colonialism as well as Arab colonialism disguised as so-called pan-Arab nationalism.

"Their intentions might have been true. They wanted Lebanon for the Lebanese people and began to promote a cultural identity for Lebanon linked to its Phoenician ancestors. The Phoenician trading empire ruled the Mediterranean in ancient times.

"They sought to establish an identity unique from their Arab neighbors.

"Although the party was dominated by Maronite Christians, its membership also included Sunnis, Shiites, Druze and Jews and they supported pluralistic ideals.

"As I said, they claim they are secular, but are mostly looking after Christian interests here. They are trying to promote themselves as Phoenicians and create a new identity for Lebanon that is both nationalistic, and independent of Muslims and Palestinians.

"They are very powerful, so you should see them. They know everyone here. But I don't have much hope for their vision."

"Why is that?" Ketch asked. "Makes sense to me."

"As I said, the Middle East is tribal. Always was and always will be.

"Bottom line. The Phalange present a good face to the West, but they are very right-wing Christian and very unforgiving in the execution of their beliefs," the Major added. "The Muslims will never buy into their vision, because it doesn't have a place for them."

"As I said, I've been around the region and it's the same problem everywhere, not just here. You can't get a sergeant to salute an officer in the same command, if the officer and the sergeant are from different sects.

"We are wasting our time, men and resources here," the Major said. "Let them squabble among themselves.

"Have you heard about the Hamma Massacre in Syria? the Major continued.

"No," Ketch replied.

"Well, that sort of sums it up for me," the Major explained.

"Muslims on Muslims. In Syria. Nothing to do with the West. It seems that an up-and-coming Muslim organization known as the Muslim Brotherhood, started to challenge the president of Syria for power. Both Muslims, but different sects.

"The president of Syria squashed them like a bug. He surrounded their neighborhood with artillery and tanks, shot the shit out of them, then sent in demolition teams to bring down their buildings, even while there were people inside. Men, women, children. Then they poured diesel fuel into the cracks of the rubble and set it on fire to insure there'd be no survivors.

"After they flattened the place, they bulldozed away the rubble like nothing had happened.

"Killing children is important in this part of the world, because children all grow up to be fighters or gunmen avenging their families. The taste for revenge is more passionate when planted as a seed in a child. The kid makes it his mission in life. It gives meaning to his life. It becomes his destiny. Killing women is also important, because women give birth to more fighters and provide the logistical support for the ones already on the ground.

"Their PR loves to play on Western attacks that kill women and children, and they love to show blooded bandages of kids they probably shot themselves for the news value. But they have no qualms about killing women and children. It is total war out here.

"The West doesn't get it.

"Meanwhile, while these people are slaughtering each other, our politicians handcuff us with Rules of Engagement to make them feel better chatting over drinks in their country clubs back home, but they don't protect our men or get the job done.

"If we accidentally scrape some kid's knee out here, they make a big deal out of it because they know it tugs on Western heartstrings, makes us look immoral, grabs the headlines and fires up political and newspaper hacks.

"The best thing we could do for this part of the world is to nuke it. Sounds pretty harsh, but once you meet these people you will find that's what they would do to each other and to us, if they could.

"Without hesitation.

"Remember Hama."

Chapter Thirty

Ketch needed a drink. It was all too overwhelming.

"Hey Major, I appreciate your candor. I'm sure it's not authorized," Ketch replied. "Wish I could buy you a drink or something."

"Hey, I'll buy you a drink," Major Collins replied, reading his face.

"Listen, Kelly," the Major noted. "At first cut, I like you. What you say, we toast to Christmas."

"Sure," Ketch replied.

"I just so happen to have some brandy, courtesy of a Red Cross package. You up for it?"

"Sure."

He pulled out two small bottles from his desk drawer, hotel mini-bar size. He poured one for Ketch and one for himself into plastic cups.

"Merry Christmas," he toasted.

"Merry Christmas," Ketch toasted back.

The Major gulped his down as a shot, while Ketch sipped his.

"Hey Kelly, if you're heading into some shit, call me. I can't promise anything. So, don't expect Force Recon. It's all very political. All our activity needs to be cleared by politicians and diplomats these days.

"And they don't answer their phones that quickly. Then they need to have a meeting and argue about it for a few days. However, if you do get into trouble, I'll see what I can do, off the record. But you need to rely on yourself. Consider us a bonus surprise."

Ketch knew he was talking with a no-bullshit warrior who just wanted to do the right thing. But he also knew that he was on his own, just like the Major said.

"Come up to the roof and let me show you something," the Major instructed.

They walked up a few stairs and onto the roof. It was littered with jagged bits of sharp metal. Some small, some big. Mostly big.

"This is what they drop on us every night," the Major continued. "Any of these pieces could rip your leg off, or take your heart out.

"The bad guys are all up in those hills over there. But we're not allowed to shoot at them."

"Why not? I thought under the Rules, you could shoot back if fired upon."

"Maybe. But the Rules are a crock of shit. Their firing positions are in the middle of small villages up there. Typically mosques, hospitals, schools. That would mean civilian casualties which we are not allowed to incur.

"If the Israelis come under sniper fire from some building, they'd just pull up a tank and bring down the whole building. End of story. That's what we used to do in WWII and Korea. And that's the way to fight this war.

"Now, if we come under sniper fire we're supposed to risk the lives of our men, by sending in a small team to try to take out the guy with a rifle. We could clean up this whole place with a couple of Cobra gunships. However, we're not allowed to do that.

"In the meantime, the various militias drop heavy artillery on us and each other. If we respond, we're accused of taking sides when our mission is defined as peacekeeping. How are you supposed to keep the peace if you're not allowed to shoot guys who are shooting at you or shooting at each other?

"Nobody thought about that in World War II, either the West or the Nazis.

"In fact, it was Churchill who provoked the Germans into bombing London.

"The Germans had been planning an invasion, but offered the Brits a chance to surrender. In return, Churchill gave his 'fuck you, we will fight you on the beaches' speech.

"So, the Germans initiated their plans to invade Britain across the English Channel.

"Anyway, their strategy was to first bomb the fighter bases in England, knowing that's what would be the biggest threat in an English Channel crossing.

"The Brits only responded defensively, sending up Hurricane and Spitfire fighters and lighting up the sky with anti-aircraft barrages.

"The irony, is that the Germans were about to achieve their objectives and pretty much subdued the British fighter forces. But then one of their bombers accidentally dropped a few bombs on London in bad weather with poor navigation.

"That sent Churchill into a fit.

"The strategic response should have been to bomb German airfields. He should have been doing that from the get go.

"But instead, Churchill followed his ego. No big news there.

"So, the next day, against the recommendation of his officers, he ordered the bombing of German cities, including Berlin.

"Of course, that sent Hitler into his own fit, and he then ordered the bombing of downtown London.

"Thousands of British civilians got killed because of Churchill's ego.

"Later, in World War II, he ordered the Hong Kong commanders to fight the Japanese to the last man for the sake of British honor while privately admitting that Hong Kong didn't stand a chance of protecting itself. The Japanese offered surrender several times, but Churchill wouldn't let the troops accept it. So, many more got killed for the sake of Churchill's ego, and those that were left starved in prison camps.

"You know, history is very ironic," Major Collins went on. "We made the Germans feel guilty about the Jews, but then they turned it around on us and made us feel guilty about bombing their cities.

"The Japanese committed huge atrocities in China. The Chinese were tortured and used in medical experiments in northern China by the Japanese. As bad as what the Nazis did to the Jews and others in their concentration camps.

"But now the Japanese make us feel guilty for dropping the bomb. Every year, they do some memorial PR blitz about it with survivors.

"But if they had the bomb, they would have dropped it. Not just on China, but on the U.S. and the rest of Asia. That was their mentality.

"I'm guessing you were in 'Nam.

"The North Vietnamese and the Viet Cong had no qualms about killing civilians. Often in the most brutal ways. But we if killed some female fighters, all hell broke loose because they were women and the North Vietnamese propaganda machine really played it up that we were killing women. However, the women fighters were more vicious than the men when dealing with civilians. They felt they had something to prove because they were women. They were extremely cruel and showed no mercy.

"That's why we're not allowed to fight back, these days. Everyone in the U.S. feels guilty. But, in my opinion, it's the rest of the world that should be feeling guilty. It's their politics that dragged us into their wars. But they don't support us in ours.

"Look at all the support we gave the Brits and the French in both World Wars, but when it came to Vietnam, they couldn't be bothered. As President Johnson said, he'd be happy if at least the Brits sent a marching band.

"Meanwhile, young Arab boys here come down from the hills throwing stones at our perimeter positions to test our locations. But we're not allowed to shoot or capture them. We can't even shoot over their heads to scare them away.

"Technically someone throwing a stone at you means you've been fired upon. But you want to fight that battle with an American Congressman looking to make a reputation for himself?

"Then, they send in teenage boys with AK-47s to take pot shots at us.

"Frankly, I can't blame them.

"Think back to when you were thirteen years old. I'm sure you got into some shit. That's what teenage boys do. But back home, you probably just blew up a few firecrackers, stole some booze, maybe joined a gang or had a few street fights.

"It's what made you a man.

"Here, they use that teenage manhood adrenaline shit to come after us. Don't tell me that if somebody in your town back home, signed you up to take on a foreign army next door, you wouldn't do it.

"All your friends would be doing it. The girls would expect it. And you'd get no respect in your town if you didn't.

"In the meantime, we're global allies with the Israelis, but we we're not allowed to support them here, because we'd be accused of taking sides. Yet, the Israelis know how to fight this war. Someone shoots at you, then you respond with massive retaliation. Power is the only thing that the militias respect. If we were allowed to partner with the Israelis here, we could clean this place up in a month. But after the Israelis were forced to pull out by global politicians, then everything returned to chaos.

"As I said, the best we could do for Beirut is to nuke it."

Chapter Thirty-One

The Major took Ketch back to his office and they shared another round of brandy.

Ketch was stunned by the Major's candor and now realized that he was in a big can of worms.

This time, Ketch chugged down the brandy like a shot and tried to collect his thoughts.

"What about Amal?" he asked the Major.

"Interesting question, the Major replied. "They are Shiite Muslims fighting Christians, Sunni Muslims and everybody else.

"The Shiites and Sunnis have been facing off with each other for hundreds of years, based on counter claims as to who should be the true successor to the Prophet Mohammed and spokesman for Islam.

"Sort of like Catholics and Protestants. The only difference is that Catholics and Protestants are not shooting each other over their differences. Except in Northern Ireland, of course, thanks to the Brits' mismanagement of that situation.

"Now, Amal is sending out feelers that they want to be friends since they realized that they over-played their hand.

"*Amal* in Arabic is supposed to mean "hope." They played a major role in the fighting over the last few years, mostly to get more political recognition and resources for the Shiite Muslims that they represent here. They live in the slums south of here. If you visit those areas, you can see why they are angry. I don't blame them.

"A lot of tents and concrete walls covered by plastic tarps or sheets of metal. No running water and no toilets.

"We are not sure who funds them. Maybe Syria or Iran but more likely sympathetic donors from around the region. And their politics seem very fluid. At various times, they have fought everyone. At one point, they even battled the large Palestinian encampment here.

"On another occasion, they fought with Hezbollah, a rival Shiite group funded by Iran. But now, they are trying to make friends with them, cause Hezbollah has lots of money from Iran.

"So despite what you read in the Western press, this is not a Christian versus Muslim crusade. It's South Bronx gang wars, each fighting for turf and a piece of the pie.

"Unfortunately, I can't help you with the Amal intro. Ask the Phalange or the Lebanese Armed Forces. If they say no, I'm sure your driver can. If not, get another driver."

"What about the Druze?" Ketch asked.

"Well, they are the guys that probably shelled the airport and delayed your flight. They are most likely the guys that are shelling us right now. They are up in the Shouf Mountains. They are a wild card. Both the Druze and the Phalange have their roots in the hills. The Druze, the Phalange and the Lebanese Armed forces are fighting for control of the heights in the Shouf right now. Whoever controls the hills will be able to drop shells anywhere in the city.

"The Druze are neither Muslim or Christian, though most people consider them Muslims. But, they have their own beliefs. Some combination of both, but that's all I know. The hard-core Muslims consider them infidels.

"Politically, they are just another one of the gangs in the neighborhood. They want international recognition and they think that by shelling the Marines, they can get it.

"In response to the shelling of our base here, the U.S Navy lobbed a few shells into their stronghold in the Shouf.

"They turned it around into a big PR coup accusing the immoral Americans of shelling the sacred Cedars of Lebanon. American media and politicians jumped on it, giving the Navy a lot of shit. Of course, they've been chopping down those trees for years to pay for weapons.

"There is no reason to see the Druze," the Major explained. "And it would be very dangerous for you to go into the Shouf right now," he added. "Not necessarily because of the Druze or the shelling, but because of the many checkpoints you'd have to cross and the various factions that man them. Each one of them is an opportunity for you to get taken.

"And what about the Palestinians?" Ketch asked.

"It is a very tragic situation. They are the orphan children of the Middle East. Everyone sympathizes with them, sticks up for their rights, cheers them on and gives them money, but nobody wants to give them a home.

"They were kicked out of the British Mandate of Palestine, then they took refuge in Jordan. Later, they were kicked out of there, then moved here. But nobody wants them here because the Lebanese are afraid that they will take over and set up a Palestinian state in Lebanon.

"That's why they were kicked out of Jordan. They became too much of a threat and set off a civil war there.

"So everyone in Lebanon cheered when the Israelis invaded in 1982 and pushed Yasser Arafat and his boys out.

"In fact, the Lebanese president supposedly invited the Israelis in and backed them with the Lebanese Forces.

"Ironically, the U.S. and France sent in troops to safeguard their passage out of the country.

"The Muslim militias didn't fight for the Palestinians?"

"As I said, this is South Bronx turf wars. Everyone has his own agenda. And I'd guess the other militias also felt the Palestinians were becoming too powerful here. Arab countries and terrorist organizations use them as an excuse for their own political purposes. But in reality, they are on their own. Desperate and without friends.

"Arafat snuck into Tripoli this year and tried to set up a base, but got pushed out again. This time by the Syrians. His old buddies. As I said, it's all a moveable feast out here.

"Visit them if you have time," the Major advised. "They are always looking for friends and a sympathetic ear. I don't think they have your asset, Adam Smith, but they might be able to give you a contact at Hezbollah, which is where I think you will find him."

"Hezbollah?" Ketch asked.

"Hezbollah is another one of the bad boys on the block. Maybe the baddest.

"It means 'The Party of Allah.'

"They are likely the guys who blew up my boys here. The French certainly thought so, cause they immediately sent fighter jets to hit Hezbollah militias in the Bekaa Valley."

"And we didn't?" Ketch asked.

"No," the Major explained. "The political suits back in D.C. said we didn't have enough legal evidence and any strikes would be an escalation."

"That's insane," Ketch responded. "But where did Hezbollah come from in the first place?"

"They were set up by the Iranians to resist the Israeli invasion of south Lebanon and the Israeli-funded militia, the South Lebanon Army, a buffer group to protect the territory overlooking Israel, and hopefully prevent rocket attacks and infiltration into Israel by bad guys. In fact, there's a few American West Point grads working for the South Lebanon Army."

"As mercenaries?" Ketch asked. "I thought that was illegal and you'd lose your U.S. citizenship for it."

"Yeah, well, everyone looks the other way if it suits their purpose," Collins answered.

"Historically, most mercenaries were British. The Brits had a compulsory national military service for many years, so they had a lot of men in reserve who had been through basic training, could handle a rifle and take orders.

"Given no jobs and boredom in the U.K., many signed up to fight mercenary funded wars on behalf of Britain that the government wanted to deny involvement in. Primarily Africa. It was terrible. Most of those poor slobs got shot or worse.

"The Rhodesians and South Africans then filled the mercenary ranks. It was a better solution. They were extremely well-trained and highly motivated. After all, they were desperate Whites who needed to protect their homeland or be overrun by the natives.

"Some even served in Vietnam. Particularly the Rhodesian Selous Scouts. They were the best of the best in any man's army.

"In Africa, they were dropped behind enemy lines in ancient helicopters and DC-3s with no more than a week of rations. They were expected to live off the land, eating rats, snakes, insects and whatever, while they hunted down the bad guys. Self-reliance, initiative and innovation was their story.

"They were warriors and bush experts to a degree that the rest of us can only ever hope to be. I have the highest respect for them, though I never met one. But I believe their legends.

"The funny thing is that when you look at old pictures of them, they are all wearing shorts. Short, shorts. I mean, like gym shorts, and military boots on their feet.

"I guess that's appropriate dress for the climate, but it doesn't strike a commanding military pose, I'd have to say."

"Hezbollah," Ketch said, returning to the subject.

"Very dangerous. They are very anti-Western, especially anti-American. Allegedly they report directly to the top leaders in Tehran. Their mission is plain and simple. Kill Americans. Any Americans.

"Tehran has also given them a lot of resources, because it would not only like to kick out the West but also take over from the other players and become the dominant power broker in the region.

"They stated that their mission is to kill Americans, anywhere in the world. But if America stated it was our mission to kill Iranians anywhere in the world, we'd be considered criminals. Explain to me how that works. Why do we let them get away with it? " the Major continued. "America has become dominated by a majority of soft bellied, naïve, suburban, oblivious golfers with no perspective on the world who only care about their tee time."

"Iran has enough internal problems. Why would they want to get involved in this mess?" Ketch asked.

"Political ego," the Major replied. "Iran, formerly known as Persia, used to be the center of the universe in this part of the world.

"They extended their culture and learning throughout the region.

"A few hundred years ago, even India used Persian as their *lingua franca* in government.

"The Iranians want to relive that glory. It's a great rallying cry for the government. It takes peoples' minds off their daily troubles and the government's domestic failures.

"Tehran is doubly dangerous, because under the previous regime of the Shah of Iran, it sent many students to the U.S. to study engineering. Specifically, nuclear engineering.

"They don't have an atomic bomb yet. But I'll bet you that Iran will be the next major nuclear power in the world."

"Well, Major, I am very impressed with your insights," Ketch replied. "I apologize, but you know that the reputation of the Marines is just hard-charging guys that run up hills under machine-gun fire."

"Yeah, I know. We need a better PR company," he laughed. "But we don't think about it 'cause we know who we are and don't feel the need to explain ourselves."

"So how do I meet Hezbollah?" Ketch asked.

"Ask Amal or the Palestinians," he noted. "Although they are not on the best terms, they talk to each other.

"What else?" the Major asked.

"What about the Brits?" Ketch asked.

"Well, let me say this. When we need help, we rely on the French and Italians," he explained. "The Marines and the French compound were blown up about the same time. The French compound was also devastated. So, the French had their own problems, but when they heard about our situation, they sent a medical team to assist us anyway. We didn't even need to ask. The French are our oldest allies going back to the War of American Independence and respect that relationship. They also respect the fact that we were the only ally that came to their support in Vietnam, though they pulled out and left us holding the bag.

"When the U.S. Embassy was blown up, French forces were first on the scene with security and rescue personnel.

"The British ambassador initially offered the U.S. Embassy staff the basement of their building as temporary offices, but their Foreign Office opposed it. The British likely wanted to know how much we'd be willing to pay for it. So much for our British allies.

"The British troops here are guarding some tobacco factory," Major Collins continued.

"What?" Ketch questioned, "The British are here to guard some cigarette company."

"I assume it's big business for them," the Major suggested.

"So, I shouldn't bother with the Brits?" Ketch asked.

"I'll give you the number for the military attaché at the British embassy and you can decide for yourself," Major Collins replied. "His name is Colonel Somerset-Kent and likes to be addressed as such.

"Anything else, Mr. Ketch?" the Major said with a wink, acknowledging his real name.

"I guess that's it. Many thanks for your candor and insights."

"Last words, Kelly-Ketch. Don't be afraid to run. I don't think they gave you a candid briefing on this. And as the poem goes. Run, run, run away. Live to fight another day."

"Many thanks again, Major," Ketch replied. "I can't thank you enough.

"We're American Marines," the Major said. "We often get forced to eat shit, but we never bullshit."

As Ketch got up from his seat, the Major interjected. "Hey, Kelly. Before you take off, can I give you some personal, philosophical, no bullshit thoughts?"

"Absolutely," Ketch replied in anticipation.

"I'm a soldier, so I need to follow orders for better or worse," he explained. "But you're a freelance operator, so you only need to follow your instincts.

"If the shit hits the fan and you pull out, you may lose the contract. But worst case scenario, if you don't follow your gut, then you may die, or worse. Die slowly. Very slowly. At least you have that choice. Be grateful for the choice. Soldiers don't have that choice.

"We do or die.

"I know you were a soldier before, so you understand.

"My two cents is this. You need to be a 'shadow warrior.' Do what you need to do, but stay in the background and don't look for credits, kudos or medals.

"Your satisfaction should come from what you need to do, and doing it. As soon as you look elsewhere for satisfaction, you will be compromised.

"One of my Muslim liaison officers with the local forces here explained it to me like this.

"It's all about living in the 'Crescent Shadow.'

"Ever hear that expression?" the Major continued.

"No," Ketch replied.

"It's the strategy of every militia on the ground out here," he noted. "It's derived from the crescent moon.

"The crescent moon is very important to them, because it marks the beginning of a month-long holy period, known as Ramadan.

"Isn't that a symbol of Islam?" Ketch asked.

"No," the Major explained. "The crescent moon with the star goes back to Babylonian times and is based on some love story. The Ottoman Empire adopted it to give themselves some mythical legitimacy in the Middle East and other countries adopted it because it's a good logo.

"There are no symbols in Islam. It's against their religion to worship icons, idols or images. It only marks the beginning of the month in their calendar.

"In fact, it's probably a better calendar marker than the sun, because you can see the progression of its shape. The sun is always a bright disk you can't look at without going blind. So, it makes sense that the ancients used the phases of the moon as their calendar."

"Impressed Major," Ketch returned. "You seem to know your history out here."

"I like to understand the people and places they send me to," the Major replied. "So, I read a lot in my limited downtime. Not something you'd expect to hear from a jar-head marine, would you?"

Ketch laughed.

"So, what about the Crescent Shadow?" Ketch asked.

"The crescent provides light, but the biggest part of the moon is still in shadow," the Major explained. "The light shows the way, but the shadow offers protection.

"Be a shadow warrior. Because once you expose yourself to the light, then you are subject to attack. Not just from your enemies, but also from your bosses, officers, government, girlfriends and every housewife and yuppie who has no idea what you're doing to protect their security, but who wants to make a stink about something you did just to give their own pathetic life some sense of meaning.

"Look at the lessons of history. Heroes are typically sacrificed to fulfill someone's ego or public appetites.

"Most important. And I repeat. Most important. Stay out of the light. As the light of the moon expands, the shadow retreats. This is a natural phenomenon. Learn from it. It's a message. Use the light to see what's out there and give you direction, but stay in the shadow. Retreat with the shadow.

"The Crescent Shadow."

Ketch swallowed hard and couldn't speak. In his mind, those words alone made the whole trip to Beirut worthwhile, regardless of how it played out.

Ketch was still digesting the thought when the Major interrupted.

"Hey Kelly, one last thing," the Major offered. "I shouldn't be telling you this, because it could fuck up your head for the mission. However, I take you for the kind of guy that wants to know the skinny on things. Bottom line, it's not just religion, politics and turf wars out here. It's all about the money.

"Lebanon is currently the biggest transshipment port for illegal narcotics from the Middle East. Hashish, opium, heroin. So, the fighting is not just about politics and religion, but who gets to control the ports, the land lines or seas routes to Europe. That means my boys are not just dying for democracy and freedom but for some drug dealer that the U.S. politicians like.

"I know you did narcotics before, so I think you appreciate the realities. As I'm sure you know, there are no good guys or bad guys in that game. Only good deals and bad deals. So, finish your mission and go home. Then get out of the game."

"Many thanks for that Major," Ketch replied.

"Anyway Kelly, before you go, let me give you a tour of the airport," the Major said.

Chapter Thirty-Two

Major Collins passed off Ketch to a staff sergeant outside his door and told him, "Give this man a tour of the airport. He is a special guest.

"Take him anywhere he wants and let him take any pictures he wants. Take him to see Colonel Banks." The Sergeant took Ketch down the stairs.

Waiting outside was a big-wheeled, big-sided two-and-a-half-ton military truck with a canvas top stretched over a metal rib frame. The marines called it a deuce-and-a-half. It was the kind of military truck you saw in World War II movies. It had a metal body that seemed thick enough to stop bullets.

It was very high off the ground and Ketch almost needed to do a pull-up to get himself into the front seat next to the driver.

The sergeant drove out of the front gate of the marine compound and down a makeshift road past the parking lot. As they passed the lot, Ketch noticed Nikki standing outside the car looking very irritated as the old man kept talking at her, waving his hands and smiling. Obviously, he was turning on the charm.

They drove out towards the perimeter of the airport and stopped in the middle of nowhere.

"Wait here," the Sergeant instructed. "I need to find the Colonel's bunker. We don't put flags on it for security reasons."

Ketch sat in the truck and looked out across the no-man's zone into the hills surrounding the airport. He quickly grasped the frustration of Major Collins. Instead of being shipped to Lebanon to do what marines do best, fight as marines, they were sent by politicians to make a political statement, and be sitting ducks.

The Sergeant got back to the truck and opened the door for Ketch.

"That's where they take pot shots at us," he noted, pointing at the hills. "We could take them out with one air strike but we're not allowed to do that under the Rules of Engagement.

"Let me introduce you to the Colonel."

They walked a few yards across flat ground, then down into a ditch. The ditch led to a bunker where they met a man living inside a dirty tunnel sitting on a stool. There was a small desk, a cot to sleep on and nothing else but plywood walls trying to keep the dirt at bay.

Ketch assumed from the "full bird" ensign etched onto his collar that he must be the Colonel.

"This is Colonel Banks," the sergeant noted. "He runs the show."

"This is Eric Kelly. He's on a mission from God knows where. But here alone. So, this guy has incredible balls or is incredibly stupid. But the Major likes him and wanted you to meet so we can make this personal," the Sergeant explained candidly.

"The Major knows he's going to step into the shit and when he does, would like to send in a few guys to help him out without calling Washington."

The Colonel got up from his desk and shook Ketch's hand. Even though he was in a bunker, he wore a cammie flak jacket and had an M-16 rifle propped up against his desk.

A Colt .45 was slung from his belt in a holster.

"Pleased to meet you Colonel Banks," Ketch said as the latter extended his hand. "How'd the Major get better quarters?" he joked.

"Well, his job is to meet guys like you," the Colonel replied. "My job is to be with my men.

"Wish we could do more to help but we can't take a piss without first clearing it with D.C. or the suits on the ground here.

"So I've heard."

"Anyway, if you step into some deep shit, give the Major a call. We're Marines. We take care of our people."

"Many thanks for that, Colonel. I'll try to avoid the shit so I don't trouble you," Ketch replied.

"You're in Beirut, sir. The longer you stay, the deeper the shit. So, finish your business quickly and go home," the Colonel advised.

That was the end of the conversation. It was brief, but enough for Ketch to know where he stood. He hoped, he would never have to call the Marines for their assistance, but was comforted by the fact that the Major and the Colonel might help him out, off the record, if he got in over his head.

Ketch and the sergeant got into the truck and went back to the main gate of the Marine compound where Ketch got out.

As he left, the sergeant shouted at him, "Just remember, sir. You are in Beirut. It is anarchy, insanity and chaos on steroids. There are no rules."

Ketch slipped out of the truck and found Nikki in the parking area, where she attacked him with shouts.

"Where the fuck have you been?" she snarled. "This old man is driving me crazy. He is touching me everywhere and telling me he is looking for a girlfriend.

"He is going to get us killed," she exclaimed. "I don't even feel safe going back to the hotel with him. When you were out, he was going up to all the marines trying to sell them cigarettes. They thought he had a bomb. It was very nervous for everybody."

Anyway, they were stuck with him for one last ride. Just back to the hotel.

But on some road going north, they got stuck in traffic behind a U.S. military jeep carrying four marines. Nikki shouted at the driver to move on or take another route.

"We can't stay behind then," Nikki explained. "If they get attacked, we will also get attacked."

But the driver seemed unconcerned.

Then suddenly the situation changed.

Some teenage boy ran up to the jeep and threw something inside.

"Grenade," one of the marines in the jeep shouted and they all dove out and hit the ground.

"Down, down, down!" Ketch screamed at Nikki and the driver.

But there was no explosion. Ketch poked his head over the dashboard to watch one marine retrieve a can of Coke from the vehicle while the kid laughed, pointed his fingers at them and shouted "bang, bang."

Ketch impulsively got out of the car as Nikki screamed at him to stay put. He slapped the kid hard across the face several times, knocking him to the ground. He then grabbed the can of Coke from the marine, popped open the top and poured the sticky soda all over him. Then kicked him in the groin.

"Next time I see you, I'm gonna fuckin' kill you," Ketch said to the kid. "So stay home with your momma, you little piece of shit or join a militia and die like a man."

One of the marines then intervened. "I appreciate what you did, sir," he said. "But this is just going to backlash on us."

"Just tell them I'm British. The Brits have a long history of slapping the natives around the world."

"Long live the Queen," Ketch shouted as he got back into the car.

"Are you going to be this crazy for the rest of your stay?" Nikki asked.

"I'm done," Ketch answered. "The kid got off easy. I've done worse to punks like that in the U.S."

Fortunately, they got back to the Commodore without further incident and Ketch sat down with Nikki in the hotel restaurant to explain his plans.

Chapter Thirty-Three

"Look Nikki. I need to be honest with you," he said over a coffee. "I'm not really a journalist. I'm a freelance operator. I'm working under cover.

"I'm here to find the American professor, Adam Smith, who was kidnapped, and bring him home. I apologize."

Nikki didn't even flinch.

"No need to apologize," she replied. "Most journalists here are up to something. Except the crazy photographers high on drugs, who just want to get pictures of guns going off."

"So, can I still hire you?"

"Of course. Unless you go crazy again. What is your plan?"

"Well the Marines said I need to see the Lebanese Armed Forces then the Phalange. But most likely the Amal militia will know the most."

"A big waster of time. The Lebanese Armed Forces are called the LAF. They are a joke. Get it?

"The others are all trying to make friends with the Americans right now, but don't know anything. You need to see Hezbollah. They run the hostage business here. But they are very dangerous and suspicious. They are crazy.

"They got big money from Iran to kill foreigners. They might shoot you for looking at them the wrong way," Nikki warned.

"Sounds like New York City," Ketch replied with false bravado.

"Ok. We will do your plan, just so you can get used to Beirut.

"We will see the Lebanese Forces, then the Phalange. But, to see the Phalange, you will have to cross the Green Line. That will check your reality.

"But bottom line, as you Americans say, you will have to see Hezbollah. I must be honest with you on that one.

"I can't find you an introduction and don't want to try. They might also kill me for bringing you to them and I can't go with you to see them. So, I can't help you with them.

"Right now, the most important thing for me is that I need to go home and take a shower," she continued. "I need to get that old man's hands out of my skin.

"Also, we need a new driver. I will find one.

"I will come by later to see if you need me for something," she said with a smile.

Chapter Thirty-Four

Ketch went back to his room and called the Lebanese Forces phone number that Major Collins had given him. Meanwhile, Nikki went back out onto the street to find a new driver. She found one quickly.

Mustapha.

He drove a light green Mercedes and spoke perfect English. He had also been to the Shouf, Tripoli and crossed the Green Line many times. He was Muslim, but his wife was Christian. Nikki felt that gave them the best of both worlds.

In the meantime, Ketch was able to set up an appointment with Colonel Ahmed, head of intelligence with the Lebanese Forces.

Nikki came back to the room in the afternoon and Ketch noted the appointment.

"Ok. We've got a date with the Lebanese Forces," he said to Nikki.

"Good for you. But right now, it is not safe to go up there. Everyone is bombing them, Nikki responded.

"I have an appointment, so I am going. Are you coming?"

"You want to die?"

"No. But I don't think I'm going to die today."

"Then, I go too."

They got into Mustapha's green Mercedes and drove off. As they proceeded up one of the hills to the

LAF compound, Mustapha would suddenly accelerate the car, turn right or left without any reason.

"Mustapha, what are you doing?" Ketch challenged.

"Some *wrecked*. I want to miss the *wreckeds*.

"I am listening to the radio," he replied, while turning up the volume. "They report where are the *wreckeds* so we don't go there," he explained.

Ketch assumed he was talking about traffic jams and wrecked cars until he got a better taste of it as they were driving up a hillside road through a village.

Without warning, there was a huge explosion behind the car. It lurched the car forward, but fortunately did not do any damage or break any glass.

A rocket had exploded just behind them. Ketch now knew what Mustapha meant by *wrecked*.

"Rocket."

"Shit!" Ketch exclaimed. "Who did that?"

"Nobody knows," Mustapha replied. "It could be anyone. This is Beirut."

"Who did that?" Ketch looked back over the front seat and asked Nikki.

"Like he says. This is Beirut."

Chapter Thirty-Five

Ketch made it to the Lebanese Forces command post on the top of some hill.

It was a small concrete block-style building, maybe three stories high with mesh steel screens on all the windows to protect the glass from bomb shrapnel and other flying debris.

There were explosions going off all around the perimeter. None seemed to target the command post itself, however, Ketch felt the shock waves every time an artillery shell hit the ground.

There was no getting used to an artillery barrage.

The brain-rattling noise, the concussion of the explosion and the trembling of the ground was overwhelming.

For Ketch, the shock wave was the most unsettling. Most of his combat experience involved small arms fire back and forth. That was confusing enough. Being in the middle of lots of automatic rifles going off was like being under jackhammers digging up a sidewalk. The noise and the vibration was very disorienting.

But the concussive effect of an artillery or mortar shell exploding near you was like being enveloped in a bag with someone punching you from all sides. Your head was spinning and your ears were ringing.

"Maybe you should come in," Ketch said to Mustapha as he was dropped off in front of the building. "It could be a little dangerous out here."

"I must take care of my car," Mustapha replied. "It is my life. If they take my car, then better they also take me."

Nikki accompanied him into the meeting, afraid to stay outside with the car.

A soldier was sitting behind a metal desk in the ground floor lobby reading local Arabic newspapers and underlining items of interest with a yellow highlighter.

"I'm here to see Major Ahmed," Ketch announced.

"*Colonel* Ahmed," the soldier corrected.

"Yes," Ketch replied. "*Colonel* Ahmed."

Ketch and Nikki were ushered up one flight of stairs into a room not unlike that of Major Collins.

There was a desk, a filing cabinet and a cot. Behind the desk sat Colonel Ahmed, nervously chain smoking cigarettes. Every time a shell exploded nearby, the Colonel flinched. Ketch understood and pretended not to notice.

"Mister Kelly," the Colonel said. "Sorry about the inconveniences. What can I do to help you?"

The Colonel spoke perfect English and was obviously well-educated. Ketch wanted to ask what he was still doing in this hell-hole but didn't.

"I'm here to find an American hostage, Adam Smith, a professor from the American University," Ketch replied.

"You know anything about him? You really want to find that guy?" the Colonel asked with a hint of cynicism, while stubbing out a cigarette then immediately lighting up another one.

"That's why I'm here."

"Did they tell you why?"

"No. Only he's an American that I need to get back home."

"You Americans," the Colonel responded. "You think that all Americans are all the same. This guy has been a big troublemaker for many years. Maybe you are not here to rescue him, but to capture him."

"What do you mean, troublemaker?"

"He is well known for criticizing the Americans in the Middle East, the Israelis and all the militias in Lebanon. So everyone hates him. Didn't they tell you that?"

"No," Ketch replied.

"What about the Phalange?" Ketch asked.

"What about the Phalange?" the Colonel replied.

"I was told I should see them."

"I don't know why," the Colonel said dismissively.

"I was told they might know where he is. Can you introduce me?" Ketch asked.

"I could, but I can't for political reasons," the Colonel explained. "We're supposed to be neutral to all the militias. But it is very easy to see them. Your driver can take you."

"Will they help me find Adam Smith?" Ketch enquired.

"I don't know.

"You are on a blind mission my friend, and your government is using you. My best advice is to check in with them before you get yourself killed for nothing."

"Ok. But how do I find him?"

"You don't want to find him, is my advice. He is most likely with some very bad people.

"Hezbollah."

"So, how do I contact Hezbollah?" Ketch persisted.

"You don't want to. They will kill you if you tried. Their mission is to kill all Americans."

"So what should I do?" Ketch asked.

"Go home."

Chapter Thirty-Six

"So, I guess you must go home," Nikki suggested, as they walked back down the stairs after the meeting.

"No. I don't give up that easily. Tomorrow we will see the Phalange. I am doing this step by step."

"Ok. But since you want to die, maybe you can invite me for dinner at your hotel tonight, so I have something to remember you."

"Ok."

They got back to the Commodore and Nikki followed Ketch up the stairs to his room.

"I need to take a shower before dinner," she said.

"Ok." Ketch responded, but he was still distracted by the meeting with Colonel Ahmed.

Nikki went into the bathroom, then quickly called out to Ketch.

"You need to help me," she shouted. "The shower is not working."

Ketch went into the bathroom where he found Nikki wrapped in a towel, naked underneath.

He didn't even notice. He was still focused on the mission and both aggravated and confused by the meeting with the Colonel of the Lebanese Forces. He turned on the water, checked the temperature with his hand, pulled up the plug that redirected the water from the bath faucet to the shower head, then went back into the room.

"Maybe, you should take a shower with me," Nikki called out. "You are very stressed. It will relax you."

Ketch was too stressed for even a shower with a beautiful woman, but went back into the bathroom. Nikki was naked under the stream of water, massaging her perfect body with a bar of soap.

She tilted her head to the side, and eyed him with one of her big, cat-like eyes as he came into the bathroom.

"Come. It will be good for you," she taunted with a smile.

Ketch gave in. He stripped off his clothes and joined Nikki in the shower. He took the bar of soap and mechanically began to wash himself. But Nikki intervened.

She took the soap out of his hands, then gently began to wash and massage him with it. She started with the back of his neck, rubbing and pinching it at the same time to relieve the stress. She soaped his chest and back, then moved down to his thighs. She rubbed them thoroughly, noticing that his shaft was already hard, but avoided touching it for the moment.

She then came back up face-to-face and asked, "How do you feel about kissing me?"

Ketch couldn't resist.

But when he tried to kiss her, she pushed him away. Then she gently picked at his lips with hers, and when she sensed he wanted more, she married her mouth with his.

Ketch picked her up and pulled her legs around his waist. Then, he stepped out of the shower while she was still wrapped around him, carried her back into the room and gently placed her down onto the bed.

They kissed each other fully, deeply and passionately from the bath to the bed.

Once Ketch put Nikki onto the bed, he bent down to kiss her breasts and massage her nipples with his tongue.

"This is too nice," she responded. "It will break my heart. You need to stop.

"Don't make love to me," she added. "Just fuck me."

Ketch was reluctant to give up what he felt had become a perfect union with Nikki. Mind, body and soul. But he did as he was told and just inserted himself. At one point, he pulled her legs up around his shoulders, while he was slowly pumping her.

"Wow. That feels so deep," she responded enthusiastically.

"Did you come?" Ketch asked politely.

"Twice. Now it is your turn."

Ketch put her legs back down on the bed and squeezed them together. Then he came. The effect reverberated throughout his entire body.

"You are such a little boy," Nikki laughed. "You should be seducing me, but you need a woman to seduce you."

Ketch laughed and held her tight. He didn't want to separate himself from her body for as long as possible. For that short while, he felt safe, secure and didn't care about what tomorrow would bring.

Chapter Thirty-Seven

Just as Ketch was getting used to the idea of holding Nikki all night, she exclaimed, "I need to go."

"Why?"

"I can't stay here or the hotel will arrest me as a prostitute."

"That's bullshit."

"No. This is Beirut. Don't forget we are in Muslim West Beirut. I will see you in the morning and we will visit the Phalange, according to your plan. But we need to leave very early. And we need to be back very early. Crossing the Green Line is very tricky. I will meet you at seven."

"What about dinner?

"I just had mine," Nikki laughed.

At that point, she jumped out of bed, got dressed and left in a hurry, almost as if the morality police were about to storm the room.

Ketch took a quick shower, dressed and was preparing for dinner downstairs when the knock came on the door. He was hoping it was Nikki, back after second thoughts.

"Hey man, we met before," said the kid from Connecticut. "Look. I've run out of money and need a place to stay. Can I crash at your place?"

"Go home," Ketch replied and slammed the door on him.

Ketch finished dressing and walked down to the lobby. It was full of broken glass.

The oval shaped bar, that was home to all the journalists there, looked like someone had taken an ax to it.

"What happened?" he asked one of the workers, who was sweeping up the glass from smashed bottles of spirits that had decorated the back bar.

Fortunately, for the journalists, the wine and beer was spared because it was under the counter or in the fridge.

"The militias came and said we must stop serving alcohol," he replied.

"What militia?"

"I don't know. They are all the same."

Ketch crossed over to the restaurant and looked for a seat. The maître d' quickly grabbed him and said, "Mr. Kelly. Welcome, this evening. You are a journalist, so sit with these other journalists. Let me introduce you."

Ketch joined the table and was introduced to famous American TV network faces he'd never expect to meet in real life. They filled the table with their cameramen and local "producers."

They were already very drunk and boasting about all the people they interviewed and the shots they grabbed during the day.

The Connecticut kid was also there, puffing a cigar. He sat at the end of the table, unfortunately just around the corner from Ketch.

"Hey man, thanks for nothing. I already got a room with CBS," he boasted.

"What are you drinking?" one of the network guys asked.

"Nothing. Just 7Up."

That got a laugh out of them.

"You go through war on 7Up?" another jeered.

"Yeah. I want to keep my wits about me."

The group had a big giggle over that, then ignored him. Obviously, he wasn't part of their crowd. They were hyped up, boozed or otherwise and looking for interviews, *bang bang* and other excitement.

Ketch was obviously boring in their eyes.

Ketch ordered the lamb stew with boiled potatoes and cabbage, and finished the dinner alone in his thoughts at the crowded table while the group partied around him.

The Connecticut kid made a point of blowing cigar smoke his way, noting that it irritated him.

Just as Ketch was finishing off dinner, his Canadian TV cameraman friend Liam popped in out of nowhere and rescued him.

"Hey Eric, come join us for a drink."

Ketch asked for the bill, signed it to his room, and joined Liam and a few of his friends on the other side of the restaurant.

"So, Eric. You can tell me. We go back a long way. What the fuck are you doing in Beirut? We won't tell on you," Liam said with a laugh.

"I'm here to find the kidnapped professor, Adam Smith, from the American University and get him home."

"That asshole," Liam replied. "Let him rot, wherever he is."

"I've heard that from several sources. Any idea where he is?"

"No, but probably with one of the bad guys. Likely Hezbollah."

"Is he a good guy or a bad guy? Our team or theirs?"

"I don't know. I just know that he's an asshole."

"Well, that's my job. I'm doing this on a commission basis, so I don't get paid until I bring him home."

"And what he if doesn't want to go back home?"

"Then, I guess I don't get paid."

"Look man, this is a bad gig. You should just go back home."

"Thanks. But you know me. I can't say no to a challenge."

"This isn't a challenge, man. This is a set up. Go home."

"Go home," seemed to becoming the theme of this mission, Ketch noted.

"Well, tomorrow I want to go to East Beirut to see the Phalange," Ketch noted. "The Marines and the Lebanese Forces wouldn't give me a phone number on grounds of neutrality. Any idea how to set that up?"

"Forget the number," Liam explained. "It's always busy and impossible to make an appointment.

"Just tell your driver to take you there. He'll know where it is. All the drivers know. Just walk in and ask for Major Yousef. He's their press spokesman. They're pretty laid back about Western journalists dropping in on them. Just bring your passport and a few business cards."

"Thanks, Liam. I appreciate that. But, can you get me in to see Hezbollah?"

"What the fuck are you talking about? They will kill you just because you are American. That is their mission. To kill Americans. Any Americans."

"So I've heard. But can you do it for me?"

"Call me in a couple of days. I'm in Room 609. Don't get yourself killed in the meantime. This place is a mess. It's not worth it. I'm only here for the money."

Chapter Thirty-Eight

Ketch got up a six the next morning, did some stretching and light exercises, then walked down the stairs to the restaurant for breakfast.

Scrambled eggs, bacon, toast and 7Up.

He stopped bothering about the radio updates.

Nikki was already waiting for him in the lobby as he left the restaurant.

"Let me get my stuff and I'll be right back," he told her.

He climbed the stairs, pulled his gear together, then started for the steps again. But the elevator was already open on his floor. It was a tempting convenience. Against his instincts, he got in, pushed the button for the ground floor and the doors closed.

Then nothing.

The elevator didn't move, the doors wouldn't open and he was stuck. He immediately thought about climbing out the escape hatch in the ceiling, but there was no escape hatch. The ceiling was solid metal. He then tried prying open the doors, but they wouldn't budge.

As a university student, he made a point of practicing elevator escapes in his dormitory. He'd purposely jam the elevator between floors by forcing the doors open. Then he'd jump up and punch the ceiling hatch open.

There was a crossbar a foot above the elevator ceiling. It was close enough to leap up and grab. He'd then pull himself up onto the roof of the cabin.

One time, he climbed up the cables a few flights. They were too greasy and thin to climb up individually, so he squeezed them all together, which gave him a better grip and he managed to shinny up six floors to the roof.

However, he was so covered with grease when he got back down, that he had to throw away his clothes.

It took several days of washing with industrial strength, powdered, abrasive soap to get his hands and arms clean.

He never did it again, but considered it good practice for any *Mission Impossible* task he might be called upon in the future. From a young age, for whatever reasons, Ketch was a commando at heart.

Ketch noted the irony as he remained trapped in the Beirut hotel elevator.

Then the lights went off. Ketch cursed himself for this. He sat down on the floor and waited, hoping he'd be able to get out before having to take a pee.

After twenty long minutes, the lights came back on and the elevator took him to the ground floor.

"What happened?" Nikki asked. "I've been waiting for you."

"I did something stupid and trusted the elevator. The electricity went off and I was stuck."

"That was stupid. Don't trust anything. Not even the lift. This is Beirut."

Mustapha was waiting outside and they were off to East Beirut.

En route to the Green Line, they passed through the Minet al Hosn hotel district in northern Beirut, near the seafront. It was famous for the "Battle of the

Hotels" that happened some years earlier, as well as the "ice cream massacre."

At that time, rival militias controlled one hotel or the other. Apparently, things were peaceful during the day, but after sundown the militias started blasting away at each other from the rooftops.

According to the story, in one of the hotels, after their shift, the rooftop squad went down into the basement, where their relief team was waiting to replace them. After the others went up to the roof, one of the soldiers in the basement started exploring the area, hoping to find tunnels connecting the building to others across the street.

Instead, the soldier stumbled into freezers stocked full of ice cream. He alerted his buddies about the find and they pulled out gallon containers of it.

Then, they partied on vanilla, chocolate, strawberry and pistachio. It was a great morale booster. They laughed, told jokes and kept eating until they were sick from it.

Later, the team from the roof came down to grab the guys in the basement for their second shift. They found them asleep on the floor, some covered in melted ice cream.

One of the soldiers from the roof shift kicked them one by one out of their sleep and asked them what was going on.

"We found ice cream," one of the basement boys replied, laughing.

The boy from the roof looked at them, then opened one of the freezer doors.

"Yes," he said. "But you didn't save any for us."

The boys in the basement shrugged. They hadn't thought about it.

At that point, his comrade turned around, and emptied his AK-47 magazine into all of them.

So the story goes.

The ride was pretty smooth until they got to the Green Line and its various checkpoints. Then they waited and waited and waited as guys with guns checked cars and papers.

"Why do they call it the Green Line?" Ketch asked Nikki.

"There are two different stories," she replied. "After all the bombing of the buildings, only green plants and weeds were left in the streets. So it is green. That's one story.

"The other story is that someone used a green pen to draw the line between the Muslim and Christian neighborhoods. That's the answer I think is better. The Israelis used a green pen to divide up Palestine between the Jews and the Arabs. So, I think they got it from them.

"But in Arabic, nobody calls it the Green Line," she added. "They call it the 'line of confrontation' or *Khat al Tamas*. Nothing special," she noted.

After an hour of waiting, Ketch got restless and left the car.

"Get back in the car!" Nikki screamed at him.

Ketch ignored her and started to take pictures of the gutted, bombed-out buildings. It was like something he had seen in a World War II documentary. There was nothing left of the buildings but ghost-like skeletons. Only the haunted eyes of blown-out windows and crumbling walls, pock-marked by machine gun and rifle bullets, were left standing. Big holes were torn out by rockets.

Ketch didn't see it coming because his face was behind his camera. A big body tackled him to the ground.

"Who are you?" the body challenged.

"Who are you?" Ketch shouted back, now recovering from the fall.

"No pictures!" the body responded.

Meanwhile, Nikki ran out of the car, shouted something in Arabic at the body and with the help of Mustapha, got Ketch to stand and pulled him back inside the car.

"I told you not to leave the car," she said angrily. "If you don't listen to me, then get someone else!"

Ketch settled back into the front seat and silently licked his wounds.

He wasn't sure if he had just learned a lesson in arrogance, over-confidence, naiveté, stupidity, or all four.

After another hour in line, they were subjected to a car and full body search.

The guard in charge of searching Nikki took great pleasure in it.

He felt around her breasts then slid his hands down her back to her butt and up her skirt. He then groped between her legs.

She winced a bit as he did that, but was otherwise stoic throughout the whole procedure.

Ketch was outraged, and immediately wanted to take this guy out by whatever means possible, even if he died trying. However, in the process of his body search, two other guards restrained him by pulling back his arms while another one felt around Ketch's butt and crotch.

"I'm so very sorry about that," Ketch said to Nikki after they were released.

"No need to be sorry," she replied. "This is Beirut. Get used to it or go home.

"My big worry is that these guys don't wear gloves," she explained. "Who knows how many other people they search like that without washing their hands. So, I don't like to cross the Green Line."

"Why didn't they search the driver?" Ketch asked.

"He is a professional driver that crosses the Green Line every day for something or other. They know him and they know his car. They don't need to search him. If he brings the wrong person across, or the wrong things across, they will simply shoot him," Nikki explained. "He knows that, so he wouldn't even try."

"And who were the guys doing the searching? What militia was that?" Ketch asked.

"Who knows? It changes all the time," Nikki responded, uninterested.

When they crossed into East Beirut, Ketch was caught totally by surprise.

There were a few blown-up buildings here and there but, overall, it felt like he was in Mediterranean Europe. Single family homes with red clay shingled roofs were the norm. People were out and about in sidewalk cafes and restaurants as if nothing was happening.

"Before we go to the Phalange, take me to the port. I want to see where the ferry to Cyprus leaves and make sure I know how to buy tickets."

They got to the port, which sported lots of marinas showing off nice yachts, both big and small. Mostly big.

Mustapha pulled up to the ferry dock and Ketch went to the ticket counter followed by Nikki.

"What time does the ferry to Cyprus leave?" he purposely asked by himself in English to see if he'd be understood.

"There are two a day," the man behind the window replied with a hint of a French accent. "One at nine in the morning and one nine at night."

"How long does it take?" Ketch inquired.

"It depends on conditions."

"What conditions?"

"This is Beirut. There are many conditions.

"You should buy your ticket in advance. The ferry is usually fully booked. A lot of people are leaving Beirut right now."

"Thank you."

They got back in the car and Mustapha sped off.

They quickly arrived at an apartment building that Mustapha claimed was the headquarters of the Phalange.

"Are you sure this is the right place?"

"Yes. Yes. I take many foreign journalists here. Just go in and show them your passport. But they may not let Nikki go with you."

"Why not?" Ketch asked.

"She is Lebanese and coming from West Beirut. Better she wait here. There is a café next door. We will go for coffee."

Nikki nodded, and Ketch proceeded on his own.

Chapter Thirty-Nine

Ketch walked into the building and approached the reception desk.

It was manned by an attractive Lebanese woman wearing a low cut blouse that she easily filled out. A solider in cammies and beret stood behind her. Ketch noted that an M-16 dangled from his back and a Colt .45, with the hammer already cocked and locked, sprouted from a leather holster attached to his belt.

"Good morning, sir," the woman said cheerfully with a big smile that matched her big, dark, almond eyes. "What can we do for you?" she asked with a bit of a French accent.

"I'd like to see Major Yousef," Ketch responded. "I apologize, but I don't have an appointment. I'm an American journalist and would be grateful for a few moments of his time."

"I'm sure he will be happy to see you," the woman replied graciously. "I just need your passport and a business card."

Ketch produced his passport and the fake business card from the *Detroit City News*.

The woman took both and disappeared up a staircase as the soldier stared at him intensely, sizing him up.

"Colt .45? American?" Ketch said, trying to make friendly conversation with the guard.

"No English," came the curt reply.

"Sorry," Ketch said lamely.

The woman returned quickly and said with another big smile, "The Major can see you now."

"Many thanks. And my passport?"

"I will keep it safe for you and give it back when you come down," she replied. "Just walk up to the first floor. He is waiting for you. And don't take the lift back down. They are always getting stuck."

Ketch smiled to himself on that point and walked up the stairs.

Chapter Forty

"Nice to meet you," Major Yousef announced. "Mr. Kelly is it?"

"Yes."

"Welcome to East Beirut," replied the Major, extending his hand.

The Major wore a crisp tan uniform with a European-style double-barreled belt, known as a Sam Browne belt. The kind that has two straps. A wide one around the waist to keep your pants up and dangle gear from. Another thin strap worn diagonally across the chest and over one shoulder.

The thin strap was to keep the waist belt up from whatever you hung from it. Guns, radios, other stuff. But even if you didn't hang anything from the waist belt, the shoulder belt made the uniform look more impressive and commanding.

Ketch noticed that the Major was unarmed. He sported a short but stylish haircut and a small moustache. His English was perfect, without trace of any accent that could betray his training. Ketch guessed it was either from Canada or the American Midwest.

The Major led him into a large, bright, high-ceilinged office. There was a big wooden desk facing two soft leather chairs and a sofa against the opposite wall with a coffee table in front and two more soft leather chairs on either side.

"Please, sit over there," the Major directed, motioning to the couch. "Can I get you some refreshment? Coffee, tea, beer, whisky, brandy?"

"I don't suppose you have any 7Up?" Ketch replied.

"That one, I don't have," the Major laughed. "But next time, call me first and I will be sure to get some for you."

Ketch smiled, and for the first time in Beirut, felt totally at ease.

"So, how can I help you, Mister Kelly? Where are you staying?"

"The Commodore Hotel."

"Ah, with all the other press. So, you adventured across the Green Line, just to see me.

"I am flattered," the Major replied graciously.

"It was interesting," Ketch noted.

A woman entered the room with a tray containing two thimble-sized cups of thick, gritty espresso. She was just following guest protocol and assumed the Major's guest would want one.

"Don't feel obliged to drink that if you can't take coffee," The Major suggested. "It will keep you up all night."

As the Major was sipping coffee from the thimble, Ketch made his pitch.

"So, Major. I'm here to do a story about the American University professor, Adam Smith, who was kidnapped. I'd be grateful if you could point me in the right direction."

"You are here to do a story, or to find him so you can win a Pulitzer Prize?"

Ketch laughed at his directness.

"Both, I guess."

"It seems you know nothing about him," the Major continued. "Nobody likes him here. The Lebanese don't like him, the militias don't like him, the Syrians don't like him, the Israelis don't like him, the Palestinians don't like him. Even the Americans don't like him."

"Why doesn't anyone like him?"

"First. He calls himself Adam Smith and everyone thinks that is not his real name. It is too obvious. He picked it to sound like the famous economist. So, that tells everyone that he is not honest. He is just a self-promoter.

"Second. He both sympathizes with and criticizes everyone. One minute, he's telling them he understands their troubles, then the next minute, he is telling them they have bad political strategy and are immoral and selfish. They thought he was their friend, but then he became their big critic."

"Sounds like he is an independent free thinker."

"No. Maybe that is ok in your country, but not here. This is Beirut. You must choose sides.

"Did you play sports in school? What are you supposed to do? Beat the other team!

"What would you do if you played against a team from a poor neighborhood with bad equipment and torn uniforms? Would you let them win out of sympathy? No. You would win because it was your job to win.

"You are responsible to your team," the Major added. "If you don't like that, then don't join a team. Take up chess.

"Also, Adam Smith was not an economist. He was an engineering professor. Chemical, I think. So, he had no business in politics."

"Can you help me find him?" Ketch asked.

"Mr. Kelly. Unless your newspaper is paying you very big money to be here, I recommend you go home. Beirut is very dangerous. There are no battle lines. Random bombings and shootings happen all the time for no reason. Nobody knows who is shooting who and why. It is anarchy."

"Some of my friends claim that anarchy is the best form of government because it is no government," Ketch replied with a smile.

"Well, I assume that they are American or British intellectuals who have no experience in the real world, but like to preach their theories from soft leather chairs and antique desks in libraries stacked to the roof with old books.

"Send them to Beirut. And they will experience anarchy. Everyone is changing sides all the time. It is insanity and causing much suffering.

"Hopefully, they will come here and get shot," he added. "We've had enough of these arrogant, academic intellectuals from the West telling us how to run our country and preaching the idealism of anarchy.

"If I meet them, maybe I will shoot them myself."

"Maybe, me too," Ketch laughed.

"So, how much are they paying you to find this guy, Adam Smith?" the Major asked, going back to the original subject. "I hope it's a lot."

"Well, I don't do my job for the money."

"What then?"

"To be part of history."

The Major laughed heartily.

"Are you sure I can't offer you some whisky?" he asked. "This could be an interesting conversation."

Ketch declined gracefully.

"Well, let me tell you this," the Major continued. "Because you are here now, you are already part of history. You already have your place in history. I will sign a letter confirming it if you like.

"So, now you can go home."

"So, you can't help me find this guy?"

"I can give you some direction, if you are willing to die for this. Maybe even tortured first.

"First, they will fuck you up the butt.

"Then, they will shock you with electricity.

"Then, they will cut off your balls.

"They will not cut off your penis, because they know if they do that, you will just want to die and will yourself to die. As long as you have your penis, you can still have sex, even with no balls. But you can't have children, of course."

"Maybe, better than a condom," Ketch interjected with a smile.

"But if you don't give them what they want, they will just shoot you," the Major added.

"And what do they want?"

"Who knows?" the Major returned. "Whatever has value in their eyes at that moment. If you don't have value, they will shoot you. It is too much trouble for them to keep you and feed you. They are very practical about their prisoners."

"Ok. I get it," Ketch returned, unfazed. "Bottom line, can you help me find Adam Smith?"

"I will give you the address of the Amal militia. Sorry, but I don't have a contact name.

"The Americans are claiming they are responsible for the U.S. Marines bombing at the airport, simply because they live nearby and because Amal was shooting at them before. But everyone knows they were bombed by Hezbollah.

"Hezbollah has big money from the Iranians and a big base in the Bekaa Valley run by their own elite national guards.

"Amal is trying to make friends with them because they have money and power. Hezbollah has a lot of money from Iran and a clear mission to kill Americans. Many Amal fighters have already joined them.

"Amal is a weak player right now, so they are trying to make friends with the West as well as Hezbollah.

"They see Hezbollah as a stronger force and want to be on the winning side. But they don't want to become someone else's servants. They would probably prefer to work with the West, but the West is not going to support a Muslim organization, so they need to play their bets. It is very stupid of the West. Western intelligence is very stupid out here and the politicians even more stupid.

"Amal are idealists and have been fighting everyone at one time or another. We don't know where their money comes from. Maybe only small donations from overseas Arabs.

"But I must tell you, the kidnapping business is very popular here. People are kidnapped all the time. You Americans only think about Americans, but rich Lebanese businessmen are the ones most at risk because their families will quickly pay up to get them back.

"The militias know this. So, it is an easy transaction.

"You Americans think it is all about politics. Christians, Muslims, Israelis. But it is not. It is about money. And with money, you can get power. And with power you can get more money."

The Major wrote something in Arabic on a slip of paper and passed it to Ketch.

"Here is the address for Amal," he noted. "But your driver may not want to take you there."

Ketch thanked him and left.

He collected his passport at reception and found Mustapha and Nikki enjoying coffee and croissants next door under a bright, sunny Mediterranean sky.

"So, how was your talk?" Nikki asked.

"Very good," Ketch replied. "He helped me set up a meeting tomorrow."

"Where?" Nikki pushed.

"Don't worry, we don't have to cross the Green Line," Ketch assured.

"Yes, but where?" Nikki insisted. "There are also many dangerous places on the West side. You saw it yourself. A rocket just missed our car before."

"Don't worry. We're not going up that hill again," Ketch replied confidently. "I will tell you tomorrow."

Nikki and Mustapha looked at each other nervously.

Mustapha drove them back to the hotel. Ironically, crossing the Green Line back into West Beirut was not that difficult and cumbersome. There was no line and no body searches.

"That was quick," Ketch noted.

The soldiers at the checkpoints just waved them past.

"Of course, nobody cares who comes into West Beirut to kill Muslims," Mustapha said cynically.

"Even the Muslims."

"Ok. Let's meet tomorrow at seven a.m.," Ketch instructed.

"To go where?" Nikki insisted.

"I will tell you tomorrow," Ketch replied. "I need to make some phone calls and confirm some things."

Chapter Forty-One

Ketch got up at six, took a quick shower, then called Major Collins at the Marines. When they first met, the Major had suggested that he call in to report on his whereabouts, especially if he was going to visit Amal, which was in the Marines' backyard, close to the airport.

"I'm sorry, Major Collins cannot come to the phone right now," the voice at the other end replied.

"Can I wait?" Ketch replied. "My name is Eric Kelly. I'm an American journalist. I was with the Major the other day and he asked me to keep him informed of my whereabouts. Especially, if I'm going to visit Amal, which I'm going to do today."

"Sorry Mister Kelly. Let me transfer you," the voice replied.

Ketch held the phone for several minutes. When he was about to hang up, another voice came onto the phone.

"Hello, this is Captain Walters. "Who is this?"

"Hello Captain. My name is Eric Kelly. I am an American journalist. I met with Major Collins regarding a project I'm doing in Beirut. He suggested, I might need to talk with Amal but advised I call him before doing that.

"I'm going to meet with them later this morning."

"Well, I'm sorry to inform you, but the Major is dead," the Captain returned.

"What do you mean dead?"

"He accidentally shot himself while cleaning his sidearm," the Captain replied.

"What!?" Ketch shouted. "Marines don't accidentally shoot themselves. What happened?"

"Sorry, Mr. Kelly, that's all I know," the Captain replied. "Sorry, I can't be of further assistance."

He then hung up.

Ketch was stunned. He held onto the phone for a minute, then slammed it down.

"Fuck," he shouted at no one.

He then went downstairs for breakfast in the dining room.

Nikki spotted him there and joined him for a coffee.

"You look very upset," she offered. "What happened?"

"Nothing," Ketch replied, not wanting to spook her. "I just learned that a good friend got killed."

"I am sorry. I won't bother you about it, but everyone gets killed here. This is Beirut.

"Where are we going today?" she asked anxiously.

Ketch pulled out the slip of paper from Major Yousef and showed it to her.

Nikki flinched.

"That is Amal," she responded nervously. "They will kill you.

"Ok. You don't care about you, so I don't care about you. But maybe they will kill me too."

"The Major said they are no longer hostile to the West and trying to be friends, Ketch reassured her, though very unconvincingly."

"He say, you say, everybody say. There is no say. Minute by minute the situation is changing. Anything can happen all at once. This is Beirut."

"Yes. But the major said it would be Ok," Ketch repeated.

"Did you call them?" she challenged.

"No. The Major said it is just easier to show up," he replied lamely.

She looked down disgustedly and said something to herself in Arabic.

They went out into the street where Mustapha was waiting for them.

"He wants to go to Amal," Nikki shouted. "He is crazy."

Mustapha was also visibly concerned.

He and Nikki debated the issue in Arabic for several minutes.

"Ok. I will take you. But today's price will be double," Mustapha volunteered.

"Me too," Nikki chimed in.

"Ok. Fine. Let's go."

The address was in southern Beirut. Mustapha took them back along the coast road which allowed Ketch to once again take in the beauty of the beaches along the Mediterranean seaside. This time, he not only noticed the beaches, but the bikinis nonchalantly prancing around in the sand as if nothing was happening.

"That is a big resort," Nikki said, pointing at what appeared to be a big seaside hotel.

"It is where rich Lebanese people go for a weekend of peace," she explained.

"The hotel has its own militia and negotiates with all the other militias to leave them alone. They pay them money, so it costs a lot to buy your weekend escape by the pool.

"Like everything else here, it is all about money and business, not religion or politics as you Western journalists report," she added sarcastically.

Mustapha then turned inland onto a maze of streets into a ghetto-like environment. Worse than a ghetto. Square, box-like concrete modules that had been constructed with no attention to design or human amenities. Garbage was piled up in the streets everywhere and the air stank of urine and feces.

Women wearing the *hijab* head scarf as well as the more conservative veiled *niqab* head covering, were filling up buckets with water from open fire hydrants. Small, unwashed boys ran naked in the streets, kicking tin cans with dirty, bare feet for amusement.

Some of the women's faces revealed touches of makeup. A bit of eyeliner and lipstick. It would not have passed the approval of the truck driver at the Pakistan-Afghanistan border. Mustapha found the address and stopped the car across the street.

Two men wearing *balaclavas* were standing at the doorway, behind a three-foot high pile of sandbags, AK-47s at the ready.

Balaclavas.

Not to be confused with the famous sweet Middle Eastern pastry *baklava.*

The *balaclava* was essentially a ski mask made of wool and designed for the British soldiers during the Crimean War in the nineteenth century to protect them against the cold. It rolled up to the top of the head, or could be pulled down with holes exposing only the mouth and eyes.

They were named after the city of Balaclava, near Sevastopol, and the Battle of Balaclava fought there.

The war was a slugfest by the British, the French, the Turks allied against the Russians in another demonstration of European nationalistic arrogance and failed diplomacy. The alliance claimed they were protecting Catholic rights in the Middle East while the Russians claimed they were protecting Eastern Orthodox rights. Christians fighting Christians over political supremacy.

Geographically, the Russians attacked the Turks to gain control of the Crimea, a strategic peninsula in the Ukraine on the Caspian Sea that would give the Russian fleet a warm water port to the Mediterranean. Britain supported the Turks, but it might have been more for business than religious reasons. Allegedly, British banks held a significant amount of loans to Turkey and wanted to make sure they got paid.

Florence Nightingale, a nurse born in Italy but trained in Britain, made her name there, attending to wounded allied soldiers in the field. Day and night.

The war was also famous for the poem, *The Charge of the Light Brigade,* based on a real battle by lightly armed British cavalry.

The British Light Brigade was armed only with lances and sabers and assumed it was attacking a retreating Russian artillery unit. However arrogant officers, who refused to question muddled orders from above, sent their men against the wrong position. They directed them into a gauntlet of cannons and riflemen of Russian troops defensively dug in. The charge was so senseless and casualties were so enormous that the Russians assumed that the Brits must have been drunk.

The *balaclava.*

In modern times, it became popular among skiers. Ketch had worn one himself for skiing. Even when not skiing, as a kid, he wore a *balaclava* when winter storms hit. He only knew it as a ski mask.

Unfortunately, in later years it became a symbol of Palestinian terrorists. Particularly during the 1972 Munich Olympic killings.

During the 1972 Summer Olympics in Munich, a Palestinian terrorist group known as Black September breached the chain link fence around the Olympic Village where the athletes were quartered.

They found their way into the Israeli dormitory.

Obviously, they were helped by someone on the inside to identify the rooms of the Israeli athletes. Allegedly, they were given logistical support and intelligence by German neo-Nazi groups.

Israeli athletes who fought back were simply shot. The rest were taken as hostages.

The terrorists presented themselves to the world press wearing their *balaclavas* from a dormitory balcony, with fists raised as a sign of triumph.

The German government agreed to their demands to fly them out of the country with the hostages. However, the government had covertly planned to take them down with snipers at the airport as they were boarding the aircraft.

Sadly, the plan went awry. All the Palestinians were killed, but so were the hostages. As the German snipers started firing on the terrorists, the terrorists simply turned their guns on the hostages. In their mind, they had nothing to lose. Dying in a glorious defeat was better than giving a victory to your enemy.

Ketch, stared at the men in the doorway for a moment, then announced, "Ok. Time to go."

"I can't go in there with you," Nikki responded, obviously very scared.

"You have to," Ketch replied coldly. "They probably don't speak English."

"Remember, you are paying me double for this," she noted. "You are lucky I keep the *hijab* in my bag. But I also keep a bikini in there. If they find the bikini, they will shoot me."

"Ok. Stay in the car for now," Ketch responded. "I will go first and don't bring your bag. Also, wipe off your lipstick."

Nikki quickly pulled the *hijab* scarf from her bag and wrapped it around her head. She took Ketch's advice and wiped off the little bit of lipstick she wore. She also remained in the car, but watched Ketch carefully.

Ketch approached the guards very slowly and cautiously. They just stared back, but raised their rifles at him as he got closer.

He left his backpack and camera gear back in the car, so they wouldn't fear a bomb. Anyway, he didn't need pictures, he needed information.

When he got close enough, he presented the paper from Major Yousef with the address.

"Hi. I'm Eric Kelly, a journalist here to speak with Amal."

One of the guards took the paper, looked at it, then walked around the sandbag barrier and immediately kicked Eric in the stomach with his military boot.

Ketch quickly dropped to the ground, doubled over in agony, clutching his stomach and gasping for his breath. The kick gave him a severe cramp in his gut that wouldn't go away or let him breathe.

Nikki immediately sprang out of the car, rushed to Ketch and intervened, standing over him and screaming at the gunmen in Arabic while he groaned in the fetal position along the road.

Nikki fell down to her knees next to him, extended one leg forward and dragged Ketch's back across her thigh, arching his stomach upwards. Then she began intensely massaging his abdomen.

Very quickly, the cramp went away, and Ketch was able to stand up again.

"Wow, Nikki," he exclaimed gratefully. "Where did you learn that?"

"It's a long story," she replied.

The guards watched impassively, then one grabbed Nikki and dragged her into the building by the arm as she tripped over herself trying to keep up. The other threatened Ketch over the sandbags with the barrel of his AK-47.

Ketch now regretted this meeting and felt very bad for getting Nikki involved. But there was nothing he could do about it at this point. Events were already playing out and he needed to make his next move. Quickly. As he regained his senses, he tried to figure out a way to disarm the guard, get into the building and rescue Nikki.

Just when he thought he had a plan, the guard who took Nikki inside emerged back onto the street with her.

"You are very lucky," she said. "They will see you."

The guard took them up two flights of stairs. The hallway stank of urine.

"Catch me if I pass out," Nikki interjected.

They were shown into a room and the guard put his hands on their shoulders and forcefully pushed them down onto two metal chairs with no cushions facing a gray metal desk with a man behind it. There was nothing else in the room except a sleeping bag off in the corner.

The plaster walls were peeling and the room stank of sweat.

"Why do you want to see Amal?" the man questioned in perfect English.

"I'm a journalist and want to write a story about you," Ketch lied.

"You're an American," the man replied threateningly. "I could sell you for lots of money."

"You could. But then I wouldn't be able to tell your story. Don't you want someone to tell your story?"

"Since you come here, you see how my people live. Can your story change that?"

"You don't know if you don't try," Ketch responded. "Look at the Palestinians. They didn't let anyone tell their story. They have a very important and just story. But, instead, they went for violence. It turned the whole world against them, even their brothers in the Middle East.

"If they let someone tell their story, maybe things would be different.

"Let me tell your story."

"You are a journalist. You never tell the real story, only your story," the official returned. "What else do you want? Journalists always want something."

"I also want to write a story about the American University professor that was kidnapped. Adam Smith," Ketch added.

"Of course, you are not here to tell my story, only to find your American friend," the official responded.

"He's not my friend. I don't know him and never met him." Ketch continued. "But I was also sent here to tell his story. You asked me what I wanted. That's it. You help me find him, I will help you tell your story. Otherwise, I will go home. I've only been in Beirut a short time, but I am already very tired."

"Well, how tired would you be living here?" the official replied angrily. "What kind of life is this? For me, my family, my children? We are everybody's toy. The Americans, the Israelis, the Syrians, the other militias, and my big money brothers in the Middle East.

"They all pay everyone to fight each other like we are teams playing in your Super Bowl. Lebanon is a big spectator sport with lots of killing. Like the Roman Coliseum and the gladiators.

"That is the story. Why is everyone paying everyone to fight each other in Lebanon? What do they want? Tell me that. What do they want in Lebanon?" the official concluded.

"I don't know, but I promise to tell that story," Ketch responded. "Can you help me find this guy?"

"I can. But I'm sorry to say, it may get you killed," the man replied solemnly. "He is with Hezbollah. In Tripoli. You will need a big suitcase full of money. Also, they may just take your money, then hold you for more money. You are a rich American. They know you will pay."

"Not all Americans are rich," Ketch retorted.

"It doesn't matter. That's what they think," the official returned. "So, if you don't pay, they will think you are trying to cheat them and just shoot you. They don't care. Nobody cares. This is Beirut.

"Hezbollah belongs to the Iranians. They hate Americans. It is not just about the money but about the Iranians wanting to humiliate the Americans."

"Why is he in Tripoli when he was taken from the American University in Beirut?" Ketch asked a bit confused.

"I don't know. But that's where he is," the official replied bluntly. "You accept this deal? I help you find your professor and you help me tell the story of my people."

"Deal," Ketch reaffirmed.

"But you must cross the Green Line," the official noted.

"Already done that," Ketch replied confidently.

"Ok. But the road to Tripoli is controlled by the Syrians, so you will need a Syrian pass to get through their checkpoints," the official advised.

"How do I get that?" Ketch asked.

"If you have a good driver, he can get one for you," the official continued.

Nikki nodded.

"You will recognize them by their tiger-striped uniforms. Whatever you do, don't show them your American passport. Don't even bring it with you," the official warned.

"And if they ask?" Ketch inquired.

"Tell them you left it at the hotel. The pass should say you are Canadian. Make sure your driver understands that.

"Meanwhile, please tell your American Marines friends that we are very sorry about the bombing. I can't say who it was. But it was a bad strategy whoever did it," the official noted apologetically.

"Thank you," Ketch replied and left.

Chapter Forty-Two

Ketch and Nikki got back to the car.

Once they got in, they both expelled a big sigh of relief.

"You don't really want to go to Tripoli, do you?" Nikki asked with hesitation.

"It seems that's the next stop on the tour," Ketch replied. "If you don't want to go, you don't have to. I'll pay you for the day anyway.

"And thank you for keeping me from getting beat up by those bastards back there."

"That's my job," Nikki laughed. "But I can't promise I will join you to Tripoli. I don't want to cross the Green Line again, and I don't want to meet Hezbollah."

"I understand," he replied. "Mustapha? What about you?"

"I will take you, but it will be double," he noted.

Ketch now felt he had a plan and looked forward to a relaxed lunch with Nikki back at the hotel.

But instead of taking the coast road back, Mustapha decided to take inner-city side streets.

"Why not the coast road?" Ketch asked.

"Too much traffic at this time."

Mustapha maneuvered through the small streets of south Beirut which gave Ketch a better look at the life there. Overall, pretty grim.

When Mustapha finally got them onto a main road, he noted, "This road takes us past the Sabra and Shatila refugee camps. Many killings there before. You don't want to visit."

Mustapha drove up the road, but then stopped just before approaching an overpass near the Shatila camp.

"Mustapha, why are you stopping? A *wrecked?*" Ketch queried, assuming another rocket attack.

"This is Beirut. Minute by minute the situation is changing. You need to know when to stop. Let's wait one minute."

Mustapha pulled over and they waited alongside the road. Ketch watched other cars pass by, but his patience was wearing thin. Ketch hated waiting. For anything. Girls, friends, meetings. Anybody who made him wait was quickly off his list.

"Mustapha. Nothing is happening. Let's go."

"One more minute."

"Just go!"

"Maybe one more minute."

"Mustapha, just go! I hate waiting," Ketch shouted aggressively.

Mustapha looked over the back seat at Nikki. She nodded and he obediently put the car in gear and started to drive up the overpass, but slowly. Another car passed them along the way and nothing happened. That gave Ketch reassurance.

Then more cars. However, the moment they got to the top of the overpass, machine gun fire opened up around them. It was from across the street, but close enough for Ketch to see the gunner's face and the size of the weapon.

.50 caliber.

The gunfire blasted apart the car in front of him. The driver tried to run out but his body just exploded in the barrage of high-caliber ammo.

Ketch's immediate instinct was to roll out of the car onto the street, off the overpass and take cover. But a little voice inside of his head said "No! You got Mustapha and Nikki into this. So, you are going to stay with them until you get them out of it or they die, or you die."

Ketch listened to the little voice, stayed in the car and prepared to die.

Under the circumstances, Ketch could do nothing. He just stayed in his seat, accepted the situation and accepted his death. He relaxed and meditated on it. If you're relaxed it doesn't hurt as much, he reassured himself.

Nikki dropped to the floor in the back seat and Ketch could hear what he assumed was her cursing. Even without knowing Arabic, he got it.

Ketch could see the gunner's face through the front windshield and reached for his Canon. However, as soon as he grabbed it, the little voice in his head said, "Don't even think about it."

So, Ketch let go of the camera and perhaps an award-winning shot, but one that could have gotten them all killed by attracting attention to their car. If he could see the face of the gunman, he reasoned, the gunman could also probably see him.

Meanwhile, Mustapha was in a panic. The .50 caliber was chewing up big holes in the road around them. He put the car in reverse and rapidly tried to spin the car around and get out. However, while he did that, another car behind them smashed into his left fender.

They were sandwiched.

Mustapha didn't bother to stop and ask for the guy's license or insurance card. Instead, he rammed his way through what was now a lethal traffic jam. They bumpered their way out and as soon as they got clear, Mustapha headed for the coast road.

Once they got in sight of the Mediterranean, Mustapha pulled the car over.

"I need to pee," he apologized.

"I also need to pee," Ketch laughed.

"I also need to pee," Nikki added, "But I don't want you to watch me, so I will wait until we are back at the hotel."

They all laughed. Escaping sudden death is no laughing matter, but the laughter relieved the tension.

"I am sorry for that," Mustapha said.

"For what?" Ketch asked.

"Taking you on the wrong road. It was my fault."

"It's nobody's fault," Ketch replied. "This is Beirut."

"Anyway, I will invite you for lunch," Mustapha said.

Ketch surveyed Mustapha's nice green Mercedes and it was a mess. Both fenders were slammed in, the front grill was dangling and the back end was crushed.

"I hope you have insurance," Ketch bantered.

"I have better," Mustapha replied. "I have a brother-in-law who is a car mechanic."

Mustapha drove up to a delicatessen near the coast road. He ordered spicy cold-cuts, thinly sliced grilled lamb, pita bread, hummus, falafel, tzatziki, tabbouleh and olive oil on the side with cold beers. Meanwhile, Nikki ran into the deli to use their toilet.

Hummus and falafel were both made from chickpeas but very different.

Hummus was a chickpea paste that you scooped up with the pita bread, while falafel was deep fried chickpea cakes. The tzatziki was a dipping sauce made of yoghurt, cucumber and garlic. Tabbouleh was a salad of minced parsley, mint, tomatoes, onions, olive oil and *couscous*, which was made from semolina wheat.

It was more than a lunch. It was a feast.

"What? No *baklava?*" Ketch joked.

"I will get some," Mustapha responded. He sprang up and was ready to drive back to the shop for some.

"No. No." I was just joking," Ketch returned. "Sit. Sit. This is more than enough. Let's just enjoy this."

"That was a very bad joke," Nikki scolded. "He just saved your life."

"I'm sorry," Ketch apologized. "Stupid American humor."

They sat along the roadside overlooking the clean waves of the Mediterranean, the blue sky above, and ate slowly, trying to make the moment last forever.

"You are lucky you came after Ramadan," Nikki said. "Everyone would be fasting from dawn to dusk, so all the restaurants are closed. You can't even have sex until the sun goes down," she noted, winking at him.

Ramadan was an annual month-long tradition practiced by Muslims throughout the world, not just in the Middle East, but wherever they were, just like Jews and Christians practiced their own holidays wherever they lived. Unlike the lunar calendar of other traditions, the Islamic calendar was pure and did not add months or days to bring it in line with the solar calendar.

It was based on the date of the revelation of the Quran to the Prophet Mohammed and marked the beginning of the Islamic calendar called the *Hijri* calendar.

Since it was purely a religious calendar and did not try to synchronize itself with the solar calendar, it was forever out of synch with the solar seasons but true to the tradition of Islam.

Ramadan was a rigorous fast. No food or drink was allowed from sunrise to sunset, not even a drop of water.

Ketch couldn't understand how Muslims even got through a day in the office without at least a sip of something.

"Fasting is good," Mustapha explained. "It cleans out your body and your head. Western people pays lots of money to go to a spa for a cleaning."

"A detox," Nikki interjected in translation.

"We just do it on our own and have the support of our families and religious leaders without paying anything or flying off to some expensive hotel."

At the end of Ramadan, Muslims greeted each other with *Eid Mubarak*, which meant something like "happy celebration," but more likely something that congratulated each other for getting through the month of fasting.

"It is a good practice of Islam," Mustapha asserted.

Ramadan started on the ninth month of the Islamic lunar calendar with the Muslim new moon. In Western astronomy, the so-called "new moon" was the dark one, the one with no light, and only the silhouette of a shadow in the sky, if you could even see it.

The moon's brightness is not from its own light, but from light reflected by the sun. So during the Western new moon, there was no reflected light because it was blocked by the moon's position between the earth and the sun.

But to the Muslims, the new moon was the first crescent emerging from its right hand side or bottom, depending on your location. This actually made more sense, because you could see it. Western astronomists called it the waxing crescent.

In Western astronomical terms, the cycle of the moon went from waxing crescent to first quarter, which some observers referred to as a half moon, because fifty percent was lighted. Then came the waxing gibbous when a bit more was exposed to the sun's rays and the lighted shape was somewhat elliptical and overlapped the half moon a bit.

After that came the waning gibbous, another lighted elliptical shape. But most of the light was on the left side and overlapped the half moon on the right side a bit. Then came the third quarter, another fifty-fifty shape of light and dark, then the waning crescent, another thin sliver of light but on the left side.

Then the cycle repeated all over again.

The cycle lasted about twenty-nine-and-a-half days, slightly less than a solar month.

The ongoing historical debate was over whether the lunar or the solar calendar made the best choice for tracking the seasons. Tracking the seasons was key for agriculture because it told farmers when to plant and harvest crops. Although, the solar calendar was eventually adopted by virtually all governments, many women would tell you that their moods and bodily functions were more tied to the cycles of the moon. And various animals and insects linked their lifecycles to the moon.

Ramadan ended with the sighting of the waning crescent moon and the yearly Muslim fast was over.

Chapter Forty-Three

Ketch and Nikki lingered over lunch along the coastal road for some time. They didn't want to let go of the moment. But finally, Mustapha prodded them back into the car, drove back to the Commodore and dropped them off.

He told Ketch that he'd be waiting for him the next morning at seven in case he still wanted to go to Tripoli.

"Can I come up?" Nikki asked as they left the car.

"Of course. I was going to ask you."

They climbed the one flight of stairs and as soon as they got into Ketch's room, they embraced. Ketch led her to the bed, but neither of them really wanted to have sex. They were exhausted by the day's events, the dangerous close call with death, and a second chance at life. They just wanted to hold each other.

As Ketch held her, he noted that her body was trembling. He held her more tightly, hoping that would make it go away and gently planted kisses on her.

They held each other for over an hour, saying nothing, doing nothing.

Then Nikki started undoing Ketch's shirt and pants.

"I want you to fuck me," she said.

"I don't want to fuck you. I want to make love to you."

"No. I just want you to fuck me."

"Ok," Ketch replied obligingly.

"Yes. But it's different this time."

"How so?"

"I want you to fuck me up the butt."

"You're kidding."

"No. Just do it."

"I've never done that before."

"A first time for everything."

"Why?"

"To make you understand Beirut."

"How is that going to make me understand Beirut?" Ketch asked, now a bit upset.

"You saw what they did to me at the Green Line," She noted.

"Yes. I was very sorry for that."

"Sorry? What means sorry?" Nikki responded. "There is no sorry in this life, only survival.

"I don't know what god you pray to, but they are all the same," she continued.

"They are not sorry. They are not sorry for creating us. They are not sorry for the suffering they cause us. And they are not sorry for our death.

"They only use us for some reason we don't know. They planted into our brains the will to survive, even though it means nothing. We all die in the end. One way or another. Life is a joke. It only ends in death.

"You know, I'm a physics teacher," she continued. "I thought studying physics would help me understand the meaning of life.

"But it didn't. Physics is all mathematics. It can describe anything. It can calculate everything. But it can't tell you the meaning of anything.

"There is no 'why.' Only 'what is.'

"That is the way it is, and that's that.

"The gods left us with nothing but hope and fear. So, you just accept it, deal with it and do things that make you feel good," she continued.

"Maybe, just raising a family, caring for your children and watching them grow," she went on. "Everyone wants to be a famous football hero, or a movie star. But maybe, you just need to have a family and share the everyday struggle with them.

"We live a very tragic life," she concluded sullenly.

"So, why not just kill yourself, and get it all over with," Ketch replied cynically.

Nikki laughed.

"I have debated that with friends for many years," she replied. "One of my friends had a good philosophy about it. He said that suicide was the coward's way out, or the hero's way in.

"He was an airline pilot. A very prestigious job. He was always very cheerful around us, but I could see from his eyes that he was a very sad, lonely person. Just like you. We also admired him for being a pilot, but he said that it was an empty job. He was only a bus driver. He committed suicide. I don't know why. But I know him to be a hero."

"So, why do I need to fuck you up the butt?" Ketch asked, returning to the original subject.

"To know Beirut," she answered.

"I was once taken by one of the militias. They dragged me into a room and pushed me over a desk.

"I expected to be raped and my big fear was that I would have a child from that.

"But they didn't really rape me. They fucked me up the butt. It is a Middle East thing.

"There were three of them. The first was very painful, but the next two not so much, because I stopped fighting them.

"I relaxed and accepted it. This is Beirut, I said to myself. You need to accept it and find pleasure among pain, otherwise you should not be here."

"I guess I shouldn't be here, then," Ketch replied. "Nikki. I'm sorry, I can't do that."

"Eric," Nikki replied lovingly. "I don't need you to fuck me up the butt. I didn't like it and didn't want you to do it. It was only a test. I am sorry for testing you. It was a bad joke."

Nikki got dressed and gave him a gentle kiss on the nose, then left.

Ketch was now afraid he lost Nikki and would never see her again.

Chapter Forty-Four

Ketch looked for his TV cameraman friend Liam in the hotel to talk with him about Hezbollah, but he was nowhere to be found.

He knocked on his room a few times and left a message halfway under the door. That way, he'd know if it was retrieved.

Finally, he inquired at the front desk.

"Mr. Liam is no longer staying at the hotel," the clerk responded.

"What? Where did he go?" Ketch demanded.

"Maybe, it is best if you talk with your journalist friends about it," the clerk replied.

Ketch went to the restaurant, but it was only mid-afternoon and nobody was around.

He went to the remnants of the bar, but it too was empty except for a slightly overweight foreigner in a safari suit nursing a drink at the far end.

Ketch wandered over and took the seat next to his.

"I didn't think you could have a drink here anymore without getting shot," Ketch offered cheerfully, trying to make small talk.

"Well fuck 'em," the foreigner replied. "If they try to shoot me over a drink, I promise I will take at least one of them with me."

Ketch laughed, "My name's Eric by the way."

"Nice to meet you, Eric," the foreigner replied. "My name's O'Hara."

"Irish?"

"Aussie," he replied curtly. "By your accent, you must be American. Maybe Canadian. But Canadians aren't stupid enough to be here."

"American," Ketch replied. "So, why are *you* stupid enough to be here?

"You wouldn't believe me if I told you."

"Try me."

"Love."

Ketch laughed out loud.

"You're right. After all the jokes I've heard about Australian lovemaking, I wouldn't believe it for a second."

"What jokes?"

"Come on. I'm sure you heard the most famous one about the French, German and Australian guy sharing stories about what turns on their ladies."

"Tell me."

"Well, I can't do it right, cause I can't do the accents."

"Tell me anyway."

"Ok. There are three guys in a bar, who are drunk and become instant drinking buddies. A French guy, a German, and an Australian.

"They start trading notes about what makes their ladies go crazy in bed. The French guy goes first.

"He says, 'Let me tell you what drives my lovely Michelle go crazy. I pour warm honey all over her body then lick it off.'"

"The German goes next. He says, 'Yah, I will tell you what drives my Hilda crazy. I wash her feet in wine, then nibble and suck on her toes like they are small sausages.'"

"Then the Australian shares his secrets. 'Right mates. I'll tell you what drives my little Lucy crazy. It's when I'm done fuckin' her, then wipe my dick off on her curtains. She goes fuckin' nuts.'"

O'Hara burst out laughing.

"That's good, mate," he responded. "My story is not so interesting.

"I met a Lebanese girl in Melbourne at university. It was love at first sight. At least for me. Something about these Mediterranean women. I can't say. I don't know why she fell for me. But, I was a pretty good in-shape bloke at the time. Captain of the rugby team.

"We got married our last year at Uni. At first, I thought she was just doing it for my passport. But she didn't want to live in Oz. She wanted to go back to Lebanon and be close to her family, so I followed.

"The family was in the trading business. Trading all kinds of shit. They put me in charge of trading nuts. Mostly almonds and pistachios.

"Then in the 1970s, the civil war broke out. I wanted to get them out, but my lady didn't want to leave. I got her parents out and they've been running a restaurant in Melbourne ever since. They are happy, but my wife found it very boring and wanted to be back in Lebanon.

"We came back and I stayed here to be with her. We also had a daughter together. She is also here. We are still trading odds and ends of stuff."

"So I assume that after years of civil war and chaos, a boring life in Australia is pretty attractive right now," Ketch replied. "Why can't you just catch the next flight out?"

"The rules have changed. She can't get a passport here for some reason. So she can't leave the country or enter another without one. Also, there are quotas for Lebanese immigrating to Australia, even if they are married to an Aussie. I'm trying to figure it all out right now."

"So, you live here?"

"Yeah, just behind the building that was bombed a couple days ago.

"And what brings an American here? You CIA?"

"No, I'm a journalist."

"Hey, don't get me wrong, mate. I have nothing against the CIA. In fact, I was hoping you were, so we could cut a deal to get my lady and daughter out."

"Sorry, but I'm here alone," Ketch replied. "And if I was working for the CIA, I probably wouldn't know it.

"By the way, you ever run into a Canadian cameraman here named Liam Williams? He was an old buddy of mine and it seems he just disappeared."

"Sorry mate," O'Hara replied. "I guess you didn't hear."

"Hear what? Was he shot?" Ketch asked anxiously.

"No. He killed himself."

"What?"

"Yeah. When he got the gig to come out here, he set up his wife in Cyprus. But it was a struggle. Not because of his cameraman shit, but because she was diagnosed with cancer. She fought it for years, but then passed away this week.

"He was devastated. She was the perfect journalist's wife. She was stunning, gracious and followed him around the world through thick and thin. Vietnam, Cambodia, China, then here.

"After they buried her, he took an overdose of sleeping pills mixed with his favorite whisky. The Famous Grouse. It's the one with the bird on the label.

"He stated in his will that he wanted to be cremated, have his ashes sprinkled with Grouse whisky, then spread over the Med from the Cyprus-to-Lebanon ferry.

"I wasn't there, but I think his mates honored that."

Ketch was shocked.

Just in the last few days, Ketch knew two good people who had died, Major Collins and Liam.

He broke his no-drinking-on-assignment rule and shared a shot of Grouse whisky with O'Hara in memory of Liam. In fact, he shared two or three. Then he disengaged.

"Good luck to you, mate," O'Hara responded as Ketch was leaving the bar. "Here's my card if you want to share another drink."

Ketch took the card, then went back to his room to map out his meeting with Hezbollah the next day.

At that point, Ketch felt very alone in Beirut without any official contacts, so he called the number for the British Embassy that Major Collins had given him.

After several rings, a female voice with that very cute British accent, picked up the phone.

"British Embassy," she answered. "How can we help you?"

"Yes, my name is Eric Kelly. I'm a journalist with the *Detroit City News* and would like to speak with Colonel Somerset-Kent," Ketch returned.

"Let me connect you," she replied.

A male voice picked up the phone and Ketch assumed it was the Colonel.

"Hi. Is this Colonel Somerset-Kent?" Ketch asked. "I'm a journalist with the *Detroit City News* and would like to talk with you about the situation in Beirut."

"No. This is not the Colonel," the voice returned very coldly. "The Colonel is having afternoon tea right now and can't be disturbed. I'm his batman."

"Batman?" Ketch replied. "You mean like the comic book hero? The caped crusader? The dynamic duo?" he added, hoping it would break the ice.

But it didn't go over well.

"No," the voice said stiffly. "I'm his valet and personal secretary. All appointments and communications go through me. But you sound like an American. Would that be correct?"

"Yes," Ketch answered.

"Then I suggest you talk with your American friends about it," Batman replied. "We are very busy with our own people."

Batman then hung up.

"Fuck you!" Ketch shouted into the phone and slammed down the receiver.

Chapter Forty-Five

Ketch woke up before the wake-up call.

He went down to the restaurant, finished his early breakfast then went out onto the street to check for Mustapha.

Mustapha was standing by his battered, green Mercedes, polishing the dust off with a damp cloth.

"Is Nikki here?" Ketch asked.

"No. I don't think she is coming."

"Ok. Let me get my stuff and I'll be back in a moment."

Ketch went back to his room, grabbed his pre-packed backpack, then went down to join Mustapha.

Ketch sat in Mustapha's car for another half an hour hoping Nikki would show up, but she didn't.

"We need to go," Mustapha said. "It is getting late."

Ketch agreed and they drove off without her.

The Green Line crossing didn't seem quite as intense this time. The line was shorter, Ketch didn't try to take pictures and nobody hassled him.

They quickly got through the East Beirut suburbs and onto a coastal road north to Tripoli.

Somewhere in the middle of their journey, Mustapha turned off the road.

"You need to see this. It is Byblos. One of the most ancient cities in the world. This is the home of the

Phoenicians that ruled the seas from Lebanon to Europe. More ancient than Egypt."

They drove down a dusty road toward the coast where Mustapha introduced him to a pile of rocks.

"Byblos," he announced. "The civilization before the Egyptians.

"This is our history, our culture. Not the Arabs, the Turks or the Jews. The Phoenicians. They ruled the Mediterranean for thousands of years."

Ketch obligingly took photos, then suggested they get off to their meeting in Tripoli.

As they drove further down the road, Ketch noticed a checkpoint in the distance flanked by soldiers in tiger-striped cammies.

Syrians.

Mustapha slowed down and stopped in front of a drop-down barrier.

"Where are you going?" the guard asked in Arabic.

"Tripoli. We have a meeting there," Mustapha replied cordially.

"Who is he? You have a pass?"

Mustapha produced his driver's license and Ketch produced his pass.

"He is Canadian?"

"Yes, of course."

"What is his religion?" the guard continued.

"He is a journalist," Mustapha replied. "He has no religion."

"Ok. Go."

They passed through the checkpoint and drove on.

Ketch didn't understand the back and forth in Arabic but got a big laugh when Mustapha explained it to him.

As they entered the outer limits of Tripoli, Ketch thought about the Marine Corps anthem, "From the Halls of Montezuma to the Shores of Tripoli."

He didn't know enough about history to know why the Marines landed there in the first place. Then or now. But the song stuck in his head.

In fact, the Marines never landed there.

They landed at Tripoli, Libya. The Barbary pirates there preyed on shipping in the Mediterranean from bases along the north coast of Africa known as the Maghreb. Modern-day Libya, Tunisia, Algeria and Morocco.

The Marines went in to rescue the crew of a U.S. merchant ship that had been taken hostage.

As they drove around Tripoli, Lebanon, Ketch caught sight of a lot of guys with AK-47s dangling from their shoulders like women's purses.

"We should not stay here too long," Mustapha advised.

However, Mustapha obviously didn't know where he was going and constantly stopped for directions.

This really made Ketch nervous because Mustapha tended to ask directions from guys with long Islamic beards, slinging AK-47s across their backs.

"Mustapha. Why are you asking guys with guns for directions?" he challenged.

"Because they will know where to go."

They finally found the address.

Two guys with AK-47s at the ready, wearing black and white checkered *keffiya* head scarves were at the door. They also wore AK-47 magazine web belts across their chests. It gave them easy access to the banana-shaped magazines for reloads, and the metal magazines also acted as a basic, light-weight, flak vest.

Ketch hoped it would go a lot smoother this time, because his introduction came from Amal.

It didn't.

Ketch approached slowly, introduced himself and presented the slip of paper from Amal. In response, one of the guards hit him in the stomach with the butt of his rifle, which sent Ketch to the ground in agony. And Nikki wasn't there to massage his tummy.

The guard took the note, leaving Ketch on the sidewalk.

After a few minutes, the guard came back, dragged Ketch into the building, but left him in the lobby hall on the floor, still in agony.

Some minutes later, another man came down into the hall. He had short, cropped hair and a tightly trimmed full-face beard like the so-called Iranian "students" who had taken over the U.S. Embassy in Tehran several years earlier. He was dressed in a long-sleeved, white, cotton shirt, tan trousers and leather sandals.

He waved the guards aside and seemed to command some authority as the guards now bowed and retreated away from him, almost apologetically.

"This man is not here," he shouted at Ketch. "He came with the Palestinians, but left when they were chased out. He is in Beirut."

"How can I find him?"

"Why do you want to find this man?"

"I am a journalist. I want to interview him."

"Well. I will tell you how to find this man. Only because your note from Amal says I should. They are now our brothers.

"But I must tell you, this man is a nuisance and no use to anybody anymore. He is in Beirut. I will give you the address.

"But if you try to protect him, it could be bad for you.

"Get him out of Lebanon or shoot him," the man shouted. "If you don't, somebody else will do it first. If you are his friend, they will shoot you too."

The man then dropped a slip of paper on the floor next to Ketch. It was in Arabic. Ketch couldn't read it, but assumed it was an address.

Ketch massaged his own stomach until the cramp went away, then found his way outside back to Mustapha.

"Good meeting?" Mustapha asked.

"Yes. Back to Beirut."

Chapter Forty-Six

As they were driving back to Beirut, Mustapha announced, "I would like to invite you for dinner."

"Really?" Ketch responded. "But it's not necessary."

"No, it is," Mustapha replied, "So you can see the beauty of Beirut. You must report that to your newspapers. This is a beautiful place that has been taken over by madmen."

They got back through the Tripoli checkpoints without incident and Mustapha drove up to a hillside restaurant overlooking the Med. It was in East Beirut just before the descent back down the road to cross the Green Line.

Mustapha parked the car in front of a small bungalow along the cliff road and they walked through a garden to a patio full of tables overlooking the sea. A lovely woman greeted them at the entrance with smiles and menus in hand.

The restaurant was empty and she sat them at a table on the edge of the property overlooking a blue Mediterranean sea and a bluer sky.

"This is the Lebanon from before," Mustapha noted. "No politics, no foreigners. Only beautiful people and beautiful food."

"So, what happened?" Ketch asked

"Everyone used to live in peace here," he replied. "All kinds of people. Muslims, Jews, Christians. Then the foreigners came. The French, the Israelis, the Palestinians, the Syrians and now the Americans are playing their politics.

"The Palestinians came because they had nowhere to go," he explained. "So, after the Palestinians came, the Israelis came. After the Israelis came, then the Syrians. It is a game for them. Now the Americans.

"We don't know why the Americans even came. They say they came to make peace. But no foreigner can make peace in Lebanon.

"And if the foreigners can't control Lebanon, they are happy to see everyone fighting each other. They would like a weak country between Israel and Syria.

"The foreign press calls Lebanon a buffer state.

"Before, a client of mine was a Russian diplomat," Mustapha continued. "I was his driver every day for six months. And after we became more friendly, I asked him the same question.

"You know what he said?" Mustapha continued. "The Jews and the Arabs deserve each other. Better they fight it out in Lebanon than the rest of the world."

"That made me very sick. We are not Arabs. We are Phoenicians, my wife is Christian and my cousins are Jewish," he added. "And we all celebrate each other's holidays. It makes our lives very special."

The waitress came back and Ketch ordered the seafood chowder and the catch of the day. Mustapha ordered vegetable soup, grilled lamb and pita bread with a side sauce of tzatziki, and Lebanese wine.

Red for him. White for Ketch.

"You need to try Lebanese wine," Mustapha explained. "Lebanon was making wine before the Greeks and the Romans. They got their wine secrets from us. Our red is like a Cabernet Sauvignon. Our white is like a Chardonnay."

As they waited for the food, two low-flying jets screamed over their position.

The noise and vibration was so intense that it knocked all the cutlery off the table.

"Israelis," Mustapha replied knowingly. "You come here to take your pictures and they come here to take theirs," he said with a laugh.

The wine arrived and Ketch and Mustapha toasted.

"What should we toast to?" he asked Mustapha.

"To friends and family," he responded. "That's all we have in the world."

"Yes," Ketch replied, and they touched glasses.

The food arrived shortly thereafter and it looked magnificent. The fish smelled very fresh and Ketch asked the manager about it.

"The boys catch it in the sea everyday and bring it up the hill. We pay them, then they spend their money on hamburgers," she laughed.

The fish was served whole, complete with head, and steamed Chinese style with spring onion and ginger.

"You know how to eat this?" the manager asked. "If you flip it over, you will flip over your boat."

"I lived in Hong Kong before," Ketch returned.

She then watched him carefully as he used his fork to scrape the meat off of the topside. Then he slid his fork underneath the bone and scraped the meat from the bottom side.

He broke off the head with the fork and pushed it to the side for later, then removed the bone and placed it on the side of the plate.

"You are a master," the woman replied. "You must have a Chinese girlfriend."

"Not now," Ketch replied. "But I was taught by one of the best."

Mustapha was also impressed and raised his glass in another toast.

"To girlfriends, in the past and in the future," he exclaimed with a smile. "What would we be without them?"

"Yes," Ketch replied and they touched glasses again.

Ketch started on his chowder, which was thick with fish, clams, oysters, and squid. A meal in itself. As he was savoring it, Mustapha interrupted.

"Have you heard about the casino?" Mustapha asked Ketch.

"No. Tell me."

"The Casino du Liban. It is just down the road, but closed now because of the fighting. So we are not going," Mustapha replied. "But, it was the crown of all casinos in Europe. Even Monte Carlo.

"And the night club show was better than anything in Las Vegas.

"Every night, it was host to the world. British, French, Spanish, Italians, Germans, Lebanese, Arabs, maybe even a few Americans. The champagne flowed like water and the chips like pocket change.

"But the big event was the midnight show.

"At midnight, they lowered a naked blonde woman on a white horse from the ceiling. Her hair was down to her waist. All naked like Lady Godiva. As they lowered her down, she'd throw out betting chips into the casino. Not big money chips, but still chips.

"When she got to the floor, she rode off, still throwing chips like women throwing rice at a wedding.

"Her legs were a bit fat, but she had very nice breasts," Mustapha added. "Like a Greek goddess."

Chapter Forty-Seven

Mustapha got Ketch back to the Commodore and Ketch invited him in for a drink in return for the dinner.

When they entered the lobby, Ketch noted that the reception clerk was staring at him very anxiously, so he went to the desk, assuming another friend had been killed or died.

"Any messages?" he asked.

"Yes. An important one," the clerk replied nervously. "Some dangerous men came and said you need to read this immediately."

Ketch took the envelope, then joined Mustapha back at the lobby bar.

Ketch opened the envelope and read the paper inside. It was inscribed in very bad handwriting with the following message:

> *"We have your girlfriend. Her name is Nikee. Give us one hundred thousand dollars, American or we kill her. We know you are rich American and you can pay. So don't try to talk about it. Stay in your room and we will call you later."*

Ketch now felt guilty for thinking hard thoughts about Nikki because she didn't show up for the trip to Tripoli.

"Mustapha," Ketch said, "I'm sorry, but we need to have this drink in my room. I will explain there."

Separately, Ketch's paranoia now shot up way beyond the red zone. He immediately assumed he was being played by Nikki or Mustapha or both for a hundred grand, but he gave them the benefit of the doubt.

They went upstairs and Ketch explained the letter to Mustapha.

Mustapha looked down at the floor, despondent.

Ketch pulled out the room service menu.

"Might as well order something to eat," Ketch offered, trying to be cheerful.

"I'm not hungry," Mustapha returned. "You go ahead."

"Actually, I'm not hungry either," Ketch replied, dropping the menu on the bed.

Ketch went to the mini-bar and poured himself a whisky. Mustapha asked for the same.

But Ketch had a plan. Maybe not a good plan. It came to him while walking up the steps to his room. But it was the only plan he had.

He briefed Mustapha over the whisky.

Ketch's brain now burned furiously.

Finally, the phone rang.

"Is this Mr. Kelly?" the voice asked in halting English.

"Yes," Ketch replied. "Who is this?"

"It is no matter," the voice returned. "We have your girlfriend and you must pay one hundred thousand dollars American or we kill her."

"No problem, but I don't speak your language," Ketch replied tactically. "Please talk to my friend about it."

He then turned over the phone to Mustapha.

After chatting on the phone for a while, Mustapha covered up the receiver and turned to him.

"There is nothing to talk about," he said tearfully. "They want the money by tomorrow or they will kill Nikki. Cash. No discount."

"Ok Mustapha," as we discussed, Ketch said, "Tell them that I don't have the money. And my newspaper company is not going to pay that much for a local translator. But they will pay twice that for me.

"Tell them, that you will kidnap me, meet them tomorrow and exchange Nikki for me. They can force me to call my newspaper, who will pay much more than one hundred thousand dollars. Maybe half a million."

Mustapha talked with the kidnappers for twenty minutes. Given the guttural tones of the Arabic language, Ketch didn't know if they were arguing or negotiating.

Finally, Mustapha put down the phone.

"Ok. We can trade you tomorrow. Six o'clock in the morning," Mustapha explained.

"The road along the coast beach. We went there before. They gave me a spot to meet. Close to where we had lunch.

"But I had to guarantee you or they will shoot me. So, you can't change your mind. Are your sure you want to do this?"

"Yes, without question," Ketch replied. "Promise me you won't say anything to Nikki, but I'm in love with her."

"I promise not to tell," Mustapha replied. "I also love Nikki, but not like you. I love her like a daughter.

Then they rehearsed the plan.

Chapter Forty-Eight

Mustapha slept in his car that night, while Ketch tried to fall asleep in his room.

But he couldn't.

He spent the entire evening, doing meditative breathing exercises while he visualized the plan that was to unfold and his role in it.

At five a.m. he got out of bed and physically walked himself through the scenario. The dining room was not open yet, so he grabbed some nuts and crackers from the mini-bar for breakfast, washed down with a 7Up.

Then he went downstairs and met Mustapha. They sat in the car for a while and rehearsed the plan one last time, then Mustapha drove out to the coastal road. The morning sun was just rising and shed twinkling rays of light along the Med. As soon as he got to the coastal road, Mustapha stopped the car and they both got out.

"For Nikki," Ketch said, looking sternly into Mustapha's eyes.

"For Nikki," Mustapha replied.

They embraced, then went to the rear of the car. Mustapha unlocked the trunk and Ketch climbed in.

Mustapha returned to the driver's seat and slowly drove the car down the coast to the rendezvous point.

As he approached the location, he noted two men in a blue Mercedes parked along the opposite side of the road in the other direction. He stopped his car and pulled off the road. They all stared at each other for a while, then Mustapha got out.

"I have the American," he shouted across the road. "Where is the girl?"

"In the trunk," one shouted back. "Where is the American?"

"Also in the trunk," Mustapha replied. "I see the girl. You see the American, then we can go have a nice breakfast."

The two bad guys laughed at that and got out of the car.

Mustapha noted that they were well dressed in suits and did not carry Kalashnikovs as he would have expected. Maybe too obvious on the open street. But when their jackets opened in the light breeze, he could see that they wore shoulder holsters, but they did not seem ready to draw their pistols, perhaps noting that Mustapha was unarmed.

Mustapha walked across the street to their car and was taken around the back to the trunk. They popped open the lid and Mustapha saw Nikki inside. She was crunched up with her knees against her chest. Her ankles and wrists were tightly bound with rope and her mouth was sealed with wide duct tape. She had a bruise on one of her cheeks indicating someone had hit her across the face but otherwise seemed to be unharmed.

She glared at Mustapha like a trapped animal and a tear slipped down her cheek.

"Ok, you see girl," one of the bad guys said as he slammed shut the trunk. "Now, we see American."

Mustapha led them to the back of his car, unlocked the trunk, then stepped to one side as he opened it.

As soon as Mustapha lifted the trunk, two shots rang out. Ketch's Browning spit two bullets into the guts of the unsuspecting bad guys. He then pushed the trunk all the way open and pumped two more rounds into their chests. One bad guy, not yet dead, reached for his pistol but wasn't fast enough. Ketch put a round through his forehead. He then put another round into the head of his partner who was crouched on the ground, but also not yet dead.

"Assholes," Ketch shouted at the bodies.

Ketch and Mustapha then dragged the corpses across the street and stuffed them into the front seats of the blue Mercedes. Ketch found the keys on one of the bodies and sprang open the trunk. Nikki was staring at him in disbelief as tears rolled down her face.

He carefully peeled the tape from her mouth and she burst out crying.

Ketch gently lifted her out of the trunk, carried her across the street and put her in the back seat of Mustapha's Mercedes.

"Get my bag," Nikki shouted, "I brought something special for you."

"Ketch went back to the blue Mercedes, retrieved Nikki's bag and joined her in the back seat.

Meanwhile, Mustapha pulled out a can of gasoline from his trunk and started emptying it inside the blue Mercedes. Mustapha then lit a cigarette with a Zippo lighter and tossed it into a puddle of gasoline inside the front seat of the vehicle. Then he ran back to his own car, waited for the blue Mercedes to catch fire, and drove off.

There were no dramatic explosions, but the blue Mercedes was soon engulfed in flames. Nothing unusual for the streets of Beirut.

Ketch tried to free Nikki from the ropes, but they were very tight.

"Mustapha," Ketch said urgently. "Give me a knife."

"I don't have one," he replied. "You didn't tell me to bring one."

"Damn it!" Ketch shouted, then reached into his pants and took out his wallet. He pulled out his American Express card and cracked it in half along the diagonal, creating a sharp, serrated cutting blade. He then used it to work on the ropes binding Nikki.

"Don't leave home without it," Ketch smiled at Mustapha.

Cutting the rope was slow going, but he finally freed Nikki.

Ketch looked back at the car up in flames as Mustapha lit another cigarette.

"I didn't know you smoked," Ketch said to Mustapha.

"Marlboro," he replied and inhaled deeply.

Chapter Forty-Nine

Mustapha got Ketch and Nikki back to the Commodore without further incident.

Ketch helped Nikki climb the stairs back to his room and led her to the bed.

"I'm sorry for causing you so much trouble," she said tearfully.

"Take a rest," Ketch replied, kissing her on the forehead.

"Sorry, but I first need to take a pee," she answered. "You want to watch?" she smiled.

Ketch declined, but was curious how she ended up in the trunk of a car.

"What happened?" he asked.

"Just near the hotel," Nikki explained. "I was thinking about you all night. I thought I didn't want you to get killed by Hezbollah alone. Dying alone is the worst thing. So, I decided to come with you. And I brought you a present. But they took me just behind the hotel.

"One guy came up to me and asked for directions. When I tried to explain, he hit me in the face. Another guy then grabbed me from behind and they pushed me into the trunk of their car. Then we drove off somewhere to some garage and they tied me up. I told them they could fuck me up the butt, but they just told me to shut up. And left me in the trunk all night with nothing to eat or drink. I had to pee, but they wouldn't let me. I held it all night long. If you have to pee, but can't, it is torture.

"I spent the whole night praying to God," she continued. "Not to rescue me but to kill me. I couldn't take it and just wanted to get it over with."

"So, who were these guys?" Ketch asked.

"Who knows. Just some guys that saw me with you and thought they could get some money," she explained. "It happens all the time. This is Beirut."

"I need to take a bath," she continued. "I smell like I've been in a hot, sweaty car all night."

"So, did you meet Hezbollah?" she inquired. "Was it a good meeting?"

"Yes, but they hit me in the stomach," he replied. "And you weren't there to massage my tummy."

"Oh. I am so sorry about that," she answered, gave him a loving hug and planted some kisses on his forehead. "But I'm here now. And happy to massage you as much as you can take anywhere you like," she laughed.

Nikki then went to the bathroom and ran the bath.

"Have you ever had a bubble bath?" she asked.

"Yes. But not in Beirut," Ketch smiled to himself, remembering the last one in Thailand.

"Good. So I can be the first. As I said, I brought something special for you. It was going to be a celebration present for surviving Hezbollah."

She retrieved a small packet of powder from her bag and dumped it into the tub as it was filling with water. As the water from the faucet created bubbles, Nikki slipped in and turned off the tap when they were just about right. She seemed to be more experienced with the technology than Ketch's lady in Thailand.

"Are you going to join me, or just watch?" she taunted, as she started rubbing the bubbles on her chest.

Ketch slid into the tub and they quickly embraced. They kissed fully on the mouth and Ketch was surprised she was so passionate. After all, she typically instructed him to just fuck her, not make love.

"So, do you want to hear about Tripoli?" he asked.

"No. I just want you to fuck me," she replied.

"No. This time, I'm going to make love to you."

"I will do you first," she said.

She gently kissed his forehead, cheeks, eyes and nose. Then she fished one of his feet out of the water and started licking the bottom.

"Stop it. That tickles too much," Ketch protested.

She smiled, then started sucking on his toes. When she started sucking on his big toe, he felt the same sensation as if she was sucking on his shaft.

She looked at him as she was doing it and noticed his pleasure.

"Wow, Nikki, that is incredible," he responded. "But at least once before I get killed in Beirut, I want to make love to you."

She relented.

He gently kissed her once on the forehead, then nibbled at her lips. When she opened her mouth, he kissed her fully and their tongues played with each other passionately.

Then, he lovingly planted kisses on her chest and nipples. She groaned, which Ketch took as a good sign.

He then spun her around in the bathtub so her back was on the inclined side instead of on the faucet side. He pulled her feet up around his shoulders and put his mouth in between her legs. He then he kissed, licked, massaged and pleasured her for two rounds.

"Ok. Stop it," she cried out. "Enough. I can't repay you for this. It is too much."

"You don't need to repay me," Ketch replied. "I did it for you, not for me."

"Why?"

"Because, you deserve it."

Ketch pulled her out of the tub and gently patted her dry with one of the hotel's big fluffy towels.

"Ok. Now I will do you," she offered.

"Next time," he replied. "I am exhausted and we have a big day tomorrow. If you want to join me, that is. I'm going to see Adam Smith."

"I will join you."

"See you tomorrow then."

Nikki got dressed and gave Ketch a long, loving kiss before she left. She gave him a big full-body hug, pressing her breasts against his chest and ran her hand down to his groin as a reminder of what might come the next time.

After the bath with Nikki, Ketch lost all interest in eating dinner. He pulled the mattress off the bed and onto the floor away from the window, placed the Browning nearby, then collapsed onto the mattress and drifted into a deep, dreamless sleep.

Chapter Fifty

Ketch woke up at five a.m. to the sounds of AK-47 gunfire.

The high-pitched crack of the AK-47 was very distinctive, so Ketch knew it wasn't the good guys shooting.

He instinctively snatched the Browning, then fumbled for a shirt, trousers and shoes, not bothering about the socks. He popped out the magazine to make sure it was full, put it back in, then racked the slide to chamber a round. He kept the hammer cocked, engaged the safety and tucked the gun into the waistband against the small of his back.

He should have stayed in his room, but Ketch being Ketch, went downstairs into the street.

There were two gunmen in front of the hotel. They were hustling all the drivers that serviced the journalists there and obviously demanding something.

Kickbacks or whatever.

The drivers typically slept in their cars overnight. Either because their demanding journalist bosses expected them to be on call 24/7 or because they had no other home.

Ketch noticed that his driver Mustapha was being herded in front of the cars with the others. One gunman was pointing his AK-47 at the drivers, while the other was shooting rounds into the air to scare them.

Ketch didn't understand the Arabic the gunmen were screaming at the drivers, but it didn't matter. He knew it was some sort of shakedown.

The gunmen were so engrossed in their drama that they didn't even notice Ketch walk onto the scene. His double-action Browning Hi-Power was good to go. He slipped off the safety with his thumb then walked towards the gunmen.

He didn't engage them. He didn't try to discuss the situation with them, he didn't try to understand their problems, sympathize with their sad stories, negotiate or give them a diplomatic hug.

He just did what needed to be done.

He calmly walked up behind each one of the assholes and put a bullet into the back of his head.

One bullet, one asshole.

He didn't think about it and didn't hesitate.

"Assholes are assholes," he noted to himself. Anywhere you find them, anywhere in the world. "Nothing to discuss. Live by the bullet, die by the bullet."

Ketch caught Mustapha staring at him, shocked but relieved.

"See you at seven," he said.

"Seven," Mustapha replied dropping his eyes.

Then Ketch went back to his room as if nothing had happened.

"This is Beirut," he consoled himself.

Chapter Fifty-One

Ketch barely finished his breakfast in the dining room latter that morning when Nikki joined him at the table.

"I want to thank you again for coming for me yesterday, and I heard what you did this morning," she said with a beaming smile. "I want you to know that I am very proud to be fucking you. No matter what happens."

Ketch almost choked on his scrambled eggs.

"I will wait for you in the car with Mustapha. He is also very proud of you. But don't expect him to fuck you," she winked. "We will find this American Adam Smith."

Ketch hustled down the remains of his breakfast, returned to his room, packed up his gear and went downstairs. This time, he included the Browning. He decided that he wouldn't carry it on him, but leave it with Nikki.

Mustapha and Nikki were waiting for him outside. Nikki gave him a big hug and Mustapha gave him a nervous handshake and smile. It was either because Mustapha was feeling guilty about being rescued, like many victims, or because he no longer knew who Ketch was and what he was getting himself into.

Anyway, his only mission for the day was to take Ketch to an address.

According to Mustapha, it was not far from the hotel. A building near the coast overlooking Pigeons'

Rock. Very upscale. The area was known for its luxurious cliff-side apartments with magnificent views of the Mediterranean and trendy boutique restaurants and cafes.

Pigeons' Rock, also known as *The Rocks of Raouché*, consisted of two mammoth, stone monuments in the sea, just off the southwest coast of Beirut's Corniche. Some imagined that one rock looked like a penis, while the other rock, which had a small archway in the base, letting the sea water pass through, symbolized a woman's vagina. Allegedly, young men looking to prove their manhood would climb up to the top of the penis-shaped rock and dive off. Some made it. Some did not.

Meanwhile, the female rock was rumored to be popular with suicidal couples taking a "Lover's Leap."

They got into the car. This time, Ketch got into the back seat with Nikki.

"Nikki, I am sorry to ask you this," Ketch said apologetically. "But can you hold my gun for me?

"My gut tells me I should bring it this time. But I don't think I should carry it."

Nikki, prepared as usual, pulled out a *hijab* scarf from her bag and a loose, long- sleeved shirt that covered her down to the thighs. She took off her blouse and bra, flashing her breasts at Ketch as she did so.

"Did you have a nice look?" she asked teasingly.

"Absolutely," he replied.

"I will put your gun in my jeans under the shirt," She noted. "Nobody would dare search a woman wearing a *hijab*.

"But I don't know how to get it to you if you need it."

"We'll play it by ear," Ketch said with false confidence.

He racked the slide, chambering a round, then dropped down the hammer de-cocking it.

"Now, it is ready to shoot, but safe to carry," he explained to Nikki. "You just need to pull the trigger to start shooting."

Despite the morning traffic, it only took them fifteen minutes to get to the address.

Ketch surveyed the building from the outside. It was a modern, nicely constructed luxury apartment building and each unit had a balcony overlooking the Med. Many balconies sported flower boxes.

He didn't expect to find an apartment building. He expected to find a command center or a prison block.

It didn't seem right.

Ketch asked Nikki to confirm the address.

She asked someone on the street who said it was correct.

"It's in the penthouse," she said sarcastically. "Very nice for a professor."

Ketch was worried that the front desk security would not let them through. But Nikki's Arabic and what Ketch assumed was her chit-chat about visiting old friends got them into the elevator.

They rode the lift to the penthouse, where it opened onto a single apartment.

Ketch rang the door bell.

"Who is it?" an American voice asked from the inside.

"Hi. My name is Eric Kelly. I'm an American journalist here for a few days. I'm looking for Professor Adam Smith so I can interview him for a story."

"I'm Adam Smith," came the reply. "You're an American from where?"

"The U.S."

"I know that asshole, but where in the U.S.?"

"I grew up in Chicago, but now working for a Detroit newspaper. Lots of Lebanese there, so they sent me here."

"What newspaper?" Smith challenged.

"The *Detroit City News*."

"Never heard of it," Smith retorted.

"It was only started a couple of years ago by some rich Lebanese businessmen," Ketch lied, thinking quickly.

"I know Chicago pretty well," Smith continued. "What street did you grow up on?"

"Dearborn," Ketch replied.

"The Gold Coast," Smith answered back with a sneer. "So, you're a spoiled rich kid, looking for adventure in Beirut."

"Not at all," Ketch replied. "The house on Dearborn belonged to my grandparents. My family lived with them. We got kicked out when we couldn't afford the property taxes.

"My dad busted his ass, taking on two jobs to pay tuition for my college in New York City, and I drove a taxi there to help pay the bills."

"You drove a taxi in New York City?" Smith inquired.

"Yes. One of those big Checker cabs."

"All right, Kelly. You're invited. Come in," Smith replied.

Smith opened the door revealing an amazing penthouse suite with high windows overlooking incredible views of the Mediterranean. Ketch walked in and Nikki followed.

"Who's that?" he shouted, pointing at Nikki.

"My translator."

Smith allowed Nikki into the apartment, then put his hand up signaling Ketch to stop.

"One minute."

"Apologies," Ketch offered. "Did I offend you?"

"No. But I need to pat you down," Smith answered. "This is Beirut."

"I understand."

Smith slid his hands up and down Ketch's body, felt his crotch, grabbed his ass, but was then satisfied.

He didn't touch Nikki.

"Sorry about that."

"No problem, Ketch returned. "This is Beirut."

"How did you find me?" Smith asked.

"A friend of a friend of a friend. You know how it goes."

"All right. How can I help you?"

"Well, I'm a little surprised, because I was supposed to be doing a story about your kidnapping. But you don't seem to be kidnapped at all."

"Well man, don't let the penthouse fool you," Adam replied. "I am basically under house arrest. Someone brings me food and booze, and does my laundry once a week, but if I go out, I'll be shot. This looks good. But it's a jail."

"Why is that?"

"Because I speak the truth."

"What truth?"

"Look man. You don't know anything about me. You are obviously another naïve, stupid American who doesn't get it. I don't just speak the truth but I deliver it," Smith replied angrily."

"I'm listening."

"Well, everybody here is full of shit. Nobody is interested in Lebanon. They all have their own agendas. They fight for whoever pays them for whatever reasons, then they get the money into Swiss bank accounts while everyone is dying here.

"Everyone here is full of shit. And everyone in the States is full of shit.

"So, I deliver my services to people here who are willing to deliver the truth."

"You mean the militias?" Ketch asked.

"Whoever," Smith replied. "So what story do you want to write about me?" Smith continued.

"Quite frankly, I was sent here to find you and help you escape back to America," Ketch admitted. "Your family in Detroit called somebody who called somebody who called my newspaper," he explained. "They said you were kidnapped."

"Well, let me tell you something," Smith responded. "My family is full of shit. They couldn't care less about me. They never called me in their entire lives and never returned my letters. Whenever I tried to stay in touch and call them, they had no time to talk. Too busy watching TV, firing up the barbecue or some other shit.

"Somebody is using them to get to me.

"I got tired preaching to the powers that be, both here and there. This is my home. It's a wonderful country. I want to bring it peace.

"But everyone's got their own agenda based on who is paying them. Just like you.

"Everybody said I was a talker, not a doer, so I needed to prove them wrong.

"So, I offered my services to doers.

"I helped build the bombs that lit up the Marines and the French. I'm a chemical engineer and know how to make bombs. Big bombs. I took my idea to one of the militias and they bought it. I built the trigger mechanism and advised them on surrounding the explosives with gas tanks. The locals couldn't build a mouse trap without my help. I did it just for fun.

"You might have read it was the biggest non-nuclear explosion in the history of war. I'm very proud of that."

"Yes, so I've heard," Ketch replied.

"That's why the Americans want me," Smith continued. "Maybe they didn't tell you that. Well, the Americans have no business being here. Nobody has any business here except the Lebanese.

"I've been here for years. This is an incredible country. But the foreign politics keep screwing it up, getting people killed, and causing a lot of suffering."

"And you are trying to rescue me and get me back to America?" Smith continued in amazement. "Get me back to what? A thankless job in a car factory like my dad? I just can't believe what a fuckin' stupid, idiot, White boy, American you are.

"Why would I want to leave Lebanon?" he continued. "You don't know anything about me.

"The bombs were nothing," he went on. "They gave the Americans an excuse to go home. The U.S should have paid me for it. How many Marines did the U.S. get killed in Vietnam before they had an excuse to go home? This was nothing.

"So why didn't you bomb the Syrians, the Israelis or the Palestinians, instead of the Americans and the French?"

"Look, mister what's your name again? I bomb whoever I like. As I told you, I did it for fun.

"For your information, the bombs needed to make a statement. And the Israelis, Syrians and Palestinians are getting bombed all the time. No new news if they get bombed again."

"So, what was your statement?" Ketch asked. "Maybe I didn't get it."

"Everyone knows the new president bought his way into office, and nobody likes him, especially the Muslims. He set up the Lebanese Army and the Israelis to clean out the Palestinians and put down the Muslims, so he can establish a Christian government dominated by Christian-owned businesses. Businesses that he controls.

"Everyone knows he's a mafia thug, expect you stupid Americans. He had no problem gunning down his Christian brothers, not to mention their women and children, over turf issues in the past. He shot them at a swimming pool. And he'd have no problem doing it again.

"Meanwhile you stupid Americans think there is really a so-called elected democratic government here, so you send in the Marines to keep peace, meaning the real objective is to keep this mafia guy in power.

"And what does peacekeeping mean? That means the Marines need to shoot the poor Muslims, who are living like dogs and fighting for a slim slice of the pie. Just what this guy wants you to do.

"That makes the Americans everyone's enemy, except for the corrupt and brutal political assholes in power. The Marines took sides the minute they started training the Lebanese Armed Forces and their ships started shelling the militias fighting the Lebanese Army. They became the president's militia. That meant that the Marines just became another one of the street gangs.

"Actually, I was very impressed with the marine leaders. They are smarter than everyone thinks. The marine colonel at the time, strongly opposed the shellings cause he saw the consequences, but he was over-ruled by some diplomatic douche-bags.

"So what was the statement?" Ketch asked again. Maybe, I missed it."

"You don't listen well, do you, Kelly?" Smith said.

"My bosses have the same complaint," Ketch replied.

"The bombs needed to show everyone that the people don't want to be led by a mafia asshole, and that his American and French friends can't protect him and they can't even protect themselves. Very simple.

"There was no American retaliation for the embassy bombing and no retaliation for the marines bombing. Your government said they didn't have conclusive legal proof. That was pretty pathetic.

"Everyone knew who did it. The French bombed the Iranian funded militia camps in the Bekaa Valley. Obviously, the French have more balls than lawyers on their team.

"So when the U.S. didn't retaliate for the bombings, everyone knew that America was a joke that couldn't be counted on. The U.S. proved themselves to be the biggest limp dicks in the Middle East. Just a "Paper Tiger" like Chairman Mao said.

"And what is your role in all of this? Ketch asked. "Who do you work for? Who is the 'we' in all of this?" Ketch asked.

"There is no 'we' only 'me.' Just like all the other players in this town," Smith answered.

"When I'm motivated and paid well, I do something. When I'm not, I don't," he continued. "It's really a fun game.

"I work for whoever I want. Nobody tells me anything. I am the only voice of truth and reason in this fucked up place. I partnered with a militia that had it out for the Americans. I supplied the know-how and they supplied the poor slob who drove the truck. I'm only a consultant. I just give people ideas. It's up to them to take 'em or leave 'em.

"But this is Beirut, you stupid, suburban American idiot. I can bomb whoever I want. And I can also kill whoever I want," Smith ended menacingly.

"So who's asking half a million for your release?'

"That's a good question," Smith replied. "My real business is more interesting. I broker about ten million dollars in hashish, pot and heroin to the West every year. The U.S. knows all about the drugs going through Beirut but they don't care. I'm sure you know that the Americans worked with drug bosses in Vietnam. Nothing's changed. They're just looking to hook up with the next power broker here who is willing to play ball with them.

"One of my business associates had the idea of posing me as a hostage victim and squeezing half of million out of Uncle Sam. Very creative. So here we are. I'm not a hostage and you don't have the money.

At that point, Smith reached down behind the bar and pulled out a pump-action twelve-gauge shotgun.

"End of lecture, Kelly. I don't know who you are and where you came from but I don't care. I keep my life simple. I'm sorry, but that means you are now going to die, pointing the gun at Ketch.

"Can we talk about it?" Ketch asked, slowly raising his hands.

"No! You're an idiot American. You didn't listen to one thing I said. You're a fool being played by fools.

"You don't care about these people. You don't care about what's going on here. You have no morals or integrity. You are only here to get your commission.

"And most important, asshole, you don't have the money."

Smith pumped one round into the shotgun, and directed Ketch to the balcony.

"Get your ass outside and lean over the railing," Smith instructed. "I will make it quick. One blast to the head, you fall over the edge and it's done.

"Not a bad way to go," Smith smirked. "There are far worse ways out here."

"And what about the girl?" Ketch asked, referring to Nikki.

"Me and the girl will make friends, after you're dead," Smith replied arrogantly. "Thank you for the present."

Ketch followed the instructions and walked out onto the balcony. Initially, he didn't care anymore. Smith was right. There were far worse ways to go. He turned his back on Smith and leaned over the balcony.

Down below were foxy, sumptuous Lebanese ladies lounging and prancing about the pool. Their buxom bodies were bursting out of skimpy bikinis, while the blue Med and the blue sky met each other on the horizon. Everything was perfect for them.

Ketch was tired by all of this and felt it was a good time to give up, but he didn't. He was not revived by anger, justice or honor. When he played sports and trained in the military, his coaches and drill instructors tried to instill anger and hate into him. In their minds, it was the biggest motivator to win and stay alive. However, over the years, Ketch learned that hate was not the most important motivator and often got in the way.

On the contrary, it was Love. Love is the most powerful force in the universe. It had nothing to do with loving your enemy. It was about unconditional love. Loving someone you loved and knowing they loved you back no matter what. In 'Nam, when Ketch was pinned down in a fire fight or lost, cold and hungry in the jungle by himself, it was love that saved him. Love for the grandmother who raised and protected him. Love for the girlfriend that cared about him. In this case, it was love for Nikki. His love for Nikki would push him to survive this or die trying. Don't die until you're dead, an old friend once counseled him.

He carefully reached into his jacket pocket and gently pulled out the pistol pen he had bought in Darra, Pakistan.

Elizabeth didn't know about the pen gun, so fortunately didn't confiscate it in Cairo.

He knew it was very inaccurate and he only had one shot with a .22 caliber round that had little stopping or killing power. But it was all he had left.

He pulled back the plunger, clicked the trigger in place and held on as tight as he could. "I really love you Nikki," he said quietly to himself. He just didn't say it, but felt it with all his heart and soul.

"One last thing," Ketch asked as a distraction while twisting back around to look at Smith.

"What's that?" Smith replied.

"When was the last time you got laid, Twinkie?"

"What?" Smith replied, disoriented by the absurd question and the reference to his high school nickname.

Ketch then dropped to the ground and pressed the clip on the pen gun.

There was a weak bang as the pen fired its shot, but once again, the recoil pushed the pen back into Ketch's hand and he felt lucky he didn't shoot his finger tips off.

He didn't know if he hit Smith, or anything else for that matter, and didn't even know his next move. In the interim, within less than a second, two shots rang out. However, they were not shotgun blasts.

Nikki used the distraction to pull out Ketch's Browning from her waistband and shoot Adam Smith in the back of the head.

Twice. A double-tap. One shot to make the kill, then another to make sure. Both within an inch of each other. Ketch was impressed.

"Asshole!" she shouted angrily at Smith, then put another round in his face as he lay on the floor and two more into his chest.

Then she turned on Ketch.

"Everybody told you he was an asshole," she shouted angrily. "Why didn't you listen?"

"Wow. Nikki. Where did you learn how to shoot like that?"

"Fuck you, asshole."

"Why am I an asshole?"

"You're a stupid American asshole," she vented. "All Americans are stupid assholes. You all come out here with your bullshit good intentions, but you only get a lot of people killed. My people.

"Only the British are bigger assholes," she continued. "But they come out here acting like assholes, so we don't expect anything from them.

"You Americans, come out here smiling and trying to be everyone's friends and getting everyone to trust you," she went on. "But you're only in it for yourself, just like the British.

"But you get everyone to like you and trust you and believe in you, then you go home before you finish the job when it gets too dirty for you," she continued. "So that makes you worse. You deceive everyone with your ideals and stupidity."

Nikki dropped the gun, then threw herself into Ketch's arms crying.

They held each other tightly, then Ketch wiped away her tears and gently tried to kiss her.

She responded, and they kissed passionately.

When their lips parted, Ketch dared to speak.

"Hey Nikki," he said. "Maybe this is not the right time or place, but will you marry me?" he asked sincerely.

"Fuck you, asshole," she replied, then broke the embrace and went to the door.

Ketch jumped ahead of her and blocked the door, hoping to continue the conversation.

"Just answer my question," Ketch insisted.

"Open the fuckin' door, asshole," Nikki demanded.

Chapter Fifty-Two

Ketch opened the door to the apartment only to be surprised by a gunman in a suit pointing an AK-47 rifle at him.

"Back, back," the gunman shouted, poking Ketch in his stomach with the barrel.

"Nice suit," Ketch returned, trying to throw the gunman off guard. "Armani?"

"Up, Up, Up," the gunman commanded, motioning for Ketch to put his hands up.

Ketch didn't try to figure out the situation. He only knew that he needed to live and the gunman needed to die.

The gunman ignored Nikki. She was only a woman in a *hijab*. She would not interfere in the affairs of men, the gunman assumed.

The gunman, then continued poking Ketch's stomach with the AK-47 barrel, shouting "Back, back, back."

Ketch's hands were still up in the air, but he caught the rhythm of the gunman's commands and jabs.

After one of the pokes, Ketch's right arm sliced down along the barrel and front stock of the AK as he stepped with his left foot around the gunman and locked him in a choke hold around his neck.

It was known as a cartoid choke hold, which shut off the blood to the brain. His right inside forearm, pressed against a major artery in the neck, while his left outside forearm pressed against the back of the neck for leverage while both hands grabbed opposite forearms to squeeze the neck tight.

The gunman immediately knew he was in trouble and dropped his rifle, grasping at Ketch's arms trying to free himself.

He spun Ketch around to try to loosen the grip, but when that didn't work, shoved him up against a wall and repeatedly slammed his back into it.

Ketch knew he couldn't let go or he would die.

As he was being slammed up against the wall, Ketch brought his legs up around the gunman's stomach in a scissor lock and tried to squeeze the breath out of him as his choke hold tried to take the life out of him.

The gunman continued to spin him around, but Ketch continued to hold on like riding a bucking bronco. The gunman then threw himself backwards onto a glass coffee table, hoping it would release Ketch's grip. Ketch bore the brunt of the fall. There was a huge crash and glass splinters everywhere. He didn't know if he was cut or not, but didn't think about it.

The gunman finally passed out, from loss of blood to the brain.

Ketch knew that if he held the choke a bit longer, it would cause brain damage. He also knew that if he held it even longer, it would cause death.

Ketch held the choke even longer than longer, just to make sure.

"Asshole," he exclaimed, as he released the corpse.

Ketch stood up and delicately brushed the broken glass off his clothes.

Nikki was holding the gunman's AK-47 but stunned by the events.

"I couldn't shoot him," she explained apologetically with tears in her eyes. "The bullet would go through him and also kill you."

"I know," Ketch responded.

Chapter Fifty-Three

Nikki dropped the AK-47 and Ketch picked up his Browning from the floor.

Just as they were about to leave the apartment, three more Armani gunmen burst in, pointing their AKs at Ketch and Nikki.

"Back, back," one shouted.

Ketch and Nikki backed off.

The lead gunman kept his aim on both of them while the other two searched them.

The gunman searching Ketch found the Browning and struck him across the face with the grip. Ketch reflexively turned his head to avoid the blow and survived with only a slight gash across the cheek.

The gunman searching Nikki, ripped off her *hijab*, and when he found blond hair underneath, slapped her hard across the face and said something in Arabic, which Ketch assumed meant something like "infidel bitch." He noted her lip was now bleeding.

Then, the lead gunmen directed them towards the balcony. Ketch's mind was racing but it didn't give him a solution. He knew that if he charged the gunmen, he and Nikki would be dead in an instant and that would accomplish nothing.

He turned around and looked out over the sea. He could see Pigeons' Rock. He motioned to Nikki to take a look. She turned around, took a look, then looked back at him and grabbed his hand tightly. She knew what he meant.

He also nodded down towards the swimming pool below them. She read his thoughts. It might work. It might not. But better to die trying with the woman you love than do nothing and get slaughtered like sheep.

Ketch looked deeply into Nikki's eyes with a serious stare signaling that this was their only chance. It might free them or kill them. Either way, they'd be free. The look also told Nikki that he really loved her. She acknowledged, nodding her head and squeezed his hand even more tightly.

Just as Ketch was about to take Nikki on a "Lover's Leap" over the balcony, three more gunmen burst into the room dressed in T-shirts, turned-around baseball caps and jeans.

"U.S. Marines," the lead gunman shouted, pointing a semi-automatic pistol at the bad guys. Then he shouted something in Arabic, which Ketch took to mean either "Freeze" or "Drop your weapons."

Of course, bad guys don't listen that well. Instead, they turned on the marines, with their rifles ready to fire.

Big mistake. The marines surgically took them out, each with two shots to the head before the bastards even turned all the way around.

The team leader kept his weapon pointed forward as the other two marines raced around other parts of the apartment.

"Clear, clear," they shouted as they swept the rooms for other assholes.

The leader then pulled out a handheld radio from his belt and clicked the transmit button a few times. "Targets down, package secure," he shouted into the device.

Nikki ran up to the leader, threw her arms around his neck and gave him a big full body hug, pressing her breasts to his chest, while planting kisses on each cheek.

"Shukran," she said to him. "Thank you."

Ketch was now jealous he wasn't a Marine.

"Fuck, man," Ketch responded. "Shit. Thank you, thank you, thank you."

"Don't thank me," the lead marine responded. "Thank Colonel Banks. He was worried about you and asked us to keep an eye out. Our intel told us where you were going, and we tagged along. We found a car full of bad guys following you, so we hung out. One asshole went upstairs, then three more went in. I thought it was time for us join the party."

"Fuck, man," Ketch responded in gratitude. "I owe you guys."

"Don't worry about it, sir," the leader responded nonchalantly. "You owe us nothing. We're marines. This is what we do."

"But you don't even look like marines," Ketch replied. "Except for your muscle-ripped bodies. You have shaggy hair, beards and great tans. No offense, but I'd take you for Arabs from a body-building gym."

"Force Recon, sir," the leader replied. "We do what it takes to get around town."

"And the Arabic?" Ketch continued.

"Actually, we're all Arab-Americans, sir," the leader responded. "I'm Lebanese, and my partners are Palestinian and Syrian. We all love America but we also respect our heritage and want to see things set right. We volunteered to be here.

"Sorry sir, but we need to leave," the leader continued. "Your driver is waiting for you. We will take you to your car and escort you back to your hotel. The only bad guy left downstairs is the driver. Not a problem."

The Marines took Ketch and Nikki down the elevator and into their car. They even politely opened the doors for them. As Ketch looked back at the Marines getting into their own vehicle, he noted that one of them went right up to the driver in the bad guys' car and gave him the middle finger right in front of his face.

"Gotta' love the Marines," Ketch laughed to himself.

"Semper Fi."

Chapter Fifty-Four

During the drive back to the hotel, Ketch felt even closer to Nikki than ever before.

"I'm sorry Nikki, but I really love you," he noted along the ride back.

Nikki did not respond and was very cold.

Finally, she broke her silence.

"Listen, Mr. Kelly," she replied. "None of this matters. Let's just say, I'm not another crème de menthe girl who meets guys in bars."

Ketch was stunned, confused, and now heartbroken again.

He was in love with Elizabeth back in Hong Kong, Katrina in Cyprus, now Nikki in Beirut. But they all seemed to be "crème de menthe" girls working for his agency, or someone's agency. It didn't matter. They were all hired to watch over him, mind him and report back.

He would never know whether their feelings were genuine or just part of their job.

At that moment, Ketch knew he would never fall in love again.

Before he got out of the car, he turned to Nikki. "Well, I guess the job is done, so I will be leaving" he said. "It would be nice if we could have a farewell dinner tonight."

Nikki was still looking down at the floor of the car. She wiped some tears from her cheeks and responded,

"Fine. One last dinner tonight. But I'm not going to fuck you."

"Ok. Seven?" Ketch asked.

"Seven," she confirmed, as she continued to look down and wipe her eyes.

As Ketch walked back into the lobby of the Commodore, he saw O'Hara at the bar nursing a drink.

"Hey, O'Hara," he said. "Mind if I join you for a quick one."

"Course not mate," O'Hara responded. "But there is no such thing as a quick one."

Ketch ordered a whisky soda and continued the conversation from where they left off the previous time.

"Any luck with the family?" he inquired.

"Not yet, mate," he replied sadly. "But I believe you make your luck, so I'm still working on it."

Ketch was touched.

O'Hara didn't hustle him or press him for help. He was sincere in his mission and was resolved to do it alone.

"Look, mate," Ketch responded, patronizingly using the ubiquitous Aussie term for friend. "I'm nobody important and I don't have any important connections. But, I'm one of those idiots who will try to help a good person if I can.

"I think you're a good person. And I have an idea.

"I hate saying this to you, but you need to trust me on this one," Ketch replied. "I will tell you that whenever someone told me to trust them, I immediately did not. I learned that whenever someone said 'trust me' it meant 'fuck you,' I'm about to screw you.

"However, you have nothing to lose on this one.

"Be here tomorrow at the bar, seven in the morning tomorrow with your wife and daughter. Only one small suitcase. I suggest you only pack it with cash, if you have any.

"I will take it from there."

"Well mate, that's all very noble of you," O'Hara replied cynically. "But what do you mean take it from there? I need to give my family more confidence than the bullshit words of some Yank I met in a hotel bar."

"Look. I am leaving Beirut tomorrow for Cyprus," Ketch replied ignoring the slight. "I will try to cut a deal and bring you along. Worst-case scenario, I will know tomorrow morning if it's going to work or not. I don't want to get your hopes up and disappoint you. But bottom line, if it doesn't come through, you can just go back home.

"But don't be late. Not one second late," Ketch replied sternly. "I hate waiting. Especially for people I'm trying to help. If you are one second late, all bets are off."

"We'll be there," O'Hara replied.

Ketch, then left for his room, took a shower and got ready to meet Nikki for a last supper.

Chapter Fifty-Five

Ketch went down into the dining room at seven and waited for Nikki.

She joined him five minutes later. He broke his 7Up fast by ordering a bottle of white wine. Sauvignon Blanc. Marlborough. New Zealand. After a few glasses, Ketch felt the courage to ask.

"So, Nikki. What did you mean that you are not just another crème de menthe girl?"

"You know what I mean Mr. Ketch."

Ketch noted that she called him by his real name, not his cover name, Kelly.

Ketch's heart sank again.

"So you work for my bosses?"

"I work for whoever pays me. And that is you right now."

"And then what?"

"There is no 'then what' in Beirut. We live minute by minute."

"So, what if I wanted to stay here with you or take you home with me?"

"Eric. I like you and I like fucking, but it would never work."

"Why is that? I could take you away from this mess."

"You can't stay here, because you will never understand Beirut and you will never understand me.

"You want to make things right," she explained. "It is very American of you. But Lebanon will never be right. It will always be chaos here.

"If you want to survive here, you need to accept the chaos and make the most of it.

"You know that Lebanon has the highest per capita sales of Valium in the world? But I don't take drugs. I focus on what I can control and let the rest be the rest.

"And you can't take me home," she said. "Beirut is my life. No matter what happens and how bad it gets. This is my life.

"Did you ever try to take one of your Thai massage parlor girlfriends back home?" she asked knowingly. "Don't answer. But you know the answer. It is not their life.

"You Americans think that all life, the best life, is back in America.

"But what is the best life?

"Living in a nice, safe, suburb, taking the kids to school and baseball games? Eating American junk food and playing golf on the weekends?

"What's the point? There is no meaning in American life. You have nice boring lives and nice boring deaths.

"Lebanon is a day-to-day struggle. It is a violent struggle. But that struggle keeps me alive. I'm doing my part to make the history change. If that history changes, then I will be part of it. If it doesn't, then the struggle will keep me going."

"And what about me?"

"Eric. I really like you. They told me about you before you arrived.

"They told me you are a Romantic, but a cynical Romantic. You hope for the best, but plan for the worst. You believe in honor, truth, justice and love.

"But you fall in love with any woman who gives you a nice bubble bath and hugs you tightly in bed."

"So, they told you to give me a bubble bath?" Ketch asked, his feelings now really hurt.

"No. I gave you the bubble bath because I wanted to. And I fucked you because I wanted to, not because of the job.

"I knew I would fuck you when you opened the door to your hotel room. The second I saw you.

"I looked into your eyes and got scared. You have very sharp eyes that tell me you have seen a lot of shit in your life. But they are also very sad and lonely eyes.

"It wasn't the sharp eyes that scared me, but the lonely eyes. I thought I might fall in love with you like a little, lost puppy dog I found on the street.

"And I felt some loving, lonely energy from you. Not from your eyes, but from your heart.

"So, I fucked you that night.

"I lied. I said it was to get it out of your system. But it was really to get it out of *my* system.

"But I couldn't. And you made me cry. Especially, when we saw the children on the Corniche. That really scared me.

"I will fuck you again anytime, anyplace. But we have a problem. I am falling in love with you. And you are falling in love with me.

"I don't know if it was the bubble bath or the hugs," she replied. "But you can't fall in love with me. And I can't fall in love with you.

"There is no love in Beirut.

"Beirut will betray you and the one you love. I will betray you. And you will betray me."

"Look Nikki, I'm in love with you," Ketch responded. "Not because of the bubble bath, the hugging or the fucking.

"I'm in love with you because, you, Nikki Hassani, are the most incredible woman I've ever met in my entire life. The kind of woman that I would want as my partner.

"You are exceptionally beautiful in mind, body and soul. You are also smart, independent and you stand by your friends. You saved my life several times and stopped assholes from beating the shit out of me. You are a caring person.

"No other women I've ever met in my lifetime, in any part of the world, would have done that for me," Ketch responded sincerely.

"That is very sweet, Ketch," Nikki replied. "But look at your history. You are a bit melodramatic. They told me about your history.

"You fell in love with your handler in Hong Kong, Jennifer, just a voice on the phone.

"Then you fell in love with your Thai massage parlor girls.

"Then you fell in love with Elizabeth, who got you out of Hong Kong.

"Then you fell in love with Katrina, in Cyprus.

"Now you are in love with me, because we fucked a few times and had some adventure together.

"As I told you before, you are such a little boy. I had to seduce you, when you should have been seducing me.

"You are so much in need of love that you are grabbing any candy cane that comes along.

"But most important, you cannot love someone until you learn to love yourself.

"First learn to love yourself, Eric, then maybe you can love me or any one of those other women."

"I already love myself," Ketch replied.

"No you don't," Nikki responded. "You are always taking on assignments trying to get yourself killed."

"Not at all," he defended himself. "I take on these assignments because the challenge inspires me and tests my mind, body and spirit. That gives me a lot of personal satisfaction and meaning to my life."

"Ok, Eric. If you say so.

"Let's have a nice dinner tonight, fuck me one more time, then I will get you to the airport. If the airport is not open, then I will get you to East Beirut and you can take the ferry to Larnaca, Cyprus.

"Getting you out of Lebanon is my job.

"But fucking you tonight is my pleasure, and hopefully yours."

Chapter Fifty-Six

Ketch took a sip of wine and looked back at Nikki.

Although he found Adam Smith, uncovered him as a bad guy and, with Nikki's help, put him to an end, Ketch didn't feel like he accomplished anything in Beirut.

"Ok, Nikki. I get it," Ketch replied. "However, I'd really like to feel like I've done something here. Done something good.

"I have a plan. But I need a big favor from you."

"It could cost you your job. But it is a good thing to do and I will owe you any favor, any time, any place you ask. Even fucking you up the butt," he smiled. "I ran into a good person at the hotel bar here. He's Australian and has been trying to get his wife and daughter out of Lebanon. But it's complicated, and he's failed. "I want to help him. Here's my idea.

"Report back to whoever you report to and tell them that I have Adam Smith, his wife and daughter in custody. I want to take them out of Beirut tomorrow with me to Cyprus. And they are willing to cooperate.

"Tell them, I want special passes for all of us to get through the Green Line, at the head of the line, and on the ferry to Larnaca. I want no-questions-asked passes. I know this can be done and I want them tonight.

"After our last incident crossing the Green Line, Mustapha told me about these passes. He was surprised we didn't have them."

"Why not just take a flight?" she asked.

"Because flights are complicated," Ketch replied. "There is immigration, customs, bad guys bombing the airport and waiting forever.

"Bottom line. My plan is not to catch the ferry to Cyprus, but cut a deal with the first and fastest speedboat I find in the marina.

"I also want someone in Larnaca to meet us at the ferry pier and get us around immigration and customs.

"Also, tell them Smith has no travel documents, so the airport is not an option. It is critical someone meet us in Larnaca at the boat."

"I will try my best," Nikki responded. "But it means I need to go now and can't fuck you tonight."

"A reason for me to come back to Beirut," Ketch smiled.

Nikki smiled in return, then left.

Chapter Fifty-Seven

Ketch was back in his room, in bed with all his clothes on except for his shoes and trying to fall asleep. But his mind was awhirl and all he could do was take deep breaths while staring at the ceiling

The knock came at midnight.

Ketch cautiously opened the door and was pleased to see it was Nikki.

She walked in but didn't sit down.

"Ok, Eric," she announced. "I have passes for everyone. You, me, your friend, his wife, daughter and Mustapha."

"You are coming with me to Cyprus?" Ketch asked somewhat hopefully.

"No. I am just coming with you to the port in East Beirut, to help you find a boat.

"And I have to warn you. The bosses were very excited to hear you are bringing Adam Smith to Cyprus, so you will have some explaining to do when you arrive."

"No problem," Ketch replied with false bravado. "I am used to explaining things to bosses."

Ketch was hoping she'd stay, but she quickly put that idea to rest.

"Ok. See you tomorrow morning in front of the hotel. I will be there with Mustapha. If your friends are late, we will not wait and the whole deal is off."

"Don't worry, they won't be late," he replied hopefully.

Then she left.

Chapter Fifty-Eight

Ketch showered, shaved and packed his bags. He didn't want to waste one second on preparing himself in the morning.

He returned to bed in the clothes he expected to wear the next day and tried to doze off.

However, he got virtually no sleep that night.

He took an antihistamine tablet to make himself drowsy and chased it with a small bottle of whisky from the mini-bar in his room. However, it didn't work.

He spent the entire night flat on his back staring at the ceiling and taking deep breaths, trying to relax.

Bombs exploded in the distance, but he took no notice. They were almost a source of comfort, like thunder during summer showers as a kid, which made you feel snug and cozy at home, while your mother prepared the evening meal.

He briefly dozed off for an hour and wished he hadn't. He didn't dream about his past days in the 'Nam, but something more relevant and in the present.

In the dream, he was trying the get home from the Middle East. But he kept facing obstacles. All transportation was cancelled, so he started walking. Then he lost his money, shoes and, later, his clothes. He kept walking, though naked. People stared at him, but they didn't laugh at his nakedness. He noticed his nakedness but didn't know what to make of it and ignored it. However, he never seemed to be making any progress in getting back home. It was one of those extremely vivid dreams where you are conscious in the dream and can control your actions. As such, his dream character knew he was in a dream and when it wasn't working for him, tried to wake himself up. But it was a struggle to do so.

He didn't know what the dream meant, but it seemed ominous and, thankfully, he pushed himself out of it and woke up.

He spent the rest of the night, intentionally keeping himself awake.

The wake-up call came on schedule and, after splashing his face with cold water from the bathroom sink, he walked down the stairs to the lobby to check out.

He walked over to the front desk and presented his American Express card, explaining that he had an accident and it was broken in half.

"No problem," the desk clerk replied. "The magnetic strip is still intact."

Ketch also noted that he'd be having breakfast in the dining room with friends, so they should add that onto his bill.

As they were preparing the payment, he noted that O'Hara, wife and daughter were already at the bar, waiting for him in anticipation. He walked over to greet them.

"So far, so good," he said. "But you never know. This is Beirut. So, join me for some scrambled eggs. If it doesn't work out, then at least you go home with a nice breakfast in you."

They joined him in the dining room and Ketch explained the drill.

"You will be traveling as Americans. Mr. and Mrs. Smith.

"O'Hara, your name is Adam Smith. The names for the ladies don't matter, but what are they, anyway?"

"Angela," the wife answered.

"Nadine," the daughter replied cheerfully. "But my friends call me 'Nadi,' she added with a smile.

"The plan is to take the ferry from East Beirut to Cyprus."

"East Beirut?" O'Hara interjected. "So, we need to cross the Green Line."

"Not a problem," Ketch responded hopefully. "I have special passes. When we get to Cyprus, we'll be met at the dock and routed around immigration and put up in a hotel.

"But, you need to make believe you are this guy Adam Smith.

"Can you fake an American accent?"

O'Hara's attempts were pathetic and based on old American cowboy movies.

"I'm not going to pretend to be a fuckin' Yank," O'Hara responded.

Ketch ignored the slight, but was now losing patience.

"Ok. Forget it," Ketch replied. "Anyone talks to you, just nod and smile. Once we get you into the hotel, then everything will be ok."

"So you want me to trust your American bullshit with my family," O'Hara responded aggressively.

Ketch could not longer ignore the slight. He was trying to help someone, but their cultural ego seemed to dominate the situation.

"Look, O'Hara," he replied, losing his temper. "You took a risk coming out here for love. Now you have the opportunity to leave for love.

"I really stuck my neck out for you based on a couple of drinks at the bar and right now, I don't give a shit either way. If you want to get insulting about it, and be some fuckin', arrogant, asshole, then go fuck yourself and figure it out on your own.

"I am leaving with or without you."

At that point, Ketch got up from the table and made for the door.

Mustapha and Nikki were waiting outside the hotel and Ketch noticed that Mustapha had a new car. A current model four-door Mercedes. White.

"I see you bought a new car, Mustapha," Ketch said jokingly. "Obviously, I'm paying you too much money."

"Don't be an asshole," Nikki responded. "It's my father's car. He loaned it to us for today. You crash this one, then *you* will be paying for it."

Radio antennas sprouted from the roof like a cactus plant.

"What are all those antennas for?" Ketch asked.

"My father likes to stay in touch," Nikki replied.

Ketch got into the front seat next to Mustapha.

"Where are your guests?" Nikki asked.

"Fuck 'em," Ketch replied. "Ungrateful assholes."

As Mustapha started the engine, O'Hara and his family came running out of the hotel and raced to the car.

"Look, mate," he shouted at Ketch. "Apologies for being an asshole. We'd like to come along if you'll still have us."

"Get in," Ketch shouted back coldly.

They stuffed themselves into the back seat next to Nikki and Mustapha sped off towards the Green Line.

Chapter Fifty-Nine

After a short drive down the street, Nikki said to Ketch, "Give me your gun. Also the pen."

Ketch looked at her questioningly over the seat.

"It will only be a problem," she replied. "Don't worry, if they stop us, I will put my boobs in their guns like before."

Ketch pulled out the Browning and the pen gun. He didn't care so much about losing the Browning, but hoped to add the pen gun to his souvenir box.

He handed them across the seat back to Nikki and she immediately tossed them out the window.

As they drove on, Ketch started to hand out the passes to everyone, but Nikki stopped him.

"No. You are the holder of the passes," she explained. "They only have your name on them. You are the boss and we are your employees and servants. Under your name, they say one translator, one driver, one gardener, one maid and one chamber girl.

"They say you are a big shot here, so you must act like one. It might even be helpful if you start ordering us around at the checkpoint.

"Give them to me," she added. "I will hold them, so you don't do something stupid."

"The most important thing is the Arabic writing on the bottom which is stamped *haas* and signed by Colonel Ahmed. I had to wake him up for this, but he understands and wishes you a safe journey and is glad you are taking his advice to go home.

"What does *haas* mean?" Ketch asked noting that Nikki pronounced it with a more guttural, throaty sound you only find in Middle Eastern languages. To his ears, it sounded more like *khaas*, like she was clearing her throat and ready to spit.

"Special," Nikki replied. It is code, but it is only good for a short time. Every six hours they change the code.

"Maybe, after lunch the code is not 'special.'"

"God willing, these cards should get us through the Green Line in no time flat and through the port at Jounieh. With these passes, they don't need papers.

"God willing?" Ketch asked somewhat in disbelief at her choice of words, seeing the Muslim side of her for the first time.

"God willing," Nikki responded emphatically. "This is Beirut. There is nothing on this earth but God's will."

Ketch assumed that Nikki suddenly got touched by religion. Maybe her many scrapes with death finally caught up with her. He also noted that Mustapha had affixed the letters "TV" onto the front hood of the car with wide strips of bright red electrical tape.

"What are the TV letters about?" Ketch asked.

"That says that you are an important media person and can not be delayed," she responded.

"Why didn't we do that before?" he asked.

"Because, before, it would alert the militias that you are a good kidnapping target," she responded. "Now, we are doing it to push us through the Green Line.

"If the tape doesn't come off so good, I may need to charge you for a new paint job for my father's car," she smiled.

When they reached the Green Line, Mustapha drove around all the other cars straight up to the head of the line.

The bravado of his Mercedes with the "TV" markings gave them credibility, but it was Nikki who sealed the deal. Three guys emerged from the checkpoint, rifles drawn and banging their hands on the hood and roof of the car and shouting at them in Arabic.

Nikki immediately jumped out and presented the passes.

Nikki was shouting *haas* or *khaas* at them while waving the passes.

Ketch noted that all the guards gave her deference. But when they took Nikki and the passes into a booth and picked up a phone, Ketch became very nervous.

However, after a few calls, they all returned smiling, bowing to Nikki apologetically and waved them though.

Ketch laughed out loud.

"Nikki!" he screamed with delight. "You are amazing."

"Yes, I know," she responded dryly.

Mustapha got them to the port with plenty of time to catch the morning ferry, but Nikki objected to them taking it.

"You are *haas,* 'special' like diplomats. You cannot take the ferry or people will be suspicious. You need to take an expensive yacht or speedboat.

"How expensive?" Ketch asked, now feeling like he was getting hustled.

"We will see," she replied calmly.

Nikki then stormed up and down the docks of the marina shouting "Larnaca" at each yacht moored there.

Bleary-eyed crew stumbled onto the decks of big and small boats, looking for business but not this early in the morning.

There was everything from celebrity-style mega-yachts to open-deck runabouts with outboard engines.

Then she started shouting "Larnaca, *haas.*"

That got more notice.

Finally, a man in his mid-forties emerged from a small cabin cruiser.

"Nikki," he shouted with a smile.

"Thomas," she responded knowingly.

They exchanged some words in French, a kiss on each cheek and a big hug.

She then turned to Ketch and commanded, "You will go with him. I know his family. Only five thousand dollars cash, American for everyone."

Ketch balked, "I don't have five thousand dollars cash."

"Don't worry," she replied. "I will care of it, but I may have to fuck him. Do you mind?" she said with a wink. "I will call Larnaca and tell them you are coming."

"I love you Nikki," he said sincerely.

"I love you too," she said, kissing him on the forehead.

As Ketch was stepping down into the yacht, he felt a tear running down his cheek. He caught it between two fingers, kissed it and used it to wave goodbye to Nikki.

She waved in return.

"Before you come back," she shouted with a wink. "Get a haircut."

Ketch noted that Nikki was wiping her eyes. Ketch laughed and cried to himself at the same time.

In the meantime, the yacht's crew had cast off the lines and they were on their way to Cyprus.

Nikki watched them until they left the dock, then walked away.

Epilogue

The boat ride to Larnaca was pretty uneventful.

The sky was blue and the sea was flat. O'Hara's daughter, Nadine, was feeling seasick during the ride, so Ketch showed her how to massage the inside of her wrists to make the nausea go away.

But no one knew what to expect in Cyprus and everyone was silent and anxious. Ketch knew he was betting on the outcome and just hoped he could make it all work out.

After the boat landed, they wandered around the docks, not knowing what they'd encounter.

Out of the blue, a young man in a suit, maybe in his early thirties, came running in their direction with a signboard spelling out "Kelly."

Ketch spotted it, waved him down and introduced himself.

"Mister Kelly," the young man replied. "My name is Steven Walsh. I'll be getting you and your guests to the hotel."

Walsh did his job.

He got them through all the barriers and into a mini-van in front of the terminal exit.

Then he got them into a nice hotel in Larnaca overlooking the sea.

When everyone was settled, he said to Ketch, "Someone is anxious to see you. You need to meet him right now."

"Who?"

"Your boss."

"What boss?" Ketch asked.

"Evans."

"Shit!" Ketch replied. "What's he doing here?"

Ketch was upset, but relented. He got into a chauffeured Mercedes with Walsh and they drove off to the U.S. Embassy in Nicosia.

Walsh ushered him through security, then a quick elevator ride to the second floor and into a sparse office with only a desk and two chairs. It looked like a police interrogation room.

"Have a seat," Walsh said. "Can I get you a coffee or a soft drink?"

"You have any 7Up?" Ketch asked.

"That we do."

After a short wait, Walsh returned with a can of 7Up and Evans, his supervisor from D.C.

"Eric Ketch," Evans said as he strolled in. "I always wondered when I'd see you again and whether it would be alive or dead."

Ketch was stunned.

"What are you doing here?" Ketch asked defensively.

"I've been in the region for the last month," Evans replied. "And I couldn't resist the opportunity to talk with Adam Smith personally. But this guy is not Adam Smith, is he?" Evans continued.

"No. How did you know?"

"Because, I know you shot Adam Smith." Evans responded coolly. "Given what we knew about him and how events unfolded, that's what we wanted you to do. But we wanted you to talk to him first. However, Nikki said it was self-defense and you had no choice.

"I assume you didn't get the 'talk then terminate' radio message."

That meant Ketch was supposed to squeeze Smith for everything he knew, by whatever means, then execute him.

"No, I didn't" Ketch responded. The radio thing was a bunch of bullshit. You should have given me someone I could talk to."

"We did," Evans answered back. "Their phone number's on the business card we gave you, but you never bothered to check in."

Ketch knew he screwed up and quickly changed the subject.

"So you wanted me to take this guy down because he built the bombs that hit the Marines?" he asked.

"Who told you this guy was involved in the bombing of the Marines?" Evans questioned.

"He did," Ketch replied.

"In his dreams," Evans sneered. "He was obviously trying to impress you. That's his history in Lebanon. Bullshitting everyone about how great he is. But this fucker couldn't set off a firecracker.

"Any boasting about blowing up the Marines was pure bullshit. Everyone knows it was Hezbollah and Iran. They wouldn't need his help. All their top guys studied engineering at American universities. Yet, now they are all committed to kill Americans. So, they wouldn't want an American on their team, even if he had a nuke. Pride.

"Basically, Smith was a drug dealer that owed some bad people a lot of money. He set up this whole kidnap scam to get us to pay for his ass. He needed half a million to stay alive.

"In the meantime, he killed two of our guys. Partners that had worked narcotics in the Middle East together for five years. He did it in front of other local drug honchos presumably to show his loyalty and buy some time on the money he owed them. He sent us a video. He also sent it to their families. Very sick.

"One guy's daughter opened the mail and played the video before her mom got home from work. I can't begin to think what that did to her. Our guys were tied up with duct tape, then Smith announced their real names, pronounced them as American traitors and blasted each of their faces away with a shotgun.

"We don't know how he knew they were our guys, how he found them or got their family info. That was your job. We gave you a great sympathetic cover story. Rescue a kidnapped American professor. A soft entry for you and a media spotlight that might shake him out.

"But you fucked that up. You didn't make it happen. Instead, of bringing out a high value narcotics asset and a psycho killer, you let this chubby boy from Detroit get the jump on you.

Ketch felt like shit. He thought he was following the plan and doing the right thing. Now, he just wanted to go back to his hotel and shoot himself. He cursed Nikki for taking away his Browning.

"So, who is this guy you brought out?" Evans asked, interrupting his thoughts.

"An Australian. Just a good guy I met at the hotel bar, who was trying to get his family back home to Melbourne," Ketch replied. "He hoped I was CIA. Thought he could do a deal and they might help him. He could be a valuable asset, Ketch continued. "His years on the ground and his wife's connections could be very useful."

"My, my, my," Evans replied cynically. "I never marked you for a bleeding heart, good Samaritan sucker.

"Yes, he could be a good asset," Evans continued. "But you didn't even check him out. All you needed to do was make one phone call to the number on your card, but you didn't. You got touched by his sob story and put Nikki on the spot.

"Fortunately, Nikki is smarter than you and checked him out. He has no training, but it seems that he and his wife did some intel work on a freelance basis around the region. Not just Lebanon, but Oman, Yemen and Syria. Rumor is he shot one of his Aussie mates without permission. An Australian agent working deep cover, but maybe playing both sides for money. Maybe, O'Hara got some of the money, so the Aussies won't bring him home, except in handcuffs. That's why he was stuck in Beirut.

"Sounds like something you would do, Ketch," Evans said with the glimmer of a smile.

"If he wants to play ball, we will offer him asylum in the U.S.," Evans replied. "If he doesn't, then he's an ungrateful son-of-a-bitch and on his own. He's just another refugee hustling any soft touch who will listen to his sad story.

"I have no sympathy for refugees or defectors, Ketch. They are all opportunists. I don't care what the situation is in their country. Refugees are people who don't want to fight for their country or their ideals or work to change the politics. They just want to get somewhere else where they can make more money or avoid paying taxes.

"Do you know who are the biggest refugees in the world? The British.

"Why? To avoid taxes. Yet, overseas Brits will be the first to get into a fight with you over the Queen, Churchill or a soccer team. A lot of them live in the U.S. Have you ever been in one of the bars where they all hang out? They'll be the first to tell you how superior they are and how fucked up Americans are and they're only here for the tax relief, and how stupid Americans are for even letting them live here.

Did you know that your British friends in Hong Kong invested in U.S. stocks and property, but unlike Americans, didn't have to pay U.S. capital gains taxes?

"Anyway, we gave O'Hara three days to decide, then he will start paying his own bills. And this isn't a cheap hotel.

"He's lucky he found a stupid, American sucker like you to help him out. But don't expect him to be appreciative. In fact, you are ordered to stay away from him, so he doesn't continue to play you with his refugee sob story. The Aussies think he took a quarter of a million off the guy he offed, but don't know where the money is.

"And what do we tell Smith's family?" Ketch asked.

"We tell them, that thanks to Eric Kelly, we found their son Adam, offered the bad guys the money, but they killed him anyway," Evans responded. "They were crazy bad guys and had already killed Adam in advance and just hoped to rip off the money. We're sorry for your loss. We did everything we could. But he shouldn't have been living in a war zone in the first place. People get killed in war zones.

"Separately, Ketch, the family don't give a shit about him and haven't seen him for years. Just like you and your family. So, they'll get over it. Also, he had a half million dollar life insurance policy in their name. I'm sure that will dry some tears."

"And what next for me?"

"Quite frankly Ketch," Evans answered in a very fatherly way. "It would be good for you to go home for a bit and reconnect with America."

"By the way, your mom died."

"What?" Ketch responded.

"Yeah. Sorry you had to hear it this way. One of your sisters left a message on your answering machine in D.C., but when you didn't respond, she called the police.

"The police called someone who called someone who called someone who called us.

"She doesn't know what you do or where you are. And we couldn't inform you while you were in-country on a mission. I'm sure you appreciate that.

"Sorry, but the funeral's over, so you don't need to rush back. And better you call her from back in the States.

"I assume she doesn't get a lot of calls from Cyprus and if you call her from here, I guarantee that her phone number's going to be on somebody's list.

"Another reason to go home," Evans continued. "Your sisters resent you for living an exciting international life while they are stuck in the boring suburbs. At the same time, they are secretly hoping you get killed out here cause they are beneficiaries of your life insurance policy, which is pretty significant. None of my business, but I don't believe how much you pay into it every year to keep it going for the sake of an ungrateful family.

"Maybe you need to rethink that. I know a lot of charities who would be more appreciative and at least put your name on a brass plaque and come to your funeral.

"How do you know what my sisters think?" Ketch challenged.

"Come on, Ketch," Evans answered. "Don't play stupid with me. We not only know what your sisters think, but what your friends think and any bar girl you spend a night with. It's our job to know.

"I told you before. We own you. About time you get used to it.

"Anyway, a company jet is leaving tomorrow back to D.C. I think you should be on it. I was able to book a Gulfstream. Five-star all the way.

"Time to go home," Evans reiterated.

Again, "go home" seemed to be the theme of this mission, Ketch noted.

"I'd prefer to unwind here for a few days, then fly commercial," he told Evans.

Ketch had two things in the back of his mind. First, he wanted to see Katrina again. Second, he couldn't bear to spend a long flight cooped up with Evans, in a toothpaste tube corporate jet.

Evans read his mind.

"Katrina has left," Evans responded knowingly.

"So, don't waste your time.

"Also, you'll like the in-flight service. I think you might have met one of the flight attendants before in Hong Kong or Cairo.

"Her name is Elizabeth."

Ketch made the flight.

Fortunately, the cabin layout was all single seating and Evans didn't try to sit nearby.

As Ketch settled back into his seat, the Gulfstream took off at a steep angle, almost like a fighter jet. Once it reached cruising altitude, an air hostess emerged into the cabin.

Elizabeth.

She was wearing a light, white and blue polka-dotted cotton mini-dress that barely covered her. A narrow belt, tight around her waist, accentuated her figure. Her cleavage popped out of the top and her long, lean, aerobic instructor legs presented themselves from the bottom almost right up to her panties.

"Welcome aboard, Mr. Ketch," she said nonchalantly. "It's a long flight back home. I'm sure you could use a drink."

"Yes," Ketch replied, once again, taken in by her Eurasian cachet and alluring British accent.

"Glenlivet, no ice?" she asked knowingly.

"Perfect."

The drink arrived shortly.

As Ketch sipped the smooth, single-malt whisky, he looked out the window and caught the moon coming up over the horizon.

A Crescent Moon.